The Librarian's Son

Ellen Gelerman

Book design by Joe Montgomery

Author photo by Double Exposure Photos

Photo of William Munch is property of the Munch family and is used with permission.

ISBN paperback: 979-8-9876491-7-6

ISBN eBook: 979-8-9876491-8-3

This book is dedicated to two very different kinds of heroes,
storied and unsung:
Firefighters, who run toward danger when others run away,
and
Librarians, who are often on the front lines of preserving democracy

In loving memory

William ("Bill") Munch
1960-2023

ONE

The whimpering from Micah's bedroom woke Jessie immediately, even before the screaming started.

"Mama! Mama!"

With a groan, she forced her eyes, sticky with sleep, to open and focus. From experience, she knew that there was no ignoring it, no hoping it would stop on its own. The commotion came in stereo, from down the hall as well as through the baby monitor that she hadn't quite felt comfortable enough to retire when Micah celebrated his third birthday four months back. The night terrors . . . well, those had started three weeks ago on and off, and she and Cassandra already had a tag-team system set up.

"My turn, I guess," she said to Cassandra's back, pulling away a lock of her own hair that had somehow found its way into the corner of her mouth. Despite her hopes that she might be overruled—*"just this once"*—Cassandra grunted in agreement and tugged the blanket more tightly over her shoulders as Jessie slipped out of bed and put her robe on over her nightgown.

With only the dim hallway nightlight to guide her, Jessie felt along the corridor wall, the *shh, shh, shh* of her slippers against the polished hardwood floor echoing her hushing of Micah's cries as she reached his door. "Mama's coming, honey," she called in a low, weary voice. If Micah woke his brother up, that would be the end of sleep for all of them for tonight.

"You OK, sweetie?"

The nightstand lamp that Cassandra had found for him on Etsy—a cheerful, cartoonish fireman in a red jacket and black helmet, with a Dalmatian romping alongside—was already on, casting a subdued glow. Micah had been afraid of the dark almost from birth, and he wouldn't go to sleep without some kind of illumination. Now he was sitting up in his bed using his blanket to wipe his tears away. Also his snot. *Ugh. More laundry, first thing after work tomorrow.*

"Dark." Micah coughed. "So dark, Mama, can't see."

He was talking, so not a night terror. Just your run-of-the-mill nightmare. That wasn't anything she couldn't handle.

"The light's on, honey. Just like always. Look!" Jessie waved her hand in front of the lamp, causing shadows to flit around the room like a swarm of butterflies.

"Dark," he said again, insistent, and then, "Can't *see*," though his eyes were open and clearly focused on his mother's face. He rubbed a finger over the bridge of his nose where his small strawberry birthmark sat like a ladybug.

Jessie gathered him up in her arms. "You had a bad dream, baby," she said, "but Mama's here, and the light is on, and everything is fine."

He shook his head with vehemence from side to side and coughed again. "Not fine. Can't breev."

He can't breathe? Micah had never said that before—well, not unless he had a bad cold, but he didn't sound stuffy. Now Jessie was concerned, considering whether she should wake Cassandra and ask her to get out her emergency kit. Or should they bring Micah to the ER? Her mind raced, wondering whether he might have developed an allergy, and to *what*; wondering whether this was one of those situations where every minute counted and she was wasting precious time. Yet he didn't appear to be struggling for breath, and with an ear pressed to his chest, she could hear his intake, even and deep.

"De smoke!" Micah said, with a little choking noise. But his heart was no longer in it, and, pressing himself closer to his mother, he calmed. Jessie sniffed the air. The room had its usual smell of Cassandra's favorite eco-friendly household cleaner and lavender laundry detergent, overlaid with the warm scent of their son. The combination smoke/carbon monoxide detector that Cass had installed at the doorway to his room was reassuringly silent, its green light periodically flashing the message that everything was A-OK.

Jessie repeated that message aloud, to comfort both Micah and herself: "Everything's fine now, isn't it?"

He nodded against her chest. "I'm firsty, Mama," he murmured. "Wanna drink."

"Look, here's your sippy cup, right here," Jessie said, retrieving the yellow cup from its usual spot beside the lamp. It was always there, to head off the inevitable cry for water in the middle of the night. If only the nightmares were that easy to combat!

Micah took three long gulps from the cup and handed it back to Jessie. "It dark, Mama. And de smoke. Can't see anyfing but keep going up." Becoming drowsier, he sighed as he snuggled closer to his mother. "Up, up, up."

"That was some nightmare, baby," Jessie said with relief. She kissed his forehead, which was damp but cool, and helped him lie back down, settling the sullied blanket across his chest. Seeing his favorite stuffie, Dot, on the floor, she retrieved it and tucked it in next to him. The stuffed Dalmatian had been a gift from one of Cassandra's coworkers at the firehouse when Micah turned two, and he had become attached to it almost immediately, requiring it for bedtime, naps, and most outings. Despite Cass's attempts to get him to name the dog Spot, Micah couldn't manage the sound. For a while he called it Ot, but eventually he settled on Dot instead, and the name stuck.

Though Micah was asleep almost immediately with Dot beside him, Jessie stayed an extra minute, just to be sure.

Just to listen to his breathing.

She glanced around his room, much of it in shadow. At about two-and-a-half, Micah had become very vocal about his décor . . . or as vocal as a toddler with a limited vocabulary could be. He was suddenly opposed to the playful, brightly colored zoo animals that had adorned his nursery, pulling off the bedcovers and trying to yank down the wall art. Jessie and Cassandra agreed that he was growing up, and he had decided that he was too big for such baby stuff. In its place, Micah made it known that he wanted fire houses, fire trucks, firemen. So Cassandra found him a new duvet cover with big red fire department trucks on it, which led to her giving him a detailed explanation of the various kinds of vehicles—ladder trucks, rescue vehicles, pumpers. He'd listened avidly. As an EMT, Cassandra was very proud of her son's latest fascination, though she admitted to being disappointed that his interest didn't extend to the medical services arm of the department. Micah spent over an hour on his bed the first day, admiring the trucks and describing them aloud—in his own way—to no one in particular. Later, they'd added wall decals, pillows, framed art, books, and, of course, toys. Micah loved it all.

But now, as she shuffled back to her room, Jessie wondered whether it was all too much, whether his obsession was seeping into his dreams, turning them frightening. Maybe it was too easy for all this emergency equipment to create terrifying scenarios for a little boy on the cusp of sleep.

"Well, that was a new one," she said to Cassandra as she fumbled her way into bed. But Cassandra, bless her, was a sound sleeper, and as usual, once the initial disturbance had passed, she trusted that Jessie would have the situation under control. She was snoring quietly, her breath whistling through her nose on the exhale.

Jessie smiled through her exhaustion and cuddled up next to Cassandra, draping an arm around her waist. Nightmares happened, and as scary as it had been in the moment, there was nothing worth waking Cass for. Nothing unusual, nothing concerning.

And she fell easily back into the untroubled sleep of a person who had no idea her life was about to be upended.

Two

Cassandra, refreshed by a full night of uninterrupted sleep, was up earlier than Jessie the next day. As Jessie walked down the stairs in her nightgown and robe, sluggish and not entirely awake, the smell of coffee brewing lifted her spirits. In the kitchen, she accepted the cup—the "#2 Mom" mug Cass had made for her as a joke when their elder son, Eli, made Cassandra a "#1 Mom" card last Mother's Day—with a grateful sigh. Cass had already put in half-and-half and one sugar, and all Jessie had to do was drink it and recharge.

Jessie observed her wife moving around the kitchen in her blue EMS uniform with affection and incredulity that she had ended up with such a prize. When they'd first met, she'd secretly laughed at the irony of a woman so angular—from the planes of her narrow face to the sharpness of her thin body even to the spikes of her short, brown hair—bearing a name as insistently flowery and lush as Cassandra Delarosa . . . until she grew to love both the woman and, by extension, the name. But when they discussed how to manage their surnames as their wedding approached, Cassandra had insisted on taking on Jessie's and leaving hers behind: A refutation, she'd said, of everything that name and her family represented.

"Micah's not in his room," Jessie said, looking around. "What's he up to now?"

Before Cassandra could speak, the answer came from the doorway. "He's playing with Keef." Six-year-old Eli stood at the entrance to the kitchen, a comic book in his hand, still wearing his worn-out, gray T-shirt and favorite rocket-ship pajama bottoms, his brown hair sticking up like a weathervane atop a barn.

"What's a keef?" Though Jessie was puzzled, Cassandra looked alarmed. As she told Jessie later, in her EMS vocabulary, it meant something that neither Eli nor Micah could or should know about.

Eli rolled his eyes. "You know, *Keef*. His pretend friend."

"Oh. *Keith*." Cassandra laughed a little in relief.

"Huh. I didn't know he had a name," Jessie added.

Micah had always been good at entertaining himself, and it was a relief to both Jessie and Cassandra that he could play quietly on his own, particularly last year when Eli had become a bit more needy as he started first grade. Micah would talk to himself while playing, and recently, in the last month or so, they'd noticed him taking on both roles in the conversation, even providing different voices. Maybe, she would joke to Cassandra, he had mad acting skills. Or, maybe, Cassandra would reply with a smirk, he had a split personality. But to Jessie, it was charming that Micah had an imaginary friend. An only child herself, Jessie thought such a companion would have come in handy when she was growing up, lonely and feeling out of place.

"So, Eli, what are Micah and Keith doing?" She glanced at the wall clock; it was getting late.

Shrugging with one knobby shoulder, Eli shuffled into the kitchen and grabbed a banana from the bowl on the counter. "Dunno. Playing with his trucks, I guess." Dropping the comic book to the floor, he peeled the top of the banana and stuffed about a third of it into his mouth. Cassandra hustled over to make sure he didn't choke, breaking off a large portion of the part that was still protruding from Eli's mouth.

"Pick up your book, sweetie, and come sit down," she said to Eli, who complied. He finished his banana and started in on the toast and jam that Cassandra had prepared for him.

Settling her nose above her coffee and letting the familiar earthy aroma nudge her into full consciousness, Jessie wandered into the den. Mornings were more hectic on days like this one, when she and Cassandra had shifts that coincided with each other. She should have a greater sense of urgency, she knew; she should be getting ready for work, not chasing after her younger boy. But she didn't know how his mood would be after his nightmare the night before, and she didn't want to pressure him.

Micah, in one of his many pairs of fireman pajamas, was on the floor in their den, a small room that held a well-worn, dark brown leather sofa; a bookcase filled to overflowing with children's books; a toy box; and a Lego table. A flat-screen TV that was almost as old as Eli was mounted on the wall opposite the couch, and family photos—baby pictures of the two boys and their moms, visits with Santa, school portraits—took up the rest of the limited wall space. Much of the floor was filled with other toys, including the trucks Micah was currently playing with, sitting with his knees bent and his legs splayed out to the sides like a capital *M*. It was a painful-looking posture that always made Jessie cringe, but he seemed comfortable enough, mumbling to himself. His silky brown hair was exactly the same color as Jessie's but not as wavy—though you couldn't tell. He always insisted on having it cut short, almost in a buzz cut. He was pushing a truck in each hand, and in between the *vroom* noises he appeared to be making them talk to each other.

"Good morning, honey. Whatcha doing?"

"Dis is me," he replied waving a semi in his right hand. "And dis," he said, indicating the firetruck in his left hand, "is Keef. Keef is a fireman." After a pause, he corrected himself. "A firefighter."

"Wow." Despite his obsession, she'd never heard Micah use that particular term before. "That's a big word."

"De *right* word, Keef says."

"Well, we want to use the right words, don't we." Jessie was proud of him.

And yet.

After the nightmare last night, she wondered exactly when the firehouse obsession had escaped the bounds of room decoration and books and started to dominate Micah's life. She thought back to last fall. The "fireman" costume complete with helmet was his very vocal demand for Halloween, and he had expressed himself in oddly mature and specific terms: "Black, no red. Like real ones," even though Cassandra's department wore yellow. More than once, they had taken him to a Touch-a-Truck event at Cassandra's firehouse and had a hard time getting him to leave. He sat in all the trucks, running his hands over the controls and pretending he knew how to work them, and wanted to hug all the firefighters. Naturally, they all adored him, and Cass was pleased to know that Micah was always welcome there. For his third birthday, Jessie and Cassandra gave him several picture books and DVDs, but what he really loved was his one big gift, the nearly two-foot-long ladder truck with real working lights, hose, and siren. The siren had been silenced by order of Cassandra, who had enough of that kind of noise during her workday, but as a result Micah learned to make a suitable noise himself. His mothers were grateful that he hadn't figured out that the hose would work if filled with water until earlier this summer, when they had blown his mind by taking it outside for the first time and letting him play until he and Eli were soaked through.

"Keef loves being a firefighter," Micah continued, unprompted.

"And how about you? Do you want to be a firefighter?"

"No."

Jessie was taken aback, and that one word did more to wake her up than the coffee she'd been drinking. She thought that all the books, accessories, and toys were evidence that he knew what he wanted to be when he grew up. But children change their minds, and maybe she and Cassandra would be changing his room décor soon. "Well, then," she said, getting hold of herself, "you can be whatever you want to be, honey. But right now, you need to be getting ready for daycare. Come on." Her nearly empty cup still in her right hand, she extended her left down to him, and he put down the trucks to take it.

"Bye, Keef."

"I'll get him fed and dressed," Cassandra said, emerging from the kitchen. "You go have some breakfast."

"Mm, thanks, babe. Micah, go with Mommy. Eli, please go get dressed."

"I don't wanna go to camp today," Eli responded with a scowl.

Jessie suppressed a sigh. He loved the day camp at their Unitarian church while he was there, as evidenced by the growing collection of arts and crafts he proudly brought home but getting him there was often a fight. Getting him to school was usually worse. In fact, lately almost everything was a struggle. "Well, you're in luck today, buster, because there's no camp." She did not explain—because he didn't ask, and they wouldn't have wanted to explain anyway—that a boy from his group had contracted a case of head lice. While the camp was still open, Jessie and Cassandra agreed they would not be taking any chances. *Nasty things.* "You're going to Quentin's house instead."

"Oh, yeah! Woo!" Eli bolted from the room and dashed up the stairs.

Fifteen minutes later, Jessie had her purse in hand, her tote bag on her shoulder, with Micah standing close behind her in the foyer. She was ready to take him out the door when Cassandra stopped her.

"Can I trade you?" she asked Jessie. "I'll take Micah to daycare, and you take Eli to Quentin's today?"

Their sharing of parental responsibilities according to their hours usually resulted in Jessie being in charge of Micah's daycare while Cassandra got Eli to the school bus on time. During the summer it was similar, except for getting Eli to day camp.

"No problem. Care to tell me why?"

Cassandra shrugged one shoulder, in that moment charmingly reminiscent of Eli a half hour earlier. She leaned in close to Jessie so Micah wouldn't hear. "Not a fan of Dean Marshall, and you know he sometimes takes Fridays off in the summer."

"Well, I'm no great fan, either," Jessie responded in a similar low voice, "but we've known him for four years. Has something changed recently?"

"Not exactly. It's just a vibe I've been getting from him lately." Cassandra grabbed her bag and slung it across her shoulder, snatching up Micah's backpack on her way to the door. "Come on, big guy, say bye-bye to Mama, and let's get you to daycare."

"Bye, Mama," Micah said without a glance toward Jessie, who felt a pang that her independent little man couldn't be bothered to kiss her goodbye. Cassandra did, though, leaving Jessie with a smile as she called for Eli.

Quentin Marshall and Eli had been inseparable since they'd met in preschool, and the past four years hadn't dimmed their bond. The friendship between their mothers wasn't as intense—nor as obvious, on the surface. It certainly puzzled Cassandra: How did her bookish East Coast wife grow so attached to a gregarious third-generation Hadlinsburg, Ohio, native?

To Jessie, it all boiled down to one thing. When they'd moved to Hadlinsburg, where Jessie knew no one but her new coworkers, Trish had been the one who had reached out at preschool drop-off and said, "You need a friend, and that friend is going to be me." She was absolutely the right person for the job at the time: upbeat and friendly, active in the town and school, and always advocating for kids—or at least, her own kids, but the result was the same. Trish introduced Jessie to the people she should know in town, showed her the best places to eat (and the ones to avoid), and never forgot to celebrate a birthday or holiday with cards and gifts. That their boys were devoted to each other made their relationship all the more inevitable.

It wasn't all smooth sailing by any means. Without saying anything, the two women knew that they would be on opposite sides of any discussion of politics or religion and gracefully sidestepped them when they came up. And despite their long-standing friendship, Jessie could never warm up to Trish's husband, Dean. She felt he wore a constant air of disapproval and condescension and seemed to keep a tight rein on the whole family. More to the point for Jessie, whenever he was with his children in the library, Dean always escorted them as a group and frequently put back a perfectly suitable selection that Jessie could over-hear him deeming "too worldly" or "profane." As if four-, six-, and eleven-year-olds could understand the concept. Jessie had said as much to the head librarian the first time she'd seen Dean in action and had received a tart reminder that parents had the final say, and she mustn't intervene. Seeing that the Marshalls' eldest, Alanna, who'd be sixteen soon, was becoming a bit of a wild card—starting to push back on her parents—Jessie had some higher hopes for her.

Yet while Jessie tolerated Dean for Trish's sake, trying to remain cordial despite his poorly hidden hostility, Cassandra never felt the same obligation, swearing she never wanted to be in the same room with the man. In fact, she felt that Jessie was far too easy on him, giving him too much benefit of the doubt.

"Why do you let him treat you that way, like you're barely human?" Cass had grumbled when they first met Dean and his parents at a holiday party when the boys were three, a few months after they'd moved to Hadlinsburg.

Of course Jessie could see where Cassandra was coming from: Dean was a reminder of all the progress that had yet to be made. Still, she continued to hope for the best. "Oh, c'mon," she'd said at the time, "he's not that bad."

"Seriously?" Cassandra's righteous indignation, always a force to be reckoned with, was at full power. "He shook your hand like you had a communicable disease and turned away from you while you were still talking to him. You're always excusing bad behavior in the name of peaceful coexistence."

"You say that like it's a bad thing. Meanwhile *you're* always looking for a fight."

"And you're saying *that* like it's a bad thing. Sometimes you have to stand up for yourself, Jess, even if it means rocking the boat."

But Jessie, already seeing how attached the boys were to each other and valuing Trish's friendship, had chosen not to fight this particular battle. It wasn't always wise to rock the boat when there were children aboard, she felt. Nevertheless, the two families never socialized outside of major events like birthday parties despite the connections between the mothers and their sons.

So Jessie was relieved when Trish, rather than Dean, met the two of them at the door with the kind of over-the-top vitality one would expect from the prom queen she had once been. Jessie didn't know how Trish managed with four children while she occasionally felt overwhelmed with two. But her kids were pleasant and polite, and her always-spotless house—a giant brick McMansion with five bedrooms, a toy-filled play-room with all the latest electronics, and a kidney-shaped in-ground swimming pool that Trish watched with steely-eyed focus when the kids were outside—provided Eli with a safe and fun place to play: His idea of Heaven.

"Hey there, girlfriend!" Trish declared as she swung the door open.

"Good morning, Trish." Jessie smiled, while internally she was shaking her head in amusement. She couldn't possibly match Trish's energy—nor did she want to. From past conversations, she was aware that Trish was up 5:30 a.m. to do a workout in their home gym before her children woke up. There had to have been extra time built into her day for blowing out her ash-blond hair and putting on her full face of makeup, even if she was planning a day at home with the kids. Jessie always felt dowdy by comparison, despite having a figure proportional for her five-foot-four frame.

The two boys charged off and disappeared with a clatter into the recesses of the house, their yells echoing through the hallways. Jessie dropped the small tote—containing Eli's bathing suit, towel, and a couple of comic books he refused to leave the house without—in the foyer and was ready for an equally quick departure. "Well, I'm off to work. We really appreciate your having Eli over."

Waving away Jessie's expression of gratitude, Trish said, "Oh, gosh, don't be silly! It's actually easier for me to have Eli around to entertain Quentin. The others are having a special day out with their dad and grandparents, but you know Quentin: He'd rather have a visit from his bestie than go out roller-skating and for hamburgers and ice cream with the old folks." She chuckled. "My little weirdo."

Knowing the elder Mr. and Mrs. Marshall as she did, from birthday parties and school events, Jessie wanted to give Quentin a big hug and the kind of full-sized candy bar his grandparents bragged about giving out on Halloween. The Marshalls, like Trish's parents, were Hadlinsburg natives, but their family tree went back to the founding of the town, and their attitude implied that it gave them special influence there. Mr. Marshall, a tall, barrel-chested man with abundant white hair, was proud of the three successful businesses he'd built but perhaps even more so of his yearly stint as the town's official Santa, though Jessie thought his physical resemblance wasn't enough to merit the role; she considered him an ignorant blowhard and Mrs. Marshall (suitably attired but considerably less jolly than Mrs. Claus) an ego-driven bubblehead. Micah had refused to sit on his lap last Christmas, and Jessie and Cassandra didn't blame him for an instant. Maybe he'd sensed that the couple was clearly and sometimes vocally uncomfortable with his mothers' marriage, but so were several other people in the town, including their son Dean. Jessie handled any contact by being as pleasant as she could, ignoring the veiled and occasionally obvious insults, and by keeping Cassandra as far away from them as possible.

"So, Cass has a twelve-hour shift today, and if it's OK with you, I'll pick Eli up right after I get off from work. Around sixish?"

"No problem. And if the little dude gets hungry, well, there's always plenty to go around."

"Thanks so much, Trish, as always. I'll head out now and . . ."

"Oh, wait a min, won't you?"

Jessie did as requested, though she had an inkling of what was coming. While she stood in the foyer, Dean passed through the marble-floored hallway on his way from the kitchen to the living room while talking on his phone, and glanced Jessie's way. From the wedding photo prominently displayed in their dining room, Jessie knew that he had once been a good-looking man, with broad, sturdy shoulders; a full head of thick, brown hair; and strong chin and jawline framing a dazzling smile. Time hadn't been kind to him, though, and by the time Jessie met him years later, he had developed a paunch and lost almost all his hair; his face had turned puffy and devoid of definition. She gave a subdued wave as he passed, but Dean didn't even bother to return it. *Be that way!* Jessie thought with a grimace. Clearly it was too much of an effort for the man to be civil. She wondered if Trish was still as enamored of her high school sweetheart as she'd been when they'd married at nineteen.

When Trish returned from her quick trip into the kitchen, she was carrying a small, white plastic bag. She handed it to Jessie, covering her guest's hand with her own.

"Give this to your darling Cassandra, won't you? It's a little somethin'-somethin' from me to her. A couple of teensy gifts: sample sizes of our newest toner, serum, day crème, night crème—different formulations from yours, of course. You have a totally different profile. But Cass could have such glowing skin if she'd only take better care of it."

Trish was always pushing samples of the beauty products from the multilevel-marketing company she'd joined in the spring. Jessie still smarted a little at the memory of the "tea party" Trish had invited her to on a Saturday afternoon in May, thinking it was going to be a fun, even elegant, gathering of some of Trish's closest friends. Instead, she and a dozen other women—wearing their finest floral dresses, plates of tiny sandwiches balanced on their laps—had had to sit through a half-hour long presentation about cleansers, toners, and blushers, and the "unbeatable opportunity" to peddle them to others in the community.

Cassandra had laughed heartily at the story once Jessie came home, stony-faced with disappointment and embarrassment.

While she'd had no luck persuading Jessie to join the small team of salespeople she'd managed to recruit in Hadlinsburg, or to sell her the whole line of *perfect* cosmetics to enhance her complexion's reddish undertones, Trish had succeeded in making Jessie a devotee of the company's hand cream. The price had initially made Jessie choke, but by the time she'd finished her sample, she'd become enamored of its light vanilla/citrus scent—and the way it moisturized her hands, rough from frequent washing—and had adjusted her monthly budget to accommodate it.

Trish was now turning her attention to Cassandra, who was even less likely to take the bait. The smooth, unadorned skin of Cassandra's face was one of Jessie's favorite things about her. No makeup, no fancy creams, only drugstore cleanser and moisturizer. Maybe avoiding Trish was the actual reason Cassandra had bailed out of driving Eli this morning. Nevertheless, Jessie replied, "Of course. How thoughtful of you, Trish."

"Well, you know me. Anything for a friend."

Waving goodbye, Jessie opened her car door and with a flick of her wrist tossed the bag into the back seat, where it landed among other unnecessary, forgotten detritus.

THREE

Was there any smell as sweet as the accumulated aroma of thousands of books?

Jessie didn't think so and occasionally remarked on it, despite the other librarians' amused insistence that there was no such scent, the way there might be in an ancient and scholarly library in Britain, for example. In fact, they maintained if there were any smell at all in their building, particularly in her department, it would be toddler puke or—as one of her coworkers suggested, oddly—feet. As she often did, she counted herself fortunate to have found her life's work in a public library, surrounded by books. She'd discovered early that they were good friends, ones you could count on even when—particularly when—there was little else so dependable. In fact, if she could move her family into the library, and provide them with enough food—and clothes for the boys who were always outgrowing their current ones, she supposed—she could happily live there forever.

Being able to guide even the most confused elementary school student through this enchanted forest to find a particular volume felt like the greatest privilege in the world. Books had saved her during her awkward tween years as well as her parents' illnesses and the loneliness beyond, and she couldn't think of a better way to return the favor.

And every day Jessie was in the library, she was grateful that she got to spend her time with books instead of patients as Cassandra did; during her service in the Air Force, she had decided to become certified as an EMT. Oh, there were difficult library patrons to be sure: the noisy, the disruptive, the deliberately clueless. The vocal, demanding parents; the people who monopolized the computers; the ones who ate chips— or once, even fried chicken!—in the stacks when they thought no one could see them. But at least there were fewer bodily fluids, and no life-and-death circumstances involved. At least, there hadn't been yet.

Ignoring for a moment the piles on her desk that cried out for her attention, she smiled at the group of elderly people heading toward Conference Room A, and they smiled back. The senior center book club met here the third Friday of every month, regardless of the season, promptly at ten a.m. There were about a dozen of them, and Jessie guessed they ranged in age from late sixties to mid-eighties, mostly women but with a few men sprinkled in. In the mix were several highly respected citizens of the town: Diana Hadlin, descendant of the town's founder and a popular, retired high school social studies teacher who had been voted the state's Teacher of the Year back in the '90s; Dorothy Arthur, the CPA who still did probably a quarter of the population's taxes; and Charlie Duquesne, known as the Duke, the town's oldest veteran at ninety-four, who had been awarded the Purple Heart in Korea and who still walked with a limp due to the injury he sustained there. Though the other librarians agreed that they never asked for advice on their eclectic selections, Jessie had a good idea what they'd been reading based on what she'd seen being carried into the meetings. She wished she could sit in on their discussions, to find out how an elderly group ricocheted from rip-roaring bestsellers to obscure, doorstopper-length nonfiction, but they always closed the door behind them and sat away from the glass panels that separated the room from the rest of the library with their backs to the door. Their muffled voices, occasionally raised in passionate argument, could often be heard through the glass.

But Jessie loved her own department, loved passing time in the company of Dr. Seuss, A.A. Milne, C.S. Lewis, and the talented newcomers who added variety to her days. It was a great thrill to be able to introduce a new generation to authors who had inspired her as a child and to encourage a passion for the written word in a child beginning to discover it for themselves. She and an occasional intern also planned scavenger hunts, school vacation projects, crafts, even reading sessions with therapy dogs . . . anything to keep the kids interested and engaged. While it might get loud or even chaotic in the children's section, nothing that dramatic ever happened in the library, which is exactly the way Jessie liked it. Leaving her home—and the memories of her parents—in New Jersey had been a sacrifice, but getting her dream job in a town where she and Cassandra had the means to raise their children had been worth it.

Idly leafing through the memos and sticky notes left on her desk, Jessie leaned in to turn on her computer. While it booted up, she picked up an exquisite picture book—one that she had read to Eli and Micah dozens of times—and carried it into the meeting room where story time would begin at ten thirty. She set up the tiny chairs and finger puppets that would accompany the reading before returning to her station.

Among the dozen emails in her inbox, there were the usual notifications about staff time-off requests and new acquisitions. An email from the library director with the subject *A Heads-Up* caught her eye, and she clicked on it.

Library staff: It has been brought to our attention that the organization known as Patriot Parents Against Woke (PPAW) has started making challenges in the East Daniston library system. For those unfamiliar with PPAW, its members seek to remove books from the public and school library shelves that the group calls unsuitable for children due to what they deem "explicit sexual content"; "inappropriate language"; or history that "promotes Critical Race Theory or denigrates a single race, religion, or nationality."

A shiver ran through her. PPAW—which many pronounced, derisively, as Pee-Paw—was one of the most well-known of the so-called parents' rights groups that had sprung up in recent years. Jessie had been watching the spread of these organizations and had comforted herself that most of the incursions had taken place in comparatively far-away states like Texas and Florida. But East Daniston was right here in Ohio, only about twenty minutes south of Hadlinsburg.

Subsidized by wealthy conservative groups, PPAW applies aggressive pressure on libraries starting in the form of press releases, letters to the editor, and interviews with local news outlets; escalating to vocal and sometimes confrontational appearances at library and school board meetings; and occasionally taking the form of in-person protests in front of schools and other public facilities. In many cases, PPAW members have succeeded in taking control of entire school and library boards by getting themselves elected to office with promises to—in their words—"protect our children."

Current PPAW challenges to East Daniston's public library system include the following titles:

Jessie's eyes grew wide as she glanced through the absurdly long list of challenged books, particularly the children's books, almost all of which were on the shelves in her own department. While a few of them could be considered inappropriate for all but the most mature teens, those were not shelved where young children could find them. There wasn't anything remotely objectionable in any of the rest of them, and parents like Dean always had the right to veto a choice made by their own children. To remove these books outright was, in Jessie's opinion, an overreaction and a dangerous, slippery slope. She remembered a meme she'd seen on social media recently: "The book banners are never the good guys." Jessie agreed.

She read on:

We applaud the statement from library administrators in East

Daniston assuring us that they have no intention of bowing to pressure from this or any organization that seeks to put limits on free speech and the right of individuals to read what they want or to choose what they deem suitable for their families.

The Board and I will keep you apprised of any further developments, but we want you to know that the official position in Hadlinsburg is the same as in East Daniston: We will not allow a small number of individuals, no matter how vocal or well-funded, to dictate what books are available to the citizens of Hadlinsburg.

Without even pausing to close the browser, Jessie got up and strode across the library, her steps muffled by the carpeted yellow-brick road that led from the children's section to the more sedate blue-and-brown flooring in the adult area. Head Librarian Allison Franklin was in her late sixties, with a full head of straight, dark brown hair that Jessie suspected had been dyed for a long time. She'd recently had a hip replacement and was walking with a cane, which she told anyone who would listen was "only temporary." At the moment, she was seated at her desk on the phone with the door closed, but holding one finger up, she indicated through the glass to Jessie that she was almost done. Jessie paced in a tight circle outside the office.

"I suppose you're coming about that email from the director," Allison said, cane in hand, as she opened the door to let Jessie in. She sat back down with a grimace and gestured for Jessie to sit as well.

Jessie perched nervously on the edge of the chair. "Yes. I don't mind telling you I'm worried."

"I understand where you're coming from, but I want to set your mind at ease. So far, we've heard nothing about this group here in Hadlinsburg, and—"

"You *know* it's only a matter of time."

"Jessie, I don't agree. East Daniston has a totally different demographic makeup. They're a formerly majority-white town that has seen huge growth in the past five years, adding a large minority population. If you've studied the strategies of these groups, you'll see organizations like

PPAW target towns where the established population feels threatened by changes to the status quo. Our population is already much more balanced and stable, and that makes us far less of a target."

"But these books they want removed, they—"

"You know," Allison went on, as she often did, without acknowledging Jessie's objection, "in most cases, when groups like PPAW make challenges, the people making the challenge haven't actually read the books in question. It ends up being a real PR disaster for them when that gets pointed out." Allison shifted uncomfortably in her chair, stretching out her leg in front of her with a stifled groan. "Trust me, Jessie, we're prepared if these folks start knocking at our door. They won't be getting away with anything." She glanced at the time on her desktop. "You've got a bunch of preschoolers coming in soon, don't you? I think you'd better get ready for story time.

"And leave the worrying to me, OK?"

Not entirely satisfied, Jessie nodded and went back to her department to welcome the families for story time. In the noise, excitement, and happy chaos of introducing a new group of children to one of her favorite books her concerns were soon forgotten.

Four

"Mama, Mama! Guess what!" Eli threw himself into Jessie's arms the minute he reached the Marshalls' foyer.

"Oof! Whoa, back up, Eli. What's so important?"

"Quentin and I are gonna be in the same class again this year! Mrs. Marshall said so."

"What?" Taken aback, Jessie looked to Trish for an explanation. There were three second-grade classes in Hadlinsburg Elementary, and class assignments wouldn't be distributed for another two weeks, right before the start of school.

"Surprise!" Trish said, throwing her hands in the air with a flourish. She settled them back on her hips with a self-satisfied smile. "I knew you'd be thrilled."

Jessie did not yet have enough information about the situation to be thrilled, so for now she simply asked, "But how do you know?"

"You know I'm in tight with the folks in the front office, particularly Janie Morton. Well, I *happened* to mention how great it would be if Quentin and Eli could stay together for at least another year, and wouldn't it be *wonderful* if they could both be in Miss Walbert's class. Janie called me on the down-low today, and here we are!"

Eli and Quentin, a slight boy with wide brown eyes and a fringe of dark blond hair, grabbed each other by the wrists and started swinging themselves around. "Yea, Miss Walbert! Yea, Miss Walbert!" they sang as they spun.

Jessie frowned, and not only because she was afraid the boys would crash into a wall, the table in the foyer with a vintage Lenox vase, or her. She was acquainted with Miss Walbert, a young and energetic local who had three years of teaching under her belt, and supposed she was a good enough teacher, but she and Cassandra had had conversations with another second-grade teacher, Mrs. Donohue, and thought her class would be a better fit for Eli: The woman was more established in her profession, more disciplined, and seemed to take her job more seriously. "Trish, I—"

"No need to thank me, Jessie, we both know how important Eli and Quentin are to each other. Frankly," she lowered her voice and leaned in to whisper in Jessie's ear, "I'd never hear the end of it from Quentin if the boys weren't together, and this makes things more pleasant for everyone, don't you agree?"

Eli yelled goodbye to Quentin, and Jessie gave a halfhearted gesture to Trish as they left the house.

"Are you sure you want to be in Miss Walbert's class, buddy?" Jessie asked, hoping for a negative reply.

"Oh, yeah. It's gonna be fun."

Fun was important, of course, in second grade, but Jessie hoped that he would come out of the year with a more solid grasp on math, which was his weak spot. She wondered if she could make the switch without upsetting the status quo, but knowing Eli, it was unlikely. Besides, she suspected that Cass would tell her to relax and stop her constant over-thinking—which was, of course, easier said than done.

Sunday afternoon was the annual firefighter-police softball game, and Cassandra was excited to have her whole family attend this year. The prior summer, two-year-old Micah had been suffering from an ear infection, and with no one available to keep an eye on Eli, Cassandra had gone to play alone. Her game-changing stolen base existed only in the stories the department told about it afterward and in some YouTube videos posted by spectators who happened to catch the action. As she packed up a tote filled with day-out necessities—juice boxes, crackers, and grapes as well as a change of clothes for Micah, just in case—Jessie warned Cass of the challenges of keeping a preschooler and a six-year-old happy during a long day that didn't revolve around them and required them to stay seated in one place.

"I'm just saying, if you see us getting up to leave, it has nothing to do with you, your department, or the quality of the play or players."

"Understood," Cassandra said, dropping a kiss on Jessie's lips as she headed out the door with her equipment. "See you at the game."

By some miracle, Jessie was able to wrangle two unusually cooperative boys into the car and then to herd them clanging up the already-packed metal bleachers at the high school field where the game would soon be played. Sitting with familiar fire department spouses and their children helped a lot, as did the fact that Cassandra was only three players into the lineup in the bottom of the first. The promise of hot dogs after they'd had a chance to see Mommy at bat was added incentive.

"There she is!" Jessie said, as the boys jumped up and down at their seats.

"Mommy! Mommy!" they both yelled amid whoops and cheers from the department supporters. At the batter's box, Cassandra turned and waved at her family, blowing kisses at them.

The commotion grew louder as Cassandra hit a double on the first pitch and rounded first on her way to second base.

"Woo, you go, Caaasseeee!" screamed Jessie.

"Run, Mommy, run!" shouted Eli.

"Let's go Mets!" yelled Micah. "Let's go Mets!"

Jessie, pulled up short mid-shout, looked down at Micah. He was very engaged, watching the action on the field and seemingly unfazed by his mother's confusion or the amusement of the adults close enough to hear him.

"Hey, kid!" bellowed a beefy man, a retired cop, who sat two rows in front of them. He grinned at Micah and gestured at him with his beer. "We're Reds fans in this town!"

"At least he's not cheering for the Pirates!" someone behind them responded to laughter all around.

"I have no idea where he got that from," Jessie, red-faced, said to Angela Barlow, seated beside them with her seven-year-old, Oliver. Angela's husband Pete was one of Cassandra's closest friends at the firehouse, and the two families got together from time to time for pizza nights or ice cream outings. Oliver and Eli were elbowing each other. It was all good fun, of course, until someone got hurt, so without saying a word, each mother pulled their son gently in the opposite direction.

"Well, it's nice that at least one of your boys is a baseball fan, I guess."

"But is he, though?" Jessie mumbled. Micah continued reciting rhythmically to himself: "Let's go Mets. Let's go Mets. Let's go Mets."

As play continued, Jessie considered Micah's response to her and Cassandra watching baseball on TV. Sometimes he'd stay for a couple of at-bats, but usually he'd wander away to play with his toys. He'd rarely last a full inning, only when he was particularly sleepy and wanted to cuddle with his mothers and his stuffed dog on the couch. And while the Cincinnati Reds and the New York Mets did play each other several times a season, she couldn't recall a Mets home game where Micah might have stayed long enough to hear the chant.

Her thoughts were interrupted when Eli reminded her that they'd been promised lunch, and since the inning was now over—stranding Cassandra on third and another player on first—she agreed, taking each boy by the hand to lead them to the concession stand. Assuming that Cassandra couldn't have heard Micah's chant over the roar of the spectators, she'd have to discuss it with her at home . . . and maybe find out whether Micah had a secret fascination with something other than firetrucks.

"You're shitting me." Cassandra took a big swig of iced tea.

"I absolutely am not. He said, 'Let's go Mets.' No, he shouted it. Several times in fact. Ask Angela. Ask anyone who was sitting near us; they all heard it!"

Freshly showered, her hair still damp, Cassandra was standing barefoot in the kitchen after the game. The firefighters had beaten the police department 8-6, and she was feeling pretty good about it, although, as predicted, her family had only lasted a couple of innings. Jessie had put Micah down for a much-needed nap and set up Eli in the den with a movie. Now she was after some answers.

"So," Jessie continued, "all I want to know is: Has Micah been watching baseball with you, and if not, can you explain where he might have picked up an affinity for the Mets?"

"No and no. Maybe he picked it up during one of the TV broadcasts? I mean, I don't remember every moment of every game. Maybe there was a commercial for the Mets that used the chant, which you have to admit is pretty catchy. Anyway, I think it's funny as hell. What in the *world* are you so worried about?"

"I'm not *worried* about anything. I think it's . . . odd, that's all. I mean, between the nightmares and the imaginary friend, I don't want him turning into the—the weird kid who nobody wants to play with."

For a too-long period of time in middle school, Jessie had been that kid. She hadn't been really comfortable in her own skin until she accepted that she was gay. Then she found her group, her people, who were still her friends decades later. Too bad they all lived so far away, most of them still in the New York Metro area; Zoom calls could only provide so much support.

"He's got plenty of friends at daycare, right?" Cassandra asked. "And the teachers there think he's doing fine, right?"

"Right, but he'll be starting preschool in a little over a week. Everything is going to be different! He's going to have to make new friends, get used to a more structured environment . . ."

"Maybe," Cass said, finishing off the rest of her tea and putting the glass in the dishwasher, "this isn't really about Micah at all. Maybe *you're* just upset because our baby is about to start going to school, and you're afraid he won't need you so much anymore."

Jessie hadn't considered that she might be feeling particularly emotional about Micah growing up. She remembered how she'd cried the day Eli started preschool, but having an infant at home, she still felt indispensable. Maybe that was it. With Micah developing his own personality—strange as it currently was—maybe she was afraid of becoming less important to him, and to her family.

Cassandra read her expression and nodded. "Well, then, I think you can find plenty of other things to worry about."

Facepalming, Jessie said, "Oh, come to think of it, I already do."

"And what is that?"

"Our friend Trish has pulled some strings and gotten Quentin and Eli placed together in Miss Walbert's class."

"Oh. And we were hoping for Donohue, right?"

"Right. So, do we make a fuss and get Eli moved out, offending Trish and upsetting both Quentin and Eli, or do we suck it up and count this as a potentially lost year?"

"Jess," Cassandra said, moving to put her arms around Jessie's waist. "He's only six . . ."

"Nearly seven."

"Nearly seven, but it's *second grade*. Hardly AP-level stuff. Is there anything at all he needs to learn in second grade that you and your infinite educational resources can't fill in?"

"I suppose not." She slumped against Cassandra, feeling both defeated and somehow relieved.

"And anyway, didn't you tell me right off the bat that you didn't intend to request a particular teacher because you hated it when schools were forced to play favorites?"

"Yeah, but then Trish did."

"So that's on Trish. How about we count it as the way the chips fell, how the universe worked this time around, and move onto other things? OK? Good. Let's chill for a while, because you'll be pleased to know that your baby will still need you the minute he gets up from his nap."

"Oh! While we're on the subject of Trish . . ." Jessie pulled away and stepped into the foyer to grab the tote she'd carried to the ballgame. After rooting around in it, she withdrew the small, white plastic bag, which she'd rediscovered while releasing Micah from his car seat. "Think fast!" she said, and tossed it to Cassandra, who caught it with ease. "*A little somethin'-somethin'* to make your skin glow. Are you not grateful?"

Cassandra made a face and lofted the bag, unopened, right back at her. Jessie's catch was not nearly as graceful. "Thank her for me, will you?"

FIVE

Thursday evening after dinner, with a wink at Jessie, Cassandra said, "Hey, let's all watch the Reds baseball game together tonight." She plumped up the couch pillows and turned on the TV.

"Oh, boy, Mommy, who are they playing?" Jessie exaggerated her line like an eight-year-old in a school play. They both glanced at Micah, who was lying on the floor on his belly, leaning on his elbows, leafing through yet another book about fire trucks, a new release that Jessie had brought home from work the day before.

"I think it's . . . yes, it is: the New York Mets!" Cassandra announced with the same exaggerated intonation. Micah looked up at her, blinked, and went back to his book.

Jessie shrugged at Cassandra's questioning expression.

"Do we have to?" whined Eli. He was playing on the tablet again.

With a glance at the time, Jessie told him, "Yes. Tablet time is over in five minutes. You can watch the ballgame with us, or you can read quietly, or color, or play with your action figures."

"Fine," he moped, turning his back on them and cradling the tablet. Jessie set a timer for five minutes.

"Come on up, Micah," Jessie said, patting the space between her and Cassandra. Micah dropped the book and climbed onto the couch. He leaned against Cassandra, clutching his stuffed dog and from time to time biting its ear.

It was a Reds home game, so it was unlikely that Micah would be hearing a chant of "Let's go Mets" from the crowd. Nevertheless, Cassandra and Jessie were hoping to see if he would react in some way.

When the alarm sounded to indicate that his five minutes were up, Eli set the tablet on the coffee table and climbed up on the other side of Jessie. After a while, so cozy and comfortable with her family around her —and not particularly interested in the game—she closed her eyes. Without even realizing she had fallen asleep, Jessie woke up abruptly when Cassandra tapped her urgently on her shoulder. "Babe. Jess!"

"Wha . . . ? Huh?"

Cassandra tilted her head toward Micah, who was still watching the game. He was mumbling something to himself, and Jessie leaned in to listen.

"Ag. Ag. Ag-ba-ya-ni, Ag-ba-ya-ni. Where Ag-ba-ya-ni? Left?"

Was he even speaking English? Jessie debated asking Micah what he was saying but decided to see what would happen next.

"Al-fonzo a' second," Micah added. "Ventura tird."

"What is he talking about?" Jessie said over his head to Cassandra.

"Sounds like a lineup: Alfonzo at second base, Ventura at third."

Jessie looked at the screen. She hadn't been paying attention; maybe she missed the players' names?

"And no," Cassandra said, "none of those players are on either of these teams."

"Pizza! Pizza catcher." Micah chuckled to himself. "Hahaha! Pizza catcher."

As a fascinated Jessie watched their son, Cassandra was typing on her phone. "Holy sh—cow!" she exclaimed.

"What?"

Still staring at her phone, Cassandra intoned, "Benny Agbayani,

Edgardo Alfonzo, Robin Ventura, and Mike *Piazza* all played for the Mets." She turned her phone toward Jessie. "Over twenty years ago."

They both stared at Micah, who had grown silent but was still smiling.

"Mama, can I go now?" Eli broke in. "This is boring."

"Sure, honey," Jessie said, distracted. "But no more tablet. Find something else to do."

"Ugh." He slid from the couch and, after some aimless wandering, sat down at the Lego table.

"Know what else is weird?" Cassandra asked.

"I'm almost afraid to ask."

"The lineup. He's right about everyone: Agbayani played left field; Alfonzo was on second; Ventura was on third—"

"And Mike Piazza was the catcher," Jessie murmured. "I vaguely remember my dad talking about him." Jessie's father, who'd loved an underdog and had been a long-suffering Mets fan, had tried to interest her in the team when she was growing up in New Jersey. Though she'd adored him, she didn't share her father's interest in sports, and neither did her mother. Nevertheless, Jessie had humored him, watching endless replays of the 1986 World Series and keeping him company whenever there was any sort of local game on: the Mets, the Jets, the Devils. Unlike Cassandra, Jessie had a lot of fond memories of her parents and missed them with an ache that never seemed to diminish with time. They had died within months of each other before she'd even met Cass.

Jessie wondered what her father would have made of Micah's sudden fascination with the Mets and decided he would have found it endearing. No doubt he would have been buying mini jerseys, mitts, and caps for birthdays and Christmas and waiting for the day when he could teach the boys how to pitch, catch, and hit. She lamented afresh that he and her mother had never had the opportunity to meet her little family and that the boys had never known—would never know—the joys of doting grandparents.

On TV, a Mets batter hit a home run, and despite the lack of reaction from the hometown Reds crowd, Micah started chanting, "Let's go Mets! Let's go Mets!"

"And there it is," Cassandra said. "Wow."

"Mm-hm. I think the stuff with the players is more interesting, though. I mean, he could have learned the chant from a game or a commercial, but how the heck did he know about the lineup?"

"Why don't we ask him?" Smoothing a hand over Micah's hair, Cassandra said, "Hey, Micah. Hey."

Micah finally tore his attention from the TV and turned toward her. "How do you know so much about the Mets, huh, sweetie? About Agbayani, and Ventura, and the positions they played?"

His eyes wandered the room as if he were thinking. Finally, he said, "Keef. Keef likes baseball. He likes de Mets. He goes wif Dad."

"Whose dad?" Cassandra asked, sitting up straighter. They had always been clear with the boys that they had two moms, giving them the information in an age-appropriate, matter-of-fact way.

All Micah would say in reply was, "Dad has tickets for *all* the games. Home games. Shea."

Shea Stadium had been demolished long before Micah was born, but that's not what attracted Cassandra's attention. "Jessie," she said, puzzled, "did you notice the . . ."

Ignoring Cass for the moment, Jessie was determined to ask the question that had been on her mind since Micah had first started talking about this imaginary friend: "Micah, who's Keith? How do you know him?"

But Micah had lost interest in the conversation and, without answering, climbed down from the couch. "Go potty," he said. He didn't mention Keith or the Mets for the rest of the evening.

That night in bed, Jessie stared at the ceiling, thinking. She could tell by Cassandra's breathing that she hadn't yet fallen asleep either. Clearly they both had something on their minds.

She was right. "Hey, Jess?"

"Hm?" Jessie turned toward Cass, who rolled over to face her. In the dim light, Jessie couldn't see the beloved moss-green eyes or the too-sharp nose. But she could still see the outline: the narrow chin, the prominent cheekbones. The mussed-up hair.

"Did you notice anything in particular when Micah said, 'Dad has tickets to all the games'?" Cassandra asked.

"You mean the way he pronounced his *th* sound?"

"Exactly. From the moment he started talking, he couldn't pronounce *th*. And now all of a sudden he can?"

"But he didn't do it for the rest of the night. So maybe it's a fluke." Jessie thought for a moment. "Y'know, my mom had a friend whose son said a single, clear word when he was eighteen months old and then didn't say anything else for another whole year. Maybe it's like that. Or maybe he's starting to find the sound, and we'll begin to notice him using it more."

They were silent for a few moments, and then Jessie said, "I'm still a little shook by the whole Mets thing, though. An accurate lineup from twenty years ago at a stadium that no longer exists. How did he *know*?"

"He didn't know; Keith knew."

"As if that's any better!"

Cassandra whispered in a dramatic voice, "Jessie!"

"What?"

"Do you think our son is *possessed*?"

The two of them burst into loud giggles. The situation was so absurd, they couldn't help themselves.

But they were still left without an explanation which didn't sit well with either of them.

Within the week, the baseball enigma faded into the background as their family became focused on getting the boys ready for the start of school. There were last-minute supplies to buy, the first day outfits to settle upon (little-boy taste to gently guide and perhaps veto). They had received the official notification stating that Eli was in Miss Walberg's class; it still rankled. But Jessie's larger concern remained Micah: His ability to make new friends who weren't firefighter-fixated; his recent strange conversations.

"Preschool is going to be so much fun, Micah," Jessie said, trying to draw him out over dinner the night before the start of school. "Think about all the things you'll do, all the friends you're going to make!"

"I'm gonna have my very best friend with me in class," Eli said with glee. "I don't have to make more friends."

Jessie didn't like the sound of that. Neither did Cassandra, who responded, "I hope you'll rethink that, Eli. We can all use all the friends we can get." She and Jessie could attest to that: They had only a handful of friends, of varying levels of intimacy, in Hadlinsburg despite years of reaching out. To Jessie, a bit of an introvert, it didn't matter, until it did. Particularly when it meant no board-game afternoons, no girls' days out . . . or nights in with wine and chocolate. Trish might offer some of that entertainment, but it often came with a price: increased pressure to join her MLM, for example, or the presence of her other friends, full of frequently mean-spirited gossip about people Jessie didn't know (and sometimes did, which made it worse). She was friendly with her coworkers, but they were mostly older women who were at a different point in their lives, and they didn't often socialize. The Mommy-and-Me groups she'd joined when Micah was first born were useful for his socialization but somehow not for hers. On rare occasions she admitted to herself that she was a little lonely.

Cassandra, on the other hand, had Pete Barlow and the rest of her team. Once she'd started working as an EMT, she had a built-in group of friends, ones who literally had her back in all sorts of sometimes terrifying situations. They had their softball games and went out for beer and conversation at least once every couple of weeks.

"And what about your other friends from first grade?" Cassandra asked Eli. "Liam, and Noah, and Oliver?"

Eli shrugged. It was getting to be a habit with him when he didn't want to answer a question.

"How about you, Micah?" Jessie prompted. "Are you going to make lots of friends?"

"Maybe." Poking at a small piece of chicken nugget with his finger, he said, "I miss my boyfriend."

Cassandra put down her utensils, and Jessie lowered her water glass. They both looked at Micah, then at each other.

"Your boyfriend?" Cassandra came around from the other side of the table to sit beside him.

Micah nodded with his whole upper body. "My boyfriend. I miss him."

"Dork," Eli said with a rude snort, as he nibbled on a baby carrot.

"Hush, Eli! No name-calling! Do you have a boyfriend, Micah?" Jessie asked. Normalizing the conversation seemed to be the best option she had. "What's his name?"

"Joey."

"Do you know Joey from daycare?" His last day had been less than a week ago.

"No, from work."

Work? "Where's work?"

"De firehouse."

Then it clicked. This "Joey" was part of the story Micah told himself about Keith. She had no idea that a child could produce so many details for an imaginary friend and wondered if this indicated an underlying issue for which she might need to research in some child psychology books. "Oh, so Joey is *Keith's* boyfriend?"

"Uh-huh."

"And is Joey a fireman too?"

"Firefighter," he corrected. "Uh-huh."

"So what's Joey like?"

"He has nice blond hair. An' he cooks."

"Oh, that's fun! Does he have a favorite meal to cook?"

"Chili. For de firehouse."

"That sounds delicious."

"It's yummy."

In his short life, Micah had never eaten chili. He wouldn't even try it, shook his head vehemently at it, and called it "icky." He felt the same way about anything else cooked with beans, or any other food with a texture that didn't match his tastes. "Keith really likes Joey's chili, huh?"

"Keef loves chili." He laughed. "It makes him fart."

Jessie and Cassandra couldn't help but laugh along. But underneath their amusement, they were both worried. Of course, in their household, the idea of Micah having a boyfriend, however premature, wasn't cause for much alarm. At school, though, and combined with the other anomalies—his unusual obsession, the way Micah kept switching between his own personality and that of Keith—it could be a recipe for conflict.

Later, as the boys slept and she and Cassandra sat side by side on the couch in the den, idly rubbing their feet against each other's, Jessie looked up from the novel she was reading and asked, "Does Micah know a boy named Joey? Maybe from one of the play groups?" She thought she already knew the answer, but perhaps Cass knew something she didn't.

Cassandra didn't even pause the show she was streaming on her tablet, immediately shaking her head. "Not a single one. All the boys in his age group have names like, um, Braydon, Cooper, Lucas, and, uh, Maverick. There are actually *two* of those, can you believe it? No plain old Joeys among them."

"That's what I figured."

"So, let me get this straight, if you'll pardon the pun." Now she put the tablet down on her lap as the show rattled on and turned her body to face Jessie. "Micah has a gay imaginary friend? Who's in a relationship?"

"Apparently."

"Wow, and we had to meet each other through an app!" Her lips curled up in a smile.

Jessie rolled her eyes. "Can you be serious for a minute?"

"Sorry, babe. Look, I'm as concerned as you are. We seem to be at a really difficult stage with Micah. It is hard to understand him sometimes. But remember his terrible twos?"

"Ugh, how could I forget?" The defiance, the tantrums. The *screaming*. Jessie thought they'd never survive. But then he seemed to age out of it, and he was once again their delightful little boy.

"Well, we got through that OK with our sanity intact. I'm hoping that once he starts preschool and gets involved in his daily routine, maybe things will smooth out. Maybe he'll spend more time with real friends instead of imaginary ones." She picked up her tablet again, but Jessie wasn't done.

"Cass," she said, brushing her hair back behind her ears. Shoulder length, it was too short for a proper ponytail or bun, but it was long enough to get annoying. She was constantly wavering between letting it grow or getting it cut short like Cassandra's. "What if it's not his age or his imagination? What if there's something else going on with him?"

Giving up on her show, Cassandra turned off the tablet and set it on the coffee table. "I can't imagine what that would be."

Was that the problem? Jessie fretted. *Was it a failure of imagination on their part? Could they be missing something important?* "Do you think we need to call the pediatrician?"

"And say what, exactly? 'Doctor Stafford, I'm concerned: Micah somehow knows the lineup for the 2001 Mets.' What do you suppose she could do with that?"

"I know that sounds ridiculous . . ."

"My take is that we should roll with it. Worry about it if he starts saying something really—I don't know—disturbing. If he seems distressed."

"You mean, like his nightmares? Night terrors are one thing, and we've already talked about those with Dr. Stafford. I get that. But night-mares are another thing entirely, remember?"

"We have no evidence that the nightmares are related to Keith. Meanwhile, big day tomorrow for the boys. Let's focus on making it as normal as possible for them. Agreed?"

"Agreed."

Six

The first two weeks of school for the boys went as smoothly as their mothers could have wished, though Jessie—Cassandra's "favorite worrywart," as she lovingly labeled her—did speak to Micah's teacher after the first couple of days, gently probing to see if her son had made any *unusual* remarks. To her relief, the teacher, Miss Kira, declared that she found Micah to be like any other three-year-old, if perhaps a little shy and self-conscious. But she assured Jessie that the other children were trying to get him to play, and he was coming out of his shell little by little.

They had no such concerns with Eli, who came flying home each day claiming school was "so much fun." Considering the topic closed, Jessie didn't reiterate her concern to Cassandra that Miss Walbert's class wasn't going to benefit Eli much. She did get a copy of the second-grade curriculum, to make sure that Eli was getting all the appropriate instruction amid all the fun. Of course, having Quentin over Tuesday, Wednesday, and Thursday afternoons was another bonus. In gratitude for all the summer days Eli had spent over at the Marshall's house, Jessie and Cassandra agreed to watch Quentin three times a week so Trish could take care of "business-related activities": i.e., have her MLM parties and product pushes. She was popular enough in town to distribute her two younger children to friends' houses while Alanna attended field hockey practice, but Quentin insisted that *only* Eli would do.

"Joined at the hip, those two!" Trish said with a laugh when they made their arrangement. "Are you sure you can manage it?"

"Cassandra and I have arranged our schedules so that one of us is always home after school. It's really no problem at all."

"Well, thanks again for agreeing to have him. You know how it is: happy Quentin, happy mama!"

"It's the least we could do, Trish, for all your help this summer."

To be fair, what Trish had said about Eli during the past couple of months was equally true when the positions were reversed. Eli was a far more cooperative child when Quentin was around. They had a snack, did their homework—such as it was (usually a couple of simple worksheets that they both coasted through, pencils flying, without much thought)—at the kitchen table, and then played cooperatively in the den until Trish or, rarely, Dean, came to get Quentin.

It was a successful arrangement for both families.

Until it wasn't.

"Hello, Jessie." They were only into the second week of the school year, and it was Friday evening. Jessie had just put the boys to bed. It was unusual enough to get a call from Dean Marshall, but the chilliness of his phone manner was out of character for someone who managed his father's successful retail establishments—the town's largest furniture store among them—and prided himself on his people skills. Even when he was actively being obnoxious to Cassandra on a call, his distaste was always couched in a pleasant, almost smarmy voice. "Plausible deniability," Jessie called it; Cass called it hypocrisy.

He was now dropping all pretense of politeness.

So, Jessie was immediately on alert. She dealt with the public enough to recognize when an unpleasant conversation was about to begin and was filled with dread.

"Hi, Dean. What's up?"

Without any of the usual social pleasantries, Dean dove right in: "You know, Quentin told me the most *interesting* thing when I got home from work tonight."

"Oh? What's that?"

"He told me that Micah says he has . . . a *boyfriend*!" He said it with an air of both disbelief and distaste. Jessie's stomach clenched. "I thought he must have misheard, but no, Quentin repeated that Micah told him, and I quote: '*Your hair is like my boyfriend's.*'"

"I see."

"Yeah, well, *I* don't see. I *can't* see how that can be a thing. So, I thought I'd call to see if there was some simple explanation for such a frankly ridiculous statement."

"Yes, there is." Although she didn't owe Dean any sort of explanation, particularly none that would make it sound as if she disapproved of Micah's healthy emotional life, Jessie felt compelled to set him straight in this one instance. "Micah is talking about his imaginary friend." *You might understand that if you had any sort of imagination,* Jessie added to herself.

"Uh-huh, so Micah has an imaginary *boyfriend*?"

"No." She rubbed her forehead. How exactly was she to clarify this? The truth was every bit as hard for a person like Dean to understand as his initial interpretation of it was. But there was no way around it. "Micah's imaginary friend *Keith* has a boyfriend."

"*Keith*, is it? Charming." His voice indicated he thought it anything but. "As if that makes it any better. And where did Micah get the idea that *Keith* could have a *boyfriend*?" He gave a humorless laugh. "The poor kid. No wonder he's confused. I mean, with a family like yours."

Jessie sniffed in a breath. Hard. "What's that supposed to mean?"

"I mean," Dean came back in the most patronizing voice possible, "with no masculine figure in his life to teach him what it's like to be *a real man.*"

"A real—For heaven's sake, Dean, he's *three years old*. A child!"

"Exactly! It's *unnatural*, Jessie! Our children should not be raised thinking this is normal."

Hearing the disgust in Dean's voice, Jessie seethed. How *dare* he!

But it was about to get worse. Before she could think of a suitable response, Dean added, "At least, not *my* children. It's clear to me now that you're bringing your children up to be deviants just like you and your 'wife.'" Jessie could hear the air quotes.

"*Deviants? Excuse me!*" She was now breathless with anger.

"And I particularly don't want the people of this town thinking that *my Quentin* is some kind of *faggot* for spending so much time with Eli."

It was as if she'd been slapped; tears sprang to her eyes. Jessie couldn't recall hearing the "f-word" from anyone in years and dared to hope that her town, if not the country as a whole, had moved beyond it. She opened her mouth to push back, to tell him how offensive, how hurtful he was being, but by the time she could summon the words up from her roiled gut to the front of her mouth, he spoke again:

"So, I've made other afterschool arrangements with my parents. And Quentin won't be playing with Eli at all anymore."

"What?" Jessie became light-headed; Eli would be crushed. As furious as she was at Dean, as repulsive as she found him, especially now, she found no fault with Quentin, who was always polite to her and Cassandra and big-brother friendly toward Micah. "You're OK with crushing Quentin because you . . ."

"I just don't think Quentin should be exposed to such perverted ideas. I overlooked your so-called *marriage* because the boys seemed young enough not to notice the difference. But now . . . Well, I've changed my mind. Quentin is older now, old enough to understand right and wrong, and he's asking all sorts of inappropriate questions. I don't want him growing up to think that's OK. To think that *any of it* is OK."

"Any of what? You're talking about *my family*!" Another thought occurred, and with a breaking heart Jessie struggled to articulate it. "So, does—does Trish agree with you? Does she know you're going to separate the boys?"

"Trish is way too forgiving, in my opinion. Too soft-hearted for her own good, and for the kids' own good. And speaking of kids: To think *you of all people are* responsible for recommending books to *children*! Well, I'm sorry, Jessie, but that's going to change soon. It's a dangerous situation, and I can't in good conscience allow it to continue."

"What's that supposed to mean?" Jessie asked for the second time in as many minutes. "What say could *you* possibly have in—"

"I've reached out to PPAW; you've heard of them, right? They're exactly the group to deal with a situation like this one. They've established a group in East Daniston and were *very* excited to take my call. I've agreed to be their contact in Hadlinsburg. You'll be hearing from us."

And the line went dead.

Her chest heaving, Jessie stood looking at her phone after Dean hung up, as if hoping the device would provide her with some sort of comfort or at least sanity. With that out of the question, and still in shock, she paced around the house until she remembered that she had to get dinner on the table for the boys and put them to bed. She was able to hold herself together for their sake. But when Cassandra came home from her late shift at work, Jessie immediately started sobbing.

"And I just stood there with my jaw on the floor, Cass. I *just stood there* listening to him insult our family, taking the bullshit he was dishing out." Jessie was wrapped in Cassandra's arms on the couch, the tears flowing freely. A pile of used tissues rested on her stomach; a box of clean ones was within reach. "And using the fucking f-word to me! I should have told him to go fuck himself. I should have told him to take his homophobic shit and shove it up his ass!"

Jessie, with her pride in her considerable vocabulary, did not often resort to vulgar language, and she could feel Cass's concern in the way her arms tightened around her.

"I wish you'd have been there with me, Cass. *You* would have known what to say. I was . . . unprepared. Like always."

Resting her chin against Jessie's temple, Cassandra said, "No one is ever ready to be attacked like that, Jess. Some of us happen to be quicker on our feet than others. Remember, I've had more experience with people like Dean. Grew up with them." She swallowed audibly. "Lived with them.

"Anyway, he's always been an asshole, and you know it, but I can't stand the way he felt emboldened to say whatever he wanted."

"And after all that, after he insulted you and me, called us perverts, and insinuated that we're raising our kids wrong, he goes and says that Eli and Quentin can't play together at all anymore."

Jessie could feel Cassandra's quick intake of breath. "Well. We shouldn't be surprised, frankly. I mean, seeing as he thinks we're a bad influence and all. Goddamn." They sat in silence for a moment. "But that's for sure? He's breaking those two up? Have you spoken to Trish?"

"Are you kidding? Do you think tradwife Trish would go against Dean's decision?" They both figured they knew Trish well enough to guess the answer. "I did get this from her, though, about a half hour later." She turned her phone to show Cassandra the text from Trish, which said simply, *I'm sorry.*

"I'll bet she is. Quentin is going to be impossible to live with. Have you told Eli yet?"

"No, he was already asleep. And I'm still not sure the best way to approach it. He's going to be devastated, and he's not going to understand why." She sniffled and grabbed another clean tissue. "Poor little guy. Why should he have to suffer? It's not as if I'd be thrilled to have to interact with them to get the kids together, but still." Jessie sighed. "I wonder if it isn't time to move back east."

"What? This again?"

Jessie couldn't blame Cass for being irritated; it was an old discussion, rehashed every few months or so since they took up residence in

Hadlinsburg. Their most recent quarrel—she wouldn't call it a *fight*—had been in May, when Jessie had grumbled about the total lack of Pride Month recognition being planned in the town. It had hurt her, she'd acknowledged, that the library had never been willing to create even the sort of innocuous display that wouldn't have raised any eyebrows back in their old neighborhood in New Jersey.

"Remember when we first decided to move to Ohio?" Jessie said. "I was nervous about moving to a small town in a red state. *You* figured that being a veteran and an EMT would be enough to make people comfortable with us and our marriage, but we might as well be invisible, if not worse. Maybe we should have immediately nixed the idea of any place where we can't fly a Pride flag on our own front porch."

Cassandra pushed back, as she always did. The arguments on both sides were familiar ones.

"That front porch is on our dream house, babe. We wanted a renovated Victorian; we got a renovated Victorian." Cassandra played on Jessie's admitted weakness for gingerbread trim and original stained-glass windows. "Do you think we could have afforded one—never mind in such great condition—in any of the major metropolitan markets on our salaries?

"And speaking of—you wanted a library job; you got a library job," she continued. "And I found a station where I can not only be myself but really belong. I love my crew, and I'm happy here. Two perfect jobs, one perfect house.

"It's a diverse community. Well, ethnically diverse, anyway." It was true that Hadlinsburg had a sizable Black population and a handful of Hispanic families, but, compared to where they'd come from, *diverse* was a bit of a stretch. While there were at least a dozen churches of every imaginable denomination, there were no synagogues, no mosques, no Hindu temples. Jessie knew of one Sikh family. "And the boys have good teachers."

Would they be moving Eli into Mrs. Donohue's class after all now? *Another question,* Jessie added to the list.

"Up till now, have you felt at all uncomfortable?" Cassandra went on. "Because Dean aside, I haven't. Yes, I do wish there were a more robust LGBTQ community, but it's not like we're alone here. We've got Ginny and Beth, and—"

"And Jeremy and his boyfriend . . . um . . ."

Cassandra sighed. "Nicholas. Why can't you ever remember Nicholas? Tell the truth, Jessie: Besides Dean and his parents, have you met up with anyone—anyone at all—who makes you feel unwanted?"

When she didn't answer, Cass asked again. "Have you, though?"

"It's not anyone in particular. Just a general sense. Or maybe it's me being paranoid."

Even after four years, both of them kept their ears pricked up for insults, for badly timed laughter; without thinking about it, they were always on the lookout for finger pointing and disgusted looks. PPAW and their ilk had been on Jessie's radar long before the email came from the director. She could see the situation getting worse the closer it got to home. And now it was on her doorstep.

"I mean, I think we've been fine, up until now," Jessie said, putting a brave face on it.

"That's right. Even our next-door neighbors are real friendly; every year they share their zucchini with us."

"Don't read too much into that, babe. *Everyone* always has too much zucchini."

"Well, I still love this town. I love our frou-frou house and our neighborhood and my station. I even love that ridiculous Founder's Day celebration they insist on having year after year."

"Well, sure, because you get to march in the parade."

"True. So can we agree that there's no reason to uproot ourselves and the boys?"

"But then there's Dean," Jessie reminded her. "And now PPAW. You know the group Patriot Parents Against Woke?"

"Who doesn't?" Cassandra snorted. "Idiots."

"About a month ago, I got an email from the library director that they'd established themselves in East Daniston. And now apparently they're starting a chapter here, with Dean leading the whole ugly brigade."

Cassandra drew in a hiss of breath. Her whole body tightened as if in anticipation of a skirmish. *How very like us*, Jessie thought. If a situation triggered fight or flight, she could depend that Cass's reaction to be *fight*, and her own to be *flight*.

Except in one important circumstance.

"I know, I know," Jessie said. "They're exactly the sort of people you tried to escape from by running away to join the circus."

"I have told you before," Cassandra interrupted with mock irritation; it was their little joke. "I didn't run away. I *moved on*. There's a difference. The alternative might have resulted in someone getting seriously hurt. And the *United States Air Force* is not the circus! Or at least it's a totally different kind of circus. *My* circus. But I get your point: If I wanted to live among small-minded homophobes, I could have just stayed home with good ol' Mom and Dad."

One of the things that Jessie and Cassandra had in common was that they had both lost their parents young: Jessie's to kidney disease and pancreatic cancer, and Cassandra's parents to the scourge of bigotry. Cass had gone no-contact with them the moment she enlisted; it made her far more sensitive to perceived bias than she might otherwise have been. Jessie's parents, on the other hand, had greeted her coming out at fourteen with a mild, "What took you so long? We've known for two years," and an outpouring of love and support. It angered her that Cassandra didn't have a loving family like her own, one she deserved.

"Anyway," Jessie continued, "Dean reached out to PPAW and couldn't wait to sign up. And no doubt to get Trish and all her MLM clients in on the fun. I'm telling you this because things might become more . . . difficult for us here. For a while. It's actually kind of amazing this hasn't happened sooner, given the rhetoric of certain politicians. Now it depends on how much traction they get, how many quiet bigots have been biding their time to come out from under their rocks." She shivered. "It's a little scary."

"I suppose we should cancel our big plans for a Drag Queen Story Hour, then?"

"Hah. You joke, but I've always wanted to start one of those. But Hadlinsburg has never seemed ready for it, and certainly not now." She took a deep breath. "Hey, have you ever heard Micah mention Keith's boyfriend while Quentin was around?"

"Once. But I heard what Quentin heard. There was a movie on in the den, a Pixar thing that Eli had chosen, and Micah was lying with his head against his big blue pillow with his dog, kind of half paying attention because it wasn't one of his shows. He was talking to himself, making random remarks that had nothing to do with the story . . ."

"About what? About Keith?"

"Nothing that I could decipher. Anyway, Eli and Quentin were getting annoyed with him, telling him to be quiet. I came to stand by the doorway to make sure it didn't turn into an all-out brawl, when Micah suddenly turned to Quentin and said, 'Your hair's like my boyfriend.'"

"That was it, that's what Dean mentioned. How did the boys react?"

"At that moment? I didn't hear any commotion, so I figured they'd shrugged it off. Then I remembered that we needed more hand soap in the powder room, and I walked away to refill it. I guess it must've stuck with Quentin a lot more than with Eli. But of course, in our household, it would have seemed less unusual." After a pause, Cassandra added, "I'm sorry. I guess I should have warned you . . ."

"Warned me about what? Don't be silly; we can't spend our lives parsing everything that comes out of our kids' mouths."

"In the meantime, what are we supposed to do about Eli and Quentin?"

Jessie shook her head. She had no idea what to tell their son. As hurt and confused as he was bound to be, she didn't want him taking it out on his little brother.

Which, of course, is exactly what happened when she told him the next day.

"It's all your fault!" Eli screamed at Micah, who flinched and started to cry. "I hate you!" He lifted his hand to hit Micah, but Cassandra slid in and intercepted him easily.

"Hold on there, Eli," she said. "We never, ever hit. You know that. And Micah hasn't done anything wrong."

"He did! He made Quentin hate me, an' now I hate *him*." He was sobbing. "It's his fault!"

"It wasn't Micah who said you can't play with Quentin anymore, Eli." Jessie was angry, but not at her sons. "And it wasn't Quentin, either. It was his father who made that decision."

"But it's 'cause Micah was being stupid and talking about his boyfriend."

Jessie stiffened. "How do you know that?"

"'Cause after he said it a second time, Quentin said, 'That's sick. Boys can't have boyfriends.' An' I said, 'They can, too, if they want! My moms said so.' An' he said, 'Well, my dad says they can't. He says, that's sick.' An' now I can't play with him!" Red-faced, Eli looked at his brother again and yelled, "Go away, Micah! I hate you!" before breaking down into inconsolable tears.

Hearing the conversation repeated, Jessie was near tears herself. *That's sick*, Quentin had said. What a thing to teach your children.

Cassandra swept Eli up and carried him, sobbing, upstairs. Jessie knelt beside Micah, who was now also wailing. He wiped his eyes and nose on his sleeve and bit down on Dot's ear, sucking on it.

"Are you OK, sweetie? You know Eli doesn't *really* hate you. He's just sad and mad right now, and he's not really sure who to be mad at." She grabbed a napkin and dampened it, wiping away the tears and snot.

"Boys can have boyfriends. Keef's boyfriend is Joey."

"That's right, Micah. Boys can have boyfriends if they want, and girls can have girlfriends, like me and Mommy. But some people are afraid of that." *Why, I'll never know.* "Quentin's daddy is one of those people. It's silly, isn't it? But it can make people unhappy, like Eli is now. We have to give him a little time to get back to himself."

Jessie, pressing Micah against her, hoped it would be soon. Life was going to be difficult for a while.

She might have despaired if she knew what was coming the next day.

SEVEN

"It was dark," Micah announced, out of the blue. "We couldn't see."

"What's the matter, little dude?" Jessie, still in her nightgown and slippers, shuffled over to where Micah was standing in the middle of the den.

She and Cassandra were grateful for the small mercy of Dean's vicious call coming on a Friday night so the family could have the weekend to plan their strategy for the next school week. Their Saturday had been ruined—with both boys crying and no one feeling much like eating all day—and the night a misery, between Eli's late-night sobbing, Micah's most recent, intense nightmare, and their mothers dealing with the emotional fallout from both. Everyone was exhausted, and Sunday wasn't shaping up to be much better.

Jessie brushed away a couple of stray Legos and knelt beside her boy, who up until that moment had been leafing through a picture book. Transfixed in front of the television, the book forgotten, Micah raised his hand, pointing at the screen.

"That's where I died."

Jessie's head whipped around to the muted TV, where the news was playing some archival footage of the 2001 attack on the World Trade Center. In the turmoil of the day before, she'd forgotten today's date: It was September 11.

"Cassandra," Jessie called out. "CASS-*AN*-DRA!"

A clatter came from the kitchen as Cassandra, who was making breakfast, dropped whatever she'd been holding to rush into the den.

"What's wrong?" she said as she reached Jessie and Micah.

Jessie looked from the screen to Micah and then to Cassandra, wide-eyed. On the TV, the Tower was collapsing into a volcanic cloud of gray smoke; bystanders were running, panicked and screaming, in the opposite direction. It was horrific. She'd been in elementary school when the Towers fell, and her parents had tried to shield her from the worst of it. But in the years that ensued, she'd seen countless reports on TV, viewed the footage more times than she would have liked. And she'd been to New York, visited the memorial, walked through the museum. She'd emerged drained and puffy-eyed, taking hours to recover. It was nothing that a three-year-old should have to be familiar with. What would a preschooler know of death, never mind one so violent and tragic?

Every year, Cassandra watched the recitation of names that was part of the memorial broadcast. It was her way of honoring the firefighters who had sacrificed themselves. But not this year, Jessie decided. They hadn't reached that part of the broadcast yet, and Jessie didn't know if one was even planned, but she grabbed the remote and with an angry push of the power button, turned off the TV.

"Now. What did you say, Micah?" Jessie, trembling, asked into the silence that followed. She hoped that somehow she'd misheard. "Tell Mommy"—she gasped—"tell Mommy what you told me."

"That's where I died," Micah repeated.

Though he didn't seem in the least distressed, Cassandra enveloped him in her arms and held him tightly. "Oh, Micah," she said, "what a thing to say! We're all here together! You, me, and Mama."

Micah shook his head slowly. "Not Micah me. *Keith* me."

Jessie stilled, but inside, her body was still vibrating, and her head was buzzing. She rose to her feet but found she had to hold onto the back of a chair to keep her balance. The words—the whole conversation, come to think of it—had issued from Micah's mouth without any of the childish inflection she expected from her three-year-old. It was still Micah's voice, to be sure, but the enunciation was sharper, cleaner, with, of course, the correct pronunciation of the *th* sound. But the strangest part, the part that shook her to her core, was also the part that shocked Cassandra.

"What does that mean, 'Keith me'?" Cassandra pulled back from their son, searching his face, her question slow and precise. But Jessie could still hear the tension behind it.

"When I was Keith," Micah responded in an annoyed voice, as if it should have been obvious. "'Fore I was me."

Cassandra and Jessie both gaped at Micah. After a moment he added, "Joey was there, an' he died too. I miss him."

The family stood still for a minute, the air heavy with dread and disbelief. Jessie, her heart pounding in her ears, her throat constricted, could hardly breathe. Cassandra, on the other hand, was taking the sort of deep, steadying breaths that she might advise someone in the middle of a panic attack to take.

Thank God Eli was still up in his room, sulking and taking his sweet time getting dressed. If she and Cassandra couldn't understand what was happening to Micah, Eli would certainly be confused and would no doubt lash out. Again.

But then the moment seemed to pass.

"I'm firsty," Micah said, the lisp returning. "Juice, please, Mommy."

"Of course, honey," Cassandra said, but she made no move to get it. After a moment's hesitation, Jessie went instead to fill the sippy cup with apple juice and handed it to their son. She turned the TV back on, blocking the screen with her body until with shaking hands she found a streaming service with a nice, quiet children's program. Setting Micah on the couch, she pressed an emotional kiss to the top of his head, handed him his dog, and dragged Cassandra out of the room and into the kitchen.

"What the *hell* do you suppose that was about?" Jessie panted.

"I suppose that is Micah having a very vivid imagination?" But it came out as a question, and her voice was weak and wobbly. She was as uncertain as Jessie had ever seen her. "That's good, right? I mean, something we should be encouraging?"

Squeezing her eyes shut and rubbing her forehead, Jessie said, "Cass, I think we can agree that we have officially moved beyond a vivid imagination."

"Well, maybe he's repeating something that Eli said to him."

"I *suppose* that's possible." Jessie squinted at Cassandra. "I mean, sure, Eli might have learned the bare bones about 9/11 in school, in a big-picture, historical event sort of way, He's never mentioned it to us, though. More to the point, do we really think that he could explain what happened there to Micah? Let alone in a way that would make Micah...*internalize* it to such a degree?" She shook her head. "I don't buy it."

"Well, where else did he get it from?" Cassandra's voice came out at a higher pitch, desperate. "His entire TV consumption is limited to Sesame Street and Bluey, and movies we've seen together a million times. So, daycare? Preschool? His friends? Who would have told him something so grown-up? And why?"

"Exactly."

"Maybe one of his teachers?" Now she was clutching at straws. "Maybe she mentioned the date was coming up: September eleventh?"

Jessie shook her head again. "Which would still mean absolutely nothing to Micah. Never mind associate it with firefighters? And *dying*?"

The two were silent for a minute, until Jessie brought up the elephant in the room.

"And what do you think of 'Keith me'? What do you think, Cassandra, of 'When I was Keith before I was me'?"

"I . . . I have no idea," Cassandra said, throwing her hands up in frustration, admitting defeat. "None."

Jessie decided to broach the subject that had been on her mind for the past few weeks.

"Can we—can we at least consider the possibility that there's something going on here that doesn't fit neatly into our realm of experience?"

"No." The answer came far too quickly for Jessie's taste.

"No? That's it? No?"

"No, as in: I'm not going to go down the *reincarnation* road with you. That's a lot of bullshit. You know it, and I know it."

Jessie was no longer sure what she knew. "There are cultures where reincarnation is considered to be part of the never-ending circle of life."

"And neither of us is from one of those cultures. There's no evidence at all—"

"No evidence?" Jessie interrupted. "How about the Mets lineup? And now 9/11? What do you call a three-year-old who apparently remembers a disaster that happened decades ago? And claims he *died* in it?"

Cassandra paused. "A child? Our son?"

But what if he weren't just *our son? What if . . . what if he'd been someone else's son first?* It was an idea that Jessie was too cowardly to voice. Now that she had entertained the thought—opening the door and allowing it to enter—it refused to pack up its baggage and go away.

A fully dressed, but still pale and sullen, Eli took that moment to appear in the doorway, demanding the French toast that he had been too cranky to eat earlier. Jessie reheated breakfast for him and put his juice back on the table in an almost robotic way, her mind spinning with outrageous possibilities.

The day did not get much better from there. The house was alternately too quiet and too loud, depending on Eli's fluctuating mood, and

Jessie was relieved when it was over. Long after Cassandra had climbed into bed that night and—after an unusual amount of tossing and turning—fallen asleep, Jessie sat staring at the laptop she'd set up on the little vanity in their bedroom, her hand resting motionless on the mouse. She had done a search for "Twin Towers 9/11 firefighter fatalities" but had yet to scroll down the list of 343 names. The room was cool from the air conditioning that still hummed through the vents on this unseasonably warm September night, yet she was sweating.

The screen glowed. It glowered. It was impossible to look, but it was also impossible not to.

Finally, taking a deep breath, Jessie plunged in. The victims were listed by the company they'd belonged to, and, not knowing Keith's station or his surname, she would have to read them all. This was fine with her. Jessie didn't want to skim the names; she wanted to read them individually, both to make sure she didn't err, and to honor the memory of the victim-heroes. Her own version of the Recitation of the Fallen.

There were so many named Thomas. Kevin. John. Michael. She felt the tears welling up as she considered the wives they'd left behind . . . the friends, the children, the fathers, the *mothers*. Oh, God.

Her emotions in turmoil, it took Jessie longer than she expected to make her way down the list. After far too many minutes had ticked by, she found a firefighter named Keith. Her heart in her throat, she typed his name into the search bar and stared at his photo; a strong, attractive man stared back. She scanned his bio.

"Died in the collapse of the South Tower . . . Left behind *a wife and children*."

She leaned back and folded her arms across her chest, puzzled. The single thing they knew of "their" Keith didn't line up: If Micah was to be believed, *his* Keith was a gay man who had a boyfriend—not that they would have mentioned that particular fact in the official record.

Part of Jessie felt relieved. Maybe there was another, simpler reason for their baby's strange behavior, one they could laugh about a couple of months from now. The more curious part of her, though, continued to scroll.

Until she stumbled on it—almost missing it so close to the end of the list: *Keith Weyerhauser.*

The appearance of the other Keith having somewhat deflated her sense of urgency, she didn't expect much as she typed Weyerhauser's name into the search engine, and until she came face-to-face with another good-looking, square-jawed man, this one wearing a rakish grin. His very short bio did not mention a spouse or any other identifying details.

She gripped the mouse so tightly she could hear its plastic case creak. Could *this* be him? Had she finally found . . .

What? What exactly *had* she found?

This is only a name, she reminded herself. There was still no compelling evidence that this man bore any relation to Micah's imaginary friend, as they were still calling him. After all, it wasn't as if her preschooler had actually given her a last name, or any other identifying information: an age, a rank, a hometown. There were no doubt tens of thousands of Keiths in the world, if not more, including the other firefighter with that name who'd been lost on 9/11.

And many more Joeys, to be sure. There were a number of Josephs among the victims. It would be hopeless to corroborate Micah's information without more details.

It was already very late, so Jessie clicked the laptop shut. Keith Weyerhauser. Would it be better knowing more about this man, or less? The more she knew, the more easily she could verify details . . . assuming such information was available on a young man who had died early in the internet era, before everyone's life had become an open, searchable book. But it could also influence how she approached Micah, which questions she asked him. Wouldn't it be better to let Micah take the lead and compare results later?

.   .   .

"So, you found a firefighter named Keith who was killed on 9/11?" Cassandra seemed to be intrigued but wary when Jessie spoke to her about it the following morning as they were getting dressed.

"Two, actually. But one was married with kids."

"That doesn't mean anything, you know."

"Well, maybe I'm biased, but if I died in a horrific tragedy, I'd sure as hell be missing you and the boys." Jessie paused to think as she buttoned her blouse. "Or at least the boys. I mean—"

"I know what you mean."

"This other one, though, Keith Weyerhauser, appears to have been single—"

"And we think this might be Micah's Keith? How do you know?"

"I don't. Micah has given us absolutely nothing to go by except the first name. I don't think he's ever even mentioned what Keith looks like. At least we know that his boyfriend has hair like Quentin's."

"I'm being silly, right?"

"Not silly, no. So, why don't you investigate a little more?"

"Here's the thing," Jessie said, posing her question: to dig into the life of Keith Weyerhauser for clues with which to prompt Micah, or to hope he provided more details on his own?

"I'm not entirely comfortable with either option, frankly," Cassandra said, pulling her T-shirt over her head.

"Why not? What are you afraid of?"

Cassandra considered the question, leaning against the armoire. "I guess I'm not prepared to think there's something weird going on with Micah."

Jessie almost laughed. "And you think that if we find out that he has the memories of someone else's life that's somehow going to be weirder than him *pretending* that he was—oh, I don't know—a gay firefighter who died along with his boyfriend in the Towers?"

"When you put it that way . . ."

"Look. You know me, and you know I'm going to start doing

research regardless. All I'm asking is whether we start probing Micah for answers *before* or *after* I start looking for Keith Weyerhauser."

After a moment of thought, Cassandra said, "I think you're right that we have to let Micah take the lead on this one. How about we look into possible explanations for Micah's behavior and see if he'll give us more information on this Keith guy on his own. Unprompted."

It seemed as good an idea as any.

EIGHT

lthough they hadn't seen the boy since this whole disaster came down, Jessie suspected that Dean was filling Quentin's head with all sorts of terrible accusations about his best friend's family. So she and Cassandra agreed that it would be unwise to leave Eli in Miss Walbert's class with him. With Cass driving Micah to preschool, Jessie called Allison to tell her that she'd be late and drove the obviously unhappy Eli to school.

"You're not taking the bus today because you're not going straight to Miss Walbert's room, honey," she explained to him, her eyes flicking to the rear-view mirror for a glimpse at his unhappy face. "We're going to the school office to ask them to move you into Mrs. Donohue's class."

"Why? Why do I have to move?" The pitch of his voice was on the upswing, and Jessie bit her lip, fearing an explosion at any moment.

"Because, Eli, it will be hard on you seeing Quentin every day knowing that you're not allowed to be friends with him." This was the explanation that she and Cassandra had settled on as being the best for Eli. Although Quentin had always been a sweet boy and seemed devoted to Eli, they were terrified that he, egged on by his father, would torment

Eli and encourage the other children to do the same. Both mothers had been on the receiving end of bullying in school, and they were hoping to spare their children. "Mommy and I think it will be better that you're not in the same room all day long."

"No, it won't!" *Here it comes*, Jessie thought. Eli started shrieking, which was made even worse by the close confines of the car. "No! I don't wanna move! I wanna stay in Miss Walbert's class!"

"I'm so sorry, Eli, I really am. I know how much you like her class, and—and how much Quentin means to you."

"It's not fair! I don't wanna live with you and Mommy anymore! I wanna live with Quentin. I hate Micah, and I hate *you*!"

Suppressing a sigh along with her pain, Jessie pulled into the school parking lot, bypassing the drop-off line and parking in a visitor spot. She debated whether to allow Eli to cry himself out, but it was getting late, and there was no sign he'd stop soon. Grabbing Eli's backpack and tossing it over her shoulder along with her purse, she wrestled her thrashing child out of his car seat, nearly catching an elbow in her face.

Jessie first tried to walk Eli in and then, discouraged, picked him up and carried him, squirming, into the building. Although she was aware that they were quite the spectacle, Jessie also knew that almost every parent in that drop-off line had struggled with a recalcitrant child at one time or another.

Somehow being in the school office had a mollifying effect on Eli, and he sat quietly, if gloomily, his hands gripping his seat, kicking his feet against the legs of his chair as Jessie spoke to the office secretary. As Jessie was not only a mother of two children in Hadlinsburg Elementary but was the youth librarian in town, she was known and respected by school officials, and the secretary, Erin, assured her that she would get the principal's attention as quickly as possible. Out of the corner of her eye, Jessie could see Janie Morton staring at her, but she refused to acknowledge her. No doubt Trish had called Janie with her own version of events, and soon she, too, would be spreading rumors about Jessie's family in the school.

Within five minutes, Jessie was seated in Principal Campbell's office, with Erin keeping an eye on Eli. In her capacity as librarian, Jessie had frequent, mostly positive, contact with Michelle Campbell. As a parent, her contact was far less frequent, but Jessie was aware that Ms. Campbell was universally respected by parents and teachers alike. Trish, her fount of Hadlinsburg knowledge and gossip, had told Jessie that a decade or so earlier, Ms. Campbell had replaced a tired old gentleman named Sid Beecher, who had been literally counting the days to retirement on a calendar visible to any parent meeting with him in his office. Now she was old enough for the children to see her as ancient—it was mostly the gray streaks in her hair that aged her—but far enough away from retirement that parents hadn't yet started taking odds as to who her successor would be.

"I appreciate you meeting with me on short notice, and I'm sorry to interrupt your day," Jessie started, finally allowing a deep sigh to slip out. "I wouldn't ordinarily ask to make a switch like this, but there are extenuating circumstances." Because the Marshalls were such a prominent family, and because Trish was active in the PTA and her children were well-known in school, Jessie had already decided not to mention the family by name. She recited the script she had planned out in her head. "Eli's three-year-old brother made an innocent remark that was misinterpreted by a parent in Miss Walbert's class. As a result, they've taken a dislike to Eli and by extension to my family. They insulted my wife and me and made awful homophobic remarks. Much as I appreciate Miss Walbert, I'm not comfortable keeping Eli in that classroom. I hope you'll agree that, as early as it is in the school year, it shouldn't be a problem to move Eli into Mrs. Donohue's class."

To Jessie's relief, Ms. Campbell nodded along and agreed that Eli would be best served by switching classes. Checking her computer, she assessed that there was space in Mrs. Donohue's class and assured Jessie it would be no problem to make the change.

No problem for the school, that is. Eli would certainly make it a problem for Jessie and Cassandra.

As Jessie stood to leave, she extended her hand to the principal, who took it and held it. She said, "I want you to know, Jessie, that I've been made aware of the accusations that this . . . parent . . . has made, and I think it's much ado about nothing. Which is exactly what I told the individual who informed me." This, Jessie thought, would probably explain the glare from Janie. "Your family has my support, and therefore the support of the school, and I will quash any gossip that passes my way."

"I appreciate that," Jessie murmured. She hoped the superintendent would feel that way, should the issue ever rise that high.

Once the paperwork was completed and Mrs. Donohue notified, there was nothing left to do but let Erin escort Eli to class. "I'm sure you'll love Mrs. Donohue, Eli," Jessie said. "I'll see you after school, OK?" She crouched down and tried to hug him, but he wasn't having it. He pulled away and stood facing away from her. His head hanging, his backpack clutched in his arms, he refused to look at Jessie and shuffled his way down the hall next to Erin without a word, wiping his eyes with the back of his hand.

Jessie sat down on a bench outside the office to catch her breath, settle her stomach, and regroup. She hated to do this to Eli, but she'd been through enough teasing and abuse in school even before she'd come out and didn't want Eli to suffer the same sort of cruelty.

"Oh, good morning, Jessie!"

Looking up, she saw Diana Hadlin standing in front of her, smiling. There was something about the woman that always made Jessie want to smile back, but even that small gesture was proving too much for her today.

Jessie remembered the first time she had encountered her, on a trip to the supermarket about two months after the Wiltons had first moved to Hadlinsburg. She had entered the pasta aisle and had seen Trish Marshall greeted by a lovely, well-dressed woman who appeared to be in her late sixties.

"Hello, Patricia," the woman had said in a pleasant voice. "You are looking especially fresh-faced today. I have to say I love that color palette on you."

Jessie had watched with astonishment as Trish's eyes lit up and her cheeks grew pink. She wondered who would address Trish with such a combination of warmth yet formality and make her react in such a singular way.

"Thanks so much, Ms. Hadlin," Trish had replied, with the most genuine smile Jessie had seen her give outside of interactions with her closest friends and her own nuclear family. The smile she gave her cosmetics customers was something else entirely. "It's really great to see you."

As the woman moved up the aisle with the self-assurance of a model on a runway, she'd nodded and smiled at Jessie. Jessie smiled back. She could practically feel the woman's warmth, as if they had both stepped outside to find that the rain had cleared, leaving a sunny day.

Later, when she prepared to broach the subject with Trish, she didn't even have to ask. Trish said, her face still glowing, "That, Jessie, was Ms. Diana Hadlin. A direct descendant of the founders of our town, and a wonderful, wonderful teacher. I was in her class in high school, social studies. So inspiring. She started teaching in our district in the '80s, a young woman fresh out of her master's program. By the time *I* had her, of course, she was already in her forties, but she was still hot, if you know what I mean. Just look at her! Still so lovely. Well-traveled. Sophisticated in a way we didn't often see in a town like ours. She had a strut like a runway model, without even trying. Her hair and makeup were always on point and age-appropriate, and her clothes were to die for. You don't see teachers like that anymore. They're all wearing jeans, trying to be one of the kids. Not Ms. Hadlin! Plus she was dynamic and interesting. Everyone clamored to be in her class, and we considered ourselves lucky when we got in.

"Oh, my friends and I had a massive 'girl crush' on her." She giggled. "We all wanted to be like her: looks, brains, elegance . . . the whole package. She was quite the inspiration to me.

"But that wasn't all we loved about her." Trish had leaned in, and Jessie could tell that she was about to get an earful of intergenerational gossip.

"When she was young, there were rumors about her and another teacher, Mr. Jansen, who taught math. He was, apparently, also wildly attractive. My mother told me about him with almost literal stars in her eyes. Must have really been her type! But he left town suddenly in the late 80s, and we all just knew it had to be because of their torrid affair gone wrong. She must have been heartbroken, because she never married and as far as anyone knows, never even dated again." She sighed. "Star-crossed lovers. So tragic."

Jessie recalled the contents of the woman's cart, which did look as if Ms. Hadlin was cooking for one. Whether that was truly tragic or not, she wouldn't comment. Lots of people were better off alone than with the wrong person.

"But she stayed in Hadlinsburg, thank goodness," Trish went on, "teaching and volunteering. Even after she decided to retire, she joined a host of committees. I think she's still on the Beautification Committee, at the very least. I'll be sure to introduce you next time; she's absolutely the sort of person you should know if you're going to live here."

Later on, Jessie had gotten to know Diana Hadlin when she joined the library board, and she found the former teacher to be everything Trish had said. While Jessie never learned more about Hadlin's "tragic" past, her even-tempered, clear-headed point of view was definitely an asset to the board. She had a way of defusing tense situations.

But here Jessie was, sitting on a bench dabbing away tears, looking defeated. The thought crossed her mind that the vice president of the library board was probably not the person a librarian would like to be seen by in her current condition. She hastily wiped her eyes and attempted a smile again, but it wasn't happening today.

To her surprise, Ms. Hadlin sat down next to her and crossed her legs at the knee, her hands at rest on the thigh of her neatly tailored tan slacks. She waited for a moment as if to see if Jessie would say something. When she didn't, Ms. Hadlin said: "Having a bad day?"

"You could say that."

"Want to tell me about it?"

As much as Jessie would have loved unburdening herself, she couldn't bring herself to tell this scion of Hadlinsburg the absurdly dramatic story of what had brought her to this moment: about Micah's strange behavior, about Dean's cruel comments. How could Diana Hadlin of all people possibly relate?

"I'll be all right," she said instead, giving her eyes a final dab with her tissue and standing up. Her companion also stood. "Thanks so much for caring, Ms. Hadlin."

"We all need allies at one time or another, Jessie. I hope your day gets better."

"Thanks," Jessie replied, finally mustering something resembling a smile. "I should get going." She slung her purse over her shoulder.

As she walked down the empty hallway and went back out into the bright September sunshine, Jessie considered Ms. Hadlin's choice of words. "Allies," she'd said. It was a term the gay community knew well and counted on. It was one thing to have *friends*, quite another to have *allies*: People outside of the community who would be willing to take a stand against discrimination on someone else's behalf. People who'd put themselves on the line when the insults and the attacks didn't target them.

It was impossible to know what Ms. Hadlin meant by saying *allies*. Jessie thought it was likely that to Diana Hadlin, popular and privileged, the word didn't carry the weight that it did to her and Cassandra. Maybe she wasn't even aware of the more significant meaning of the word and had used a handy and less intimate synonym for friend.

Still, friend or ally—whatever Ms. Hadlin intended it to mean— Jessie hoped that she wouldn't forget that she'd offered her support. It would become even more important in the coming weeks.

·   ·   ·

The flyers started appearing like cicadas crawling out of a long dormancy, first one at a time and then in droves: on trees, telephone poles, store windows. Shortly after that came the posts on Facebook and NextDoor. The neighbors had all started to talk about PPAW.

By the time Allison approached her desk, Jessie had already heard rumblings about it from the other mothers at school, some in favor, some against. It was like the ominous sound of distant thunder that could either bring a catastrophic storm or an ineffectual, quickly passing shower.

"Jessie," Allison said, an 8 ½" by 11" sheet of paper in her hand. "I'm afraid you were right."

"Hm? About what?"

Allison spread the flyer out on Jessie's desk. Against the background of a huge American flag, it fairly shouted, "Protect our CHILDREN From Groomers!!" in crude, blood-red type. In smaller blue type, it read: "Do you Know what your Children Are reading in School? Join **Patriot Parents Against Woke** and take Back Your parental Rights!" At the bottom was a QR code that presumably led to the PPAW website.

"Oh," Jessie murmured. It would have been easy to laugh at the awful graphic design and uneven capitalization, if the message weren't so threatening. They were already trotting out the ugly, inflammatory language. She felt disquieted. Vulnerable. "I'd heard some things, but . . . Where did you get this?"

"They're everywhere all of a sudden. This particular one was handed to me in front of the dry cleaner. I would have shoved the stupid thing back in their smug faces, but I wanted to make sure you'd seen it."

"I appreciate that." She ran a finger over the edge of the sheet.

"You mean, you *hadn't* seen it before?"

"Guess my mind's been somewhere else." Allison wouldn't know about Micah's remarkable behavior or Eli's problems. Jessie had kept all these recent developments to herself, and the stress of it was starting to get to her. Her sleep had been interrupted, not only by Micah's nightmares but by her own, and no amount of coffee had been able to help with her exhaustion and headaches. "I mean, I knew it was headed our way, but I hoped we'd have more time. Or maybe that it would peter out before it even started. May I keep this? I need to show Cassandra."

"Of course. Unfortunately, there's plenty more where that came from."

Jessie, her mouth dry, could only nod. She folded the flyer in half, and then in half again, and put it in her tote bag, out of sight.

"This is going to affect the whole town, we know that already," Allison added. "Everyone here at the library and at the schools. I know the school board will be meeting to have conversations about it, and we intend to hold the library board to their promise that we'll stand up to these troglodytes." She leaned down on Jessie's desk for emphasis. "I don't want you to worry too much, Jessie. We'll beat this thing. Together."

But Jessie knew better. The moment life started getting unpleasant, when neighbors started taking sides, there would be no winners.

And where would their so-called allies be then?

NINE

It was frustrating, having a packed day ahead when all Jessie wanted to do was sit at her desk and do some research. She glanced longingly at the reference desk, wishing for the first time that it was her area of expertise, that she could spend hours traveling down various scholarly paths in search of an answer.

Instead, she needed to rehash some budget numbers, read up on a couple of new releases to which the director had called her attention, set up for the afterschool boardgames session, start planning Thanksgiving break activities—already! She'd only recently finished her evaluation of their summer program—and assist the patrons that were in and out. After saying goodbye to the harried mother of twin toddlers—Jessie didn't envy that poor woman—and making sure her paperwork and reshelving were done, she sat down at her computer, wondering where to begin.

The first thing she typed in to her search was simply "Reincarnation," and she was unsurprised at the number of hits she received on the term: too many to be practical. She read a few definitions and then delved into some surface-level explanations on its role in different religions, particularly Hinduism. Although she picked up a handful of interesting facts, she wasn't any closer to anything useful.

But then, she narrowed her focus to specific references for *children* who seemed to recall a past life. The stories made her sit up taller in her chair and rub her eyes. *Look here*: The boy who remembered a previous life in India, complete with the names of the village and cherished relatives. Or the four-year-old girl who claimed she'd drowned in 1935 while playing in a pond with her cousin. These stories, and many others, had been independently verified, with facts, dates, and names all lining up.

There was even a well-regarded, accredited university in Oregon with a whole department of scientists who specialized in this phenomenon. They produced not only books but scientific papers— peer-reviewed, *published* papers, something for which she had a healthy respect.

Jessie went so deep into the rabbit hole, she saw Wonderland: a place where everything she thought she knew about life and death was topsy-turvy. Her head swam. On one hand, she felt vindicated: Micah wasn't crazy, or possessed, or even all that alone in his apparent memories. Hundreds of children before him had been documented experiencing something similar—and who knows how many had gone unrecorded. On the other hand, the very idea ran counter to everything her very practical parents had taught her about how life and the universe worked: you're born, you live, you die. The End.

Literally.

Despite attending church as a child, she'd never believed in Heaven or Hell, much less any other kind of afterlife. While she could accept, as she remembered from freshman science, that energy could be neither created nor destroyed, in her own interpretation she would become one with God, with the fabric of the universe. In a best-case scenario, of course. The idea of *consciousness* surviving beyond death was simply unthinkable. How could there be consciousness without brain activity? What would that mean for someone who was declared brain dead and disconnected from life support? But she was self-aware enough to know the limitations of her education and comprehension. Maybe the philosophers or quantum physicists had a take on it, but there was no way she would understand it.

She was glad that the end of the workday was approaching. There was no way she could go back to *Hop on Pop* and the like today, not after all she'd read. Not wanting to use the library's resources, she emailed herself several articles to be printed out at home later.

"Do you think you can keep an open mind?" Jessie asked Cassandra that evening while Eli moped over his reading and math homework—considerably more than he had received in Miss Walberg's class—and Micah scribbled in a coloring book with a handful of animal crackers and a cup of juice at the ready.

"That depends."

"I want you to read something, honey. Read it with an open mind. Just this one paper to start," she said, grabbing a tidy stack of paper she'd set aside earlier on the kitchen counter. "Read the highlighted sections if you don't want to go through the whole thing.

"That's research there, Cassandra," Jessie added, thumbing the papers before holding them out to Cass. "Honest-to-God research by university professors, out of a peer-reviewed scientific journal."

Cassandra stared at her blankly.

Jessie looked over her shoulder to make sure her sons were otherwise engaged. "Listen to me," she whispered. "There are *hundreds* of recorded cases of children, some even younger than Micah, who seem to remember past lives.

"And one of the common threads in these reports is a traumatic death. Drownings, wars, murders . . . *trauma*. You tell me that dying in one of the Towers on 9/11 isn't as traumatic as it gets."

Cassandra touched the papers as if they were toxic but made no move to take them. Jessie grasped her hand and placed the report on it, folding her fingers around the edges.

"Please, Cass. For me. Read it."

. . .

"OK, you have a point," Cassandra said. Coming out of the bathroom after her nighttime routine, still smoothing on her hand cream, Jessie had found Cass sitting cross-legged on their bed, the article on her lap.

"Oh, good. And my point is?"

"I will admit it *seems* entirely possible that Micah is . . . *somehow* remembering someone else's life."

"And?"

"And that someone was a firefighter named Keith who died in the Towers on 9/11."

"Right. So what do we do now?"

Cassandra shrugged. "Honestly? I don't know."

Pushing the blankets aside on her side of the bed, Jessie sat down next to her. "We really don't have to *do* anything, if you don't want to. I want to make sure you understand that. If Micah follows the pattern of these other cases, he won't even remember anything about Keith—his life, his death—in a couple of years."

"And in the meantime we live with the mystery?" Cass's fingers tapped a nervous rhythm against the paper. "Nah. I don't know about you, but I'd like to know what's going on inside his head. If we did want to . . . *do* something? What would that something look like?"

"I guess first we could contact this professor, Dr. Vince Abernathy at Salem State University in Oregon. But you and I both have to agree that it's the right thing to do. It might call more attention to Micah during a time when certain people are already viewing us with suspicion."

Jessie could see that Cassandra was considering the possibility. They couldn't make this decision lightly.

"What are you thinking?" Cassandra asked. "I mean, are *you* leaning one way or another?"

"I have to admit my preference would be to email the university. Maybe they can do their research without creating too much of a fuss."

After a moment, Cassandra said, "OK, let's do this."

That night, Cassandra was the one who got up for Micah's latest nightmare, but Jessie couldn't go back to sleep. She kept thinking about Keith Weyerhauser and the Twin Towers and her poor baby boy, caught between two worlds.

Two lives.

"How is he?" she asked as Cassandra settled back into bed. "Did he say anything? What did he say?"

"Same stuff about it being dark and smoky."

"Do you think it's worse now that he's seen the footage?"

"Not for him. For me, maybe."

Jessie understood what she meant. A nightmare was just a nightmare, but when you knew that it was actually a memory, it ripped out your heart. She wondered with some anguish about the family Keith might have left behind and decided that it was a job best left to the experts; she didn't have the heart for it.

So she gathered Cassandra up in her arms and held her until they both fell asleep.

It was only two days later that Jessie received a response from Dr. Abernathy's team in Oregon: Would they talk to the professor in person if Dr. Abernathy and his assistant flew out to Ohio?

Cassandra surprised Jessie by saying, "Hell, yeah," without hesitation. "I mean, they're willing to come all the way here on the university's dime to give us some answers? It's not going to cost us anything?"

"Not according to their email; it's all part of their research."

After a couple of emails back and forth, Jessie arranged for the academic team to visit the following week.

"Next week? I'll admit I'm a little surprised at how quickly they jumped on this," Cassandra said. "I mean, don't they have schedules or appointments or anything?"

Jessie, too, was impressed by the sense of urgency with which the team worked. "Says here that they're excited about the opportunity to study such an intriguing case here in the US. From what I've read, most of their cases are in Asia.

"They sent us a questionnaire," Jessie added, her face expressing her bemusement. "The 'Child Dissociative Checklist.' It's apparently designed to see how likely it is that Micah is making this whole thing up due to some supposed childhood trauma. Can we work on it together?"

Based on their answers, Jessie was satisfied the team would find that Micah was not, in fact, making things up, nor that he'd experienced any psychological disturbance in his short lifetime. Not that she ever believed that to be the case, but it was the first step in confirming that something unusual was happening.

In the meantime, Micah was untroubled by the effect his memories were having on his family. His insistence on wearing the firefighter helmet from the classroom dress-up box and his occasional lapses into what Jessie and Cassanda privately called "Keith-speak" were accepted by the other preschoolers as normal behavior and by his teachers as a charming, creative quirk from an otherwise well-behaved child. After his mornings at school, he was tired but content, and Jessie was happy that he had started talking about classmates and their games and lessons instead of the horrors of 9/11.

Because Dr. Abernathy wanted Micah to be fresh and rested, Cassandra volunteered to rearrange her schedule and keep him home from preschool that Tuesday morning. The team would come to their house around ten a.m.

They'd told the boys only that they were going to have a visitor from far away and showed them on a map where Dr. Abernathy was coming from. Already wounded by his removal as Quentin's friend and his relocation to Mrs. Donohue's class and balking at what he perceived as even more privileged treatment for Micah, Eli resisted the idea of going to school, demanding that he wanted to be involved too.

"I wanna meet the professor," Eli complained. "I don't wanna go to school. It's not even fun anymore now that I'm in Mrs. Donohue's class. It's boring. She makes us work hard, and Quentin isn't there. I hate it!"

"I'm sure Dr. Abernathy will want to ask you some questions too," Cassandra answered, though they didn't really know that for a fact. "Maybe later."

"It's not fair!" Eli said, his face clouded.

"How is it not fair, sweetheart?" Cassandra asked.

"Everybody's treating Micah like he's something special. Like a TV star." He sniffed. "But he's just a little baby who's afraid of the dark!"

"I'm not a baby!" Micah cried.

"Are too!" Eli countered.

"That's enough, Eli," Jessie said, her voice sharper than she intended. "In this family, we support each other, even when things aren't going our way." It shouldn't have come as a surprise that Eli was acting out since Micah started showing these odd . . . symptoms. And the abrupt removal of his best friend only served to exacerbate the problem.

It took longer than usual to get Eli ready for the day. He fought them at every turn—getting dressed, eating breakfast, brushing his teeth —and Jessie's heart ached a little for him. Although he refused to talk about it, Jessie and Cassandra knew he'd been struggling at school. Mrs. Donohue reported that during his first week, he had come back from recess crying because Quentin had refused to speak to him. That, naturally, had led to him being labeled a crybaby by a crowd of other children. According to Mrs. Donohue, she'd managed to defuse the situation at the time, but Jessie knew that kids could be cruel in ways that went undetected by teachers and parents. She hoped Eli would open up eventually. There'd been so much upheaval in such a short period of time, and so much of it seemed to fall on him.

Ten

Dr. Vince Abernathy, clad in a subtly striped, pale-blue button-down shirt, sport jacket, and tailored slacks, was the very picture of a university professor, except for the short stature and slight build which gave him an almost elfin appearance. He seemed to be about Jessie's height, or maybe a little less: certainly no taller than 5'4". He had warm brown eyes behind wire-rimmed glasses, and close-trimmed, salt-and-pepper hair. His assistant, Savannah Davies, a graduate student, was taller than him by six inches, easily. She had ropes of braids that extended down the length of her back and a killer smile that immediately put the family at ease. Micah in particular seemed charmed by her, and it was largely due to her request to him that he agreed to watch a video in the den while the grown-ups had their conversation.

Before anything else, the team promised that their research would be strictly confidential, and that their identities would be protected unless the family specifically gave permission to make the information public. Having discussed it earlier, Cassandra and Jessie were on the same page: In the current environment, they preferred to remain anonymous. Savannah busied herself setting up a microphone and video camera, then—nodding her readiness to the professor—sat down with a tablet to take notes.

"I'll be doing a short interview with you two first," Abernathy said with a wry smile. "I say 'short' because I've found that you'd answered most of my questions before I'd had the chance to ask them. The notes that you've already provided were, um, very extensive."

"Detail-oriented is my middle name," Jessie said, blushing, in an awkward attempt at humor. Cassandra smothered a laugh.

"Ah, the benefits of dealing with a librarian! I wish all my intervie-wees were as well prepared and precise; it makes my job so much easier.

"We'll be filming all our interactions, if that's all right with you. We always try to be as unobtrusive and sensitive as possible, and no one outside our research team will view the videos. If Savannah is ready, we'll get started.

"What's your name?"

"Jessie Wilton."

"And how old are you?"

"I'm thirty-four."

"Who's this with you?"

"My wife, Cassandra Wilton."

"How old are you, Cassandra?"

"Thirty-six."

"Where were you born?"

"'I'm from New Jersey," Jessie responded. Without having to say a word, she knew Cassandra would let her take the lead. "I grew up near Hoboken, and Cass is from Staten Island."

"How long have you been married?"

"It was eight years in May."

"Micah Delarosa is your child?"

"Yes. Our child."

"Of course. May I ask which of you two carried him?"

"I did," Jessie said. "Cassandra is a little older, so we agreed that she would be the first to get pregnant. She carried Eli."

"And may I ask who his father is?"

"We had a sperm donor. Do you really need the name? We agreed to keep him anonymous, at least until the boys turn eighteen."

Abernathy shook his head. "No, that's fine. It's not all that important, and you can always let me know if my questions exceed your comfort zone. Now, then. How would you describe Micah?"

Jessie paused to think. "Affectionate, sometimes bordering on clingy. Usually quiet, but if you get him going on something he loves, he'll talk up a storm."

"Have you considered him a particularly imaginative child?"

"Well, he's always been able to entertain himself in a way that Eli—our elder son—can't. Give him some action figures or cars to play with and he's good for a half hour; that's a long time for a preschooler. But as far as, say, making up stories verbally, no. We never thought of him having a brilliant imagination until all this started."

"What do you mean by *all this*?"

"When he started talking about Keith."

"And who is Keith?"

After a pause, Jessie answered, choosing each word, "Keith is someone who Micah talks to, or sometimes pretends to be. We've been referring to him as Micah's imaginary friend, but we recently began to suspect that he was . . . something else."

"When did Micah begin mentioning Keith?"

"Early this summer."

"I know you've already written down this information, but could you please give me as many specifics as you can for the benefit of the video record?"

So Jessie recited all the details she'd previously provided: Micah's fear of the dark, his obsession with firetrucks and firefighters, his nightmares, their introduction to Keith, Micah's remarks about Joey, his sudden disturbing declaration on 9/11.

When she finished, after a solid ten minutes, Dr. Abernathy asked if Cassandra had anything to add. She shook her head.

"OK, then that concludes your portion of the interview. Next we'll bring Micah in. If it ever gets to be too much for him, or if you sense he —or any of you—could use a break, please don't hesitate to speak up. The most important thing is to allow Micah to express himself, and not to jump in to provide him with cues or answers.

"As with yours, all of Micah's answers get entered into a database, which not only keeps track of his responses but also allows us to see where he stands in the rubric that helps us determine the validity of your past-life claim. From what you've already detailed in your email, and in our interview, it sounds like we already have a lot to work with. I don't mind telling you that it's particularly exciting to find a case like this in America, where reincarnation isn't generally part of the religious or cultural landscape.

"But let's hear from Micah."

For now, Dr. Abernathy and his assistant set up the camera and chairs in the den, where the conversation could be casual and where Micah would likely be most comfortable. He was already sitting on the couch against his favorite pillow, gripping his dog, Dot, a sippy cup of water nearby. They turned off the video, and he didn't complain. Instead, he looked at the adults with curiosity.

"Hi, I'm Dr. Abernathy," the professor began. "And what's your name?"

"Micah."

"Nice to meet you, Micah. How old are you?"

"I'm free," he replied, holding up three stubby fingers.

"Three years old! And who are these people here?"

"Dat's my mama," Micah said, pointing to Jessie, "and Mommy," he added, pointing to Cassandra.

"Very good. Who else is in your family? Do you have a brother or sister?"

"My bruvver is Eli. He's six years old." Micah looked around the room. "He's at school."

"That's a lovely family you have, Micah! I'll bet you have lots of friends too. Do you have friends from preschool?"

Micah nodded vigorously.

"What are some of their names?"

After thinking for a moment, Micah recited, "Lucas an' Henry. Cooper. An' Emma."

"Aren't you lucky! Do you also have any grown-up friends you talk to sometimes?"

"Uh-uh." He shook his head for emphasis.

When it looked as if Jessie was about to interject, Dr. Abernathy held up a hand to stop her. He reworded his question.

"There must be some grown-ups you know a lot about, besides Mama and Mommy. How about your grandparents?"

"Got none," Micah replied, and Jessie felt a little pang. Her boys had no idea that they might have grandparents and an uncle in Staten Island: Cassandra, angry and closed off whenever someone raised the topic, never checked to see if her parents, who would be in their late sixties, were still alive or if her older brother had become more open-minded.

"I see. Well, maybe you know some grown-ups here in town? Can you think of any?"

"Miz Marshall."

"Very good. Who's that?"

"Mama's friend. Quentin's mommy."

"And who's Quentin?"

"Eli's friend."

"I see. Do you know anyone else?"

"Beff? And Ginny?"

"Sure, what would you like to tell me about Beth and Ginny?"

"Dey're nice. Mama and Mommy's friends. Dey're coming for Tanksgiving, Mama says."

"Very good. Who else?"

"Nick-las an' Jeremy."

"How come *he* can remember Nicholas?" Cassandra whispered to Jessie, who shushed her.

"Are they also friends of your mothers?"

"Uh-huh."

"Anyone else, besides your mothers' friends?"

"Um. Oh! Miss Kira and Miss Claire."

"Who are they?"

"My teachers."

"Are they good teachers? Do you like them?"

"Uh-huh."

"Micah, what other grown-ups do you talk to sometimes?"

Micah tilted his head. "You mean Keef?"

"Keith? Tell me about Keith. Is he a friend of yours?"

"I guess."

"Is he a friend of your mothers too?"

"Nuh-uh."

"Do you know Keith from preschool?"

"No."

"From daycare?"

"No."

"Really! So, where did you meet Keith?"

The question seemed to stump Micah. He gave up, shrugging, without an answer. Jessie was disappointed; she really wanted to know how Micah perceived Keith. As another part of himself? As a separate consciousness? A kind of a narrator?

"I *know* Keef," was all he could say.

"Well. Can you think back, think about the first time Keith spoke to you?" the professor asked. "Or the first time you saw him, or knew he was with you?"

"A baby."

"What baby? Who was a baby?"

"Me." There was a pause. "But 'fore dat."

"Before what?"

"'Fore I'm a baby."

"How . . . ?" Cassandra whispered to Jessie, who shook her head and put her finger to her lips. *Not now!*

"Oh, that's a long time," Abernathy said, apparently undisturbed by this extraordinary answer. "What else can you tell me about Keith? Oh! Do you know his last name?"

All eyes were on Micah as he sat back in on the couch. He squinted, patting his stuffed dog, deep in thought. "Where? Funny name. Where-house. Keith Where-house?" He laughed a little.

Close enough, Jessie thought.

"Keith Where-house." Abernathy accepted this response without question. "Very good. And what else do you know about him?"

"He's a firefighter."

Jessie had to restrain herself from interrupting. While she understood why they couldn't ask their own questions, she desperately wanted to know how Micah knew Keith and—more than that—what he could possibly tell them about the time before he was a baby. It was the question that had plagued humankind for thousands of years, had birthed religions: *What happens after we die? What, if anything, are we before we're born? Are we souls or something else?*

But to her frustration, Dr. Abernathy had his own agenda and moved on.

"A firefighter, how interesting! Does Keith have a mother or a father? How about a brother or sister?"

"A mommy and a dad. No bruvver. No sister."

"Do you know the names of Keith's mommy and dad?"

For a moment, Micah was silent, chewing on Dot's ear. Then, as if remembering there were other people in the room, he looked up. "Bill. Dad's name is Bill. Mommy is Janine."

"And where does Keith live?"

Micah looked puzzled. He blinked a couple of times. Finally, he smiled, and with both hands, he patted his chest. "Here. Keef is here."

Sitting silently across the room, Jessie and Cassandra grabbed each other's hands.

"Keith lives with you?"

"Not *wif* me. Here." And again Micah patted his chest.

"I see. And where did Keith live before he came to live right there?"

Again Micah paused, as if listening. "Queens," he said tentatively, then with growing confidence repeated it. "Keith lived in Queens."

Did Dr. Abernathy notice it? Jessie wondered, her eyes wide. The subtle change over to the proper pronunciation of the *th* sound? The appropriate use of the past tense? The sharpening of his entire tone?

"So, Keith is a firefighter who lived in Queens. That's very interesting, Micah. What else can you tell me about him? Anything at all."

"He gots brown hair. Short like this." He rubbed his own head.

"Very good."

"He likes music loud. *Loud.* An' hot dogs with lots of stuff." He giggled. "He eats *a lot.*"

He said it with such emphasis that the adults in the room couldn't help but laugh.

"An' he died in the Tower."

The laughter ended abruptly. Cassandra gasped; Jessie's hand flew up to cover her mouth.

Again Dr. Abernathy seemed unmoved. He glanced Cassandra and Jessie's way but continued the questioning as if it were the most natural conversation in the world. "Oh, he died in a tower? What tower was that?"

"North Tower."

"The North Tower of what? What kind of building?"

"World building. There were two." Micah held up two fingers in much the same way he did when asked his age.

"Two towers? In the World building?"

"Uh-huh."

"And where was that?"

"New York."

"What happened there, Micah? Do you know? How exactly did Keith die in the Tower?" Without thinking, Jessie and Cassandra both leaned in, anxious to hear how Micah described the catastrophe.

"Lotsa smoke. We couldn't breathe, so much smoke," Micah said without much emotion. Jessie, on the other hand, thought she might pass out from the intensity of her feelings, hearing these words come out of her baby's mouth *in context*. "Stuff was heavy. It was hot. An' dark. An' then everything fell down. That's all he 'members."

"How old was Keith when he died?"

"Twenny-eight."

So young. He was so young. Jessie's throat tightened.

"Keith was very brave, wasn't he?" Abernathy asked.

"Yup. The bravest." Micah nodded in an exaggerated way. "That's what they call us. New York's Bravest."

Us.

ELEVEN

Jessie wasn't sure how much longer she could hold herself together. Micah seemed to be unaffected by the story he was telling, but Dr. Abernathy must have determined that it was time to move on, because he took out a manila envelope from his briefcase. He withdrew a stack of 8x10 glossy photographs. They were group pictures of firefighters, with maybe twenty people, almost all men, in each photo. They all wore New York's standard black uniform with reflective yellow stripes; Jessie finally understood Micah's insistence on a black firefighter costume. Many were wearing caps and others, helmets; some were bare headed. Most bore a serious expression, but there were always a few faces, particularly young ones, cracking a smile.

"Now, over two hundred FDNY units responded on 9/11, and what we have here are some of their official photos," Abernathy said to Jessie and Cassandra before turning his attention back to their son. "Micah, I'd like you to look at these pictures of the firefighters who were at the Towers with Keith and see if you know anyone. OK?"

Jessie could see that there were nowhere near two hundred photos in the pile, more like twenty, but she trusted that Dr. Abernathy knew what he was doing. Though she was itching to have a look at the pictures herself, the professor had asked her to stand aside while he was testing Micah. He knew that she had already identified Keith Weyerhauser as a possible match for the "previous personality," as the team referred to the individual whom the child seemed to be channeling. By now, she'd seen Keith's photo and read his official obituary, where she'd seen a couple of pictures from his childhood. Dr. Abernathy was concerned that she could influence Micah by having some kind of reaction upon seeing his photo.

At first, Micah seemed completely engaged by the photos. He leaned eagerly over the coffee table as each picture was presented to him, but his interest started to flag after looking at photograph after photograph that didn't hold anyone he could identify. He squirmed in his seat on the couch and started looking around the room.

Jessie could see Micah was growing restless. Despite her disappointment, she suggested, "Why don't we wrap up for today?"

Dr. Abernathy agreed. "How about we pick it up tomorrow when Micah is more rested?"

But Micah had other ideas. "Joey!" he exclaimed. With his finger on the smiling face of a slender young man with dirty-blond hair that fell across his forehead, he added, "This is Joey. My boyfriend. I miss him."

"Very good, Micah," Dr. Abernathy nodded and made a note on his tablet. "I'm glad you spotted Joey. Is there anyone else in the picture who looks familiar?"

Micah scanned the faces again and shook his head. "No. Only Joey."

Moving to stand behind him, Jessie felt deflated. While Keith Weyerhauser was definitely not in that photo, Micah had said that Joey worked at the same station as Keith. Jessie wondered if she'd gotten it wrong, somehow had the wrong Keith.

"Do you know Joey's last name, Micah?"

Micah looked at him blankly, then frowned. "I don't 'member."

"That's OK, Micah, you're doing great."

Dr. Abernathy pulled away the photo, preparing to put down another, but Micah started to whine.

"Wanna see Joey," he complained. "Bring Joey back." His whimpering threatened to blossom into a full-blown tantrum, and Jessie started signaling to Abernathy's assistant.

"OK, I think that's enough for today," Dr. Abernathy said, taking the hint. "We'll be back tomorrow, same time? And don't worry, Micah, I will bring Joey's picture. Plus a lot more for you to look at."

When the session resumed the next day in the Wiltons' den, right away Dr. Abernathy brought out the remaining photos to pick up where he had left off. To begin, he again showed Micah the photo in which he had identified Joey and asked, "Do you know anyone in this picture?"

"Yeah, dere's Joey." He repeated his previous gesture, putting his little index finger directly below Joey's chin. "Big smile makes me happy. Big smile."

"All right," Abernathy said. Putting the photo aside, he pulled out another picture from the stack. "Do you recognize anyone in *this* picture?"

After a moment, the answer came: "No."

"How about this one?"

"No. Bring back Joey."

And so it went until Abernathy laid down the final picture. "Is there anyone in this picture that you recognize?"

"No . . . yeah! Dere's Simon, and Tommy, and Mike!" he said, pointing to each one in turn. "And look! Dere's me! Dis me! *Keef* me."

Jessie leaned over Micah's head and looked where he was pointing. A solidly built, square-chinned, brown-haired young man in his late twenties grinned up from the photo. She recognized Keith Weyerhauser, and, finally, so had Micah.

"Tell me, Micah: Who is this person?" Abernathy pressed gently.

"I told you. Dat's me!"

"Oh, so is this Micah Wilton in the picture?"

"No!" Micah made a face and bounced in his seat as if he couldn't believe the man's stupidity. "This is *Keith me!*"

Jessie and Cassandra looked at each other. There it was again: The change in pronunciation when Micah was deep in conversation about Keith. Jessie made a mental note to speak with Dr. Abernathy about it after the session.

But that detail paled against the way Micah defined the subject of the photo: *Keith me.* Despite the reading she'd done on the phenomenon, despite knowing that Keith would likely disappear from Micah's memory by the time he reached second grade, it made Jessie shiver. Were they really one and the same? How much of her precious son was Micah, and how much was Keith Weyerhauser?

"Oh, I see." Again Abernathy proved unfazed. "That's *Keith* you."

"But wrong nose," Micah added unprompted. "That's my old nose."

"What do you mean, your 'old nose'?" Dr. Abernathy asked.

"My nose is bumpy. Here," Micah pointed to where his ruby-red birthmark flecked his otherwise perfect little nose.

"Did Keith get a nose job?" Cassandra asked Jessie, who shrugged. Her research into Keith Weyerhauser would not have revealed a personal detail like that, and all the other photos she'd seen when she first identified him showed him with the same nose.

Their session ended soon after that. "I thought Keith and Joey worked together at the firehouse," Cassandra said as the team packed up. "How come they're in different pictures?"

Abernathy got Savannah's attention, tilting his head toward Micah. Comprehending him, she nodded, and addressed the little boy: "Hey, Micah, how about you show me your toy cars! Which one's your favorite?"

He slid off the couch and, grabbing her index finger, pulled her over to the toybox, where she sat down and allowed him to rattle on about his trucks.

With Micah occupied, the professor was free to answer the mothers' questions. "You might have noticed that I've cherry-picked the photos I showed Micah. I presented him with department photos that had a Joseph of the appropriate age and rough physical description. After Micah identified twenty-four-year-old Joseph Killigrew as 'Joey' yesterday, I dug a little into the departmental records. Seems he transferred into Keith's company in February of 2001, two months after these particular pictures were taken. He did, in fact, die in the North Tower along with Keith Weyerhauser and the rest of their crew."

Jessie took a moment to absorb this. With every new piece of information, the distant tragedy became closer, more personal.

"It's possible that their relationship predated the move," Abernathy continued, "or maybe they started dating once they were in the same station."

"So, what happens now?"

"Now, I'll be reaching out to Keith's father, Bill. He still lives in Queens—Astoria, if I remember correctly.

"Here's where we'll have to be patient, folks. Sometimes this part takes a while. When an individual receives a communication like this out of the blue—'Guess what? Your beloved son has been reborn and now is a preschooler in Ohio'—as you might imagine it can take days or weeks for the person to process the information. If they're resistant to the whole idea of reincarnation or the persistence of consciousness, it may take even longer, or they may not respond at all. They may be offended for religious reasons or resent reopening old wounds which may have barely healed despite the decades that have passed.

"Obviously, family members and close friends can give us corroborating details that the average person can't. They're privy to information like favorite foods or beloved pets. Sadly, there's no one left from the firehouse where Keith and Joey worked. Keith's father is our only possibility to obtain that kind of data. But even if we don't get a response from him, we can still call the case 'solved' if enough of the information lines up. I think with the information you and Micah have provided—

particularly Keith's last name, with Micah confirming his identity in the photo—we're pretty much assured of that."

"I'm glad to hear that, for what it's worth," Jessie said. "I mean, it doesn't really change his behavior, which—I'm not gonna lie—is still unsettling, but it does explain it. Are you also going to reach out to Joey's family?"

"Only as a last resort, if I don't hear from Mr. Weyerhauser. I'd much rather stick with Keith's family, since his is the previous personality. We don't have enough firsthand information about Joey to merit that kind of contact. Through experience, we've found that it only leads to disappointment. They'll ask, why wasn't *their* loved one the personality that's coming through."

Why, indeed? Jessie knew that feeling. Although she hadn't said anything aloud, even to Cass, she wondered, *Why Keith Weyerhauser? If Micah was in fact channeling the consciousness of a deceased man, why not her own, beloved father?* What she wouldn't give to know he was out there, somewhere, reaching out. Trying to make contact with her with his own love for the Mets. Or how about her mother? From her reading, she knew that on rare occasions the child could be of a different sex than the previous personality.

Meanwhile, Cassandra asked, "Professor, what do you think about Micah's remark about his 'old nose'?"

Instead of answering, Abernathy asked a question of his own: "How long has Micah had that red spot on his nose?"

"He was born with it," Cassandra replied.

Jessie added, "There aren't any other birthmarks anywhere else on his body. Is that significant?"

Looking thoughtful, Abernathy said, "It could be. I hope to find out more from Keith's father."

"Dr. Abernathy, might you have any questions for Micah's brother, Eli?" Jessie asked. "He's almost seven and feeling a little left out of the . . . um . . . excitement."

"Possibly. Has he spent time alone with his brother when he might have had conversations that you two are unaware of?"

Cassandra and Jessie looked at each other, considering the question.

"Maybe? He did know Keith's name before we did," Jessie replied. Cassandra nodded.

"All right, then, how about you bring him in tomorrow?"

"OK," Jessie said. "But what do we tell him?"

"Does he know anything about our work? Why you've called us out here?"

She shook her head. "No. He doesn't understand; he thinks Micah has an imaginary friend and is being 'weird' about it."

"Good. Just tell him we'd like to ask him some questions about his brother and the things he talks about. I'd rather get his own point of view, unbiased. It's best if he knows nothing at all."

Jessie wished that she, too, could go back to knowing nothing at all.

Twelve

Eli, looking confident, strode into the dining room, where the professor had set up for his session. Cassandra had taken Micah out for a walk so Eli could be interviewed uninterrupted.

"I'm Dr. Abernathy. And what's your name?" the professor asked.

"Eli Wilton."

"And how old are you?"

"Six. Almost seven!"

"Oh, do you have a birthday coming up?"

"Yup, next month."

"Wow, good for you! What grade are you in?"

"Second."

"And you're Micah's brother?"

"Uh-huh."

"Do you and Micah spend a lot of time together?"

"Yeah."

"What do you do together?"

"Play and stuff."

Jessie wondered what, if anything, Dr. Abernathy could possibly get out of Eli. In his lengthy career, he must have frequently experienced the tedium of trying to carry on a conversation with a six-year-old who wasn't talking about himself or his current obsession with dinosaurs or rocket ships. It could be like pulling teeth. She began to regret asking him to waste his time like this.

"When you play with Micah, what do you play? Board games?"

"Nope. He's too little for board games, so we watch TV and play with our Legos and cars, mostly. Or we color, stuff like that."

"Oh, that's fun. Does Micah talk while you're playing?"

"Sometimes."

"And what does he talk about?"

"Nothing much." There was that one-shouldered shrug again. "Sometimes he just babbles or says what he's going to do. But sometimes he talks about Keith," he added. He was sharp enough to know what Dr. Abernathy was after, Jessie had to give him that. "I was the first one to know his name, before Mama or Mommy."

"Very good, Eli. And who is Keith?"

"Micah's imaginary friend."

"Can you remember when Micah first mentioned Keith by name?"

"Let's see." Eli squinted into the air and tapped his chin as he must have seen adults do while deep in thought. Jessie had to stifle a laugh. "Maybe when he started talking about firetrucks."

"And when would that have been?"

"I dunno."

Abernathy looked at Jessie.

"He started obsessing about fire equipment about six months ago," she said, although that information was already in the record, "right around when he turned three. We never heard him mention Keith's name until fairly recently, though Eli knew exactly whom Micah was talking about."

The professor nodded. Savannah made a note. "So, what kind of things did Micah say about Keith?"

"He called him Keef 'cause he still can't pronounce his *th* sound," Eli replied. "He'd say stuff like, 'Keef drives to the fire station, or Keef is fighting a fire.'" He thought for a moment. "One time he said, 'Keef uses the big equipment to rescue people.'"

"That's very important, Eli. Good job!" To Jessie, he added, "With another source of information about the type of work Keith did, we can go further in confirming his identity."

Jessie frowned. She doubted that Micah could come up with a sentence like that and wondered if Eli were now making things up to impress the professor. She hoped he would take that into account.

Abernathy continued with his questions for Eli: "Is Micah's talk about Keith always about firefighting?"

"Yeah. Mostly. I mean, until he started talking about his boyfriend." Eli's mood darkened. "And now I can't play with Quentin 'cause his dad doesn't like it."

"Really? And who is Quentin?"

Eli's face twisted up, and Jessie could tell he was near tears. "My best friend. But I can't play with him anymore because his dad doesn't like Micah talking about a boy having a boyfriend."

"Oh, that's too bad. What does Micah say about his boyfriend?"

"It's *Keith's* boyfriend, not Micah's." He frowned. "But Quentin's dad doesn't care. He doesn't like it anyway."

"I see. I'm so sorry to hear that." The professor looked thoughtful. But he immediately moved along. "How do you know that Micah was talking about Keith's boyfriend and not his own?"

"Because he talked about him one night at dinner. Said that he met his boyfriend at work, at the firehouse. That's where *Keith* works."

"Oh, interesting. Did he give you other details?"

"He said his boyfriend's name was Joey."

"Joey what? Did he give you a last name?"

"I dunno. He never said." Eli made a face. "Do imaginary people have last names?"

Ignoring the question, Abernathy pressed on. "And what was it exactly that Micah told you about the boyfriend?"

"He said that his boyfriend had hair like my friend Quentin. That's what upset his dad."

"And what kind of hair does Quentin have?"

"It's . . . light brown, I guess? Almost blond? Kinda straight, and it covers the top of his face like this," and he dragged his fingers down his forehead to indicate bangs.

"Excellent. You see, Eli, that's exactly the kind of information that we need: Something we haven't heard before. Well done."

Eli looked pleased. Although she knew she shouldn't have been surprised—Dr. Abernathy's credentials were as a child psychiatrist, after all—Jessie was still impressed with the way he dealt with the children. He had given Eli a much-needed ego boost during a time when the six-year-old was feeling as if the whole world were against him. When the professor finished the interview and gave him a firm, grown-up handshake, Eli skipped off to the den and sat down to play with his action figures.

"Well, I think we have everything we need from this particular set of sessions, Jessie," Abernathy said as he and his assistant packed up. "We're going to head back to Oregon tomorrow, unless you can think of a reason for us to stay."

"As a matter of fact"—Jessie glanced around to make sure that Eli was occupied—"before you leave, I have a question."

"Certainly." He addressed his assistant. "Savannah, could you please put the equipment into the car?"

She nodded. "On it. It's been nice to meet you, Ms. Wilton."

"Same, Savannah."

With Savannah out the door, Jessie gestured to the kitchen table, and Abernathy sat down. "Can I get you anything, Professor? Something to drink?"

"Thank you, no. I'm fine." He looked at her expectantly.

Jessie sat next to him, folding her hands on the table in front of her, and bit her lip.

"What's on your mind, Jessie?"

So many things. But one in particular. "That part . . . when Micah said he knew Keith before he was a baby."

"Ah, yes. Extraordinary, isn't it?"

"Well, yes. I mean, it's *so* extraordinary, why isn't it making headlines? You know: 'Proof that Life After Death Exists!'"

Abernathy leaned back in his chair. "Jessie, when it first became clear to you and Cassandra that Micah knew details of the life of a deceased firefighter, how did you react?"

She thought for a moment about her reaction and Cassandra's. *Incredulity. Fear. Discomfort. Denial.* "I think I see what you mean."

"As I've mentioned before, most Western cultures have no concept of reincarnation whereas among many Eastern cultures it's just part of life. It wouldn't make headlines in India, for example.

"And this information has been available to the public for decades. You're aware of the books that came out of our department. The earliest one was published over fifteen years ago. If people *wanted* to see it as proof of an afterlife, it's there for the asking." He gave a slight shrug. "Maybe that tells you something."

"OK, I get it." Jessie shifted her weight forward in her chair, leaning toward the professor. "But I guess what I really want to know is, can we take Micah at his word? That he somehow had a meeting of—of the . . . souls with Keith before he was born?"

"This is where we have to keep in mind that Micah is a little boy, a very little boy." Abernathy said, enlacing his fingers on the table in front of him. "He doesn't have the language to describe his experience. We can't know for sure that he 'met' Keith before birth; we have no way of knowing what that could look like. What I will tell you from my own studies, though, is that there are many, many children who report being in a sort of in-between state before they're born. I've had a few who've told me that they'd seen their mothers ahead of time, for example. That they'd somehow chosen her." He smiled. "Isn't that a lovely thought?"

It was indeed.

"But, Jessie, it would be a mistake to extrapolate the sum of human experience from these cases. As many as we've documented, for all we know, they're the exception. Perhaps there are rules beyond our knowledge that govern who comes back and how they do it. Many cultures have their own ideas about that, but to those of us in the West—within our particular scientific community—it remains a mystery, as does what the 'afterlife' or 'before-life,' if you will, looks like to each individual.

"Does that help?"

"I guess." *But not really.*

"I'm sorry I can't give you the definitive answer you're looking for. Science can only offer so much at this time." He paused, thoughtful. "I suppose that's why religion is still so popular.

"Is there anything else I can do for you?"

"No." Jessie shook her head as she got to her feet. Dr. Abernathy followed suit. "Thanks so much for your time. We'll update you if Micah says or does anything else that's interesting."

"Fine. And I'll keep you apprised if we hear from Mr. Weyerhauser. We'll be overnighting him correspondence as soon as we're back in the office. Thank you and Cassandra for bringing me in on this fascinating case. I feel privileged to be part of Micah's extraordinary experience."

Cassandra and Micah arrived back at the house as Dr. Abernathy was returning to his car. From her spot at the front door, Jessie watched as they said goodbye to the professor. Once they were back inside, and Micah was set up in the kitchen with a snack of juice and some string cheese, Cassanda asked, "How did it go with Eli?"

"Pretty well, I think. He took the opportunity to complain about Quentin, and he almost lost it, but other than that it went smoothly. Dr. Abernathy says he has everything he needs from us right now and will contact us when he hears from Keith's father."

"*If* he hears from Keith's father."

The whole family hung on that *if*.

"Is Dr. Abernathy coming back?" Eli asked that night at dinner.

"We don't know yet if he is, honey," Jessie replied without thinking. "It depends on whether he can reach Keith's father."

"Keith has a father?" Eli's fork fell to his plate with a clatter. "Can an imaginary friend have a father? And a boyfriend? What kind of doctor is Dr. Abernathy anyway? Is there something wrong with Micah? Is he sick? Or is he crazy?"

Jessie put down her own utensils and sat back in her chair, realizing her mistake immediately. She'd never explained the Keith situation to Eli, and she hadn't told him the real reason for Abernathy's visit, either. She glanced at Cassandra, who gave a slight nod.

Taking a deep breath, Jessie chose her words carefully. "A long time ago, Eli, back when Mommy and I were little girls, some very bad people used airplanes to knock down a couple of huge buildings in New York City. It was a terrible, awful day, and a lot of people were killed."

"De Towers," Micah said without pausing from his dinner. Jessie looked at him in wonder, marveling that this child could be so matter-of-fact about such an earth-shattering subject.

"The Twin Towers, they were called: two tall buildings that looked alike."

"Oh, that? Mrs. Donohue said something about that stuff last week." Eli probably felt as removed from the early 2000s as from the American Revolution. "So what?"

Jessie took a deep breath. How in the world was she supposed to explain to a child what was happening with Micah without going into the most frightening details? "Anyway, um, one of the people who died that day was a firefighter named Keith."

"Keef. Where-house."

"Keith Weyerhauser. We found out he was a real person, Eli, not an imaginary one. And for whatever reason, your brother knows all about him: his work, his family, and yes, his boyfriend, Joey. It's like he . . . like Micah has Keith's memories. Think of it as . . . um . . . a computer saving a file for later. And Micah sometimes can access it, by accident, maybe by hitting the right combination of keys. But other times he can't; he gets locked out. We can't explain why any of this is happening, but Dr. Abernathy is part of a team of scientists who study children like Micah who seem to have memories that belong to other people."

"Oh." Eli seemed baffled. He looked down at his plate before turning his attention to Micah. "What a weirdo."

"No name-calling, Eli," Cassandra said, but there was no fire in it. "We want you to know that it's not something Micah can control. He doesn't know when he'll remember something that happened to Keith, and sometimes he gets himself and Keith all mixed up. You shouldn't blame him for it."

"Well, I still think he's weird," Eli said.

Sadly, he would not be the only one.

THIRTEEN

I t was silly, she knew.

That's why, later the same night, Jessie had waited until Cassandra was taking a long bath. She was still haunted by that one thing Micah had said. That one phrase: *'Fore I am a baby.* Despite Dr. Abernathy's attempt at an explanation, she held onto one promising thought: Could it really be true that in Micah's world, he had known Keith in some amorphous time before birth? What did that mean, what did it look like? Was it something—or some*place*—that everyone went to? Why Micah, and why Keith? She looked down at the photos in her hands. Her mother, her father. Pictures of them at their wedding, at Jessie's eighth birthday party, at an anniversary gathering she'd hastily thrown together for them shortly before her father died. The photos were all in color, in perfect focus, and centered on their faces. Their expressions didn't vary much, since her parents were the sort of people who grinned almost automatically when a camera was turned their way.

She examined the final picture at length. Her father had lost so much weight, and the dark circles beneath his eyes the ominous gray-purple of an approaching summer storm, but the familiar features remained, the same ones she saw when she looked in the mirror. When had she started to resemble her folks so much? She'd always been told she had her father's deep brown eyes, but now she could see that she had his nose as well. Thank God she didn't have his hairline! Her mother's smile was identical to hers, one that didn't quite go up as high on the left as on the right. Tears sprang to her eyes, and she rubbed them away with her fingertips. What she wouldn't give to know they were all right; to know they were pleased with how her life had turned out; to know they loved her sons (she knew they would have).

The room was lit only from the nightstand table. With Dot on his lap and surrounded by his fireman paraphernalia, Micah was having some quiet time as he sat in his bed, glancing through a board book he'd long outgrown. Though Jessie couldn't make out the words, it sounded as if he was talking to himself. She wondered if Keith was on the other end of the conversation, which made her task all the more urgent.

"Hi, sweetie," she said, walking into his room.

He looked up. "Mama." The sound would always melt her heart.

Jessie sat down beside him on his bed. "Want to see some pictures?"

"Uh-huh." He leaned up against her.

"Do you know who these people are?" Jessie had debated which to show him first: the last photo of her parents, middle-aged and sickly, or their wedding photo, when they were young, healthy, full of energy and focused on the future. Which face would Micah be more likely to recognize if he saw them, in the before-time? She decided to start with the one that had sat for years on her bedroom dresser, one he'd seen frequently already but now ignored as another fixture of the house: their final photo. "Who are they?"

"Your mommy an' daddy."

"That's right. This was your Grandpa Hal and your Grandma Susan. They were wonderful parents, and I loved them very much. I'm sorry you never got a chance to meet them.

"And here they are when they were younger, at their wedding. Isn't that a pretty white dress?"

Micah nodded, and Jessie smiled to herself. Her mother's shiny white satin gown was such a product of its time, there was no mistaking the era. She used to put it on to play princess when she was little, to her mother's delight, dragging the train through the living room and hiking up the shoulders, which kept falling off her tiny frame. But when she got older, she secretly mocked the design—those huge puffy sleeves, the giant bow above the butt, that wild profusion of lace dripping with faux pearls! Still, the profound joy in her mother's face made her a timelessly beautiful bride. "See how happy they were? Didn't they have nice smiles?"

"Uh-huh."

"And look at this one: That's me with my parents when I was little! I was eight, just a bit older than Eli. Isn't my haircut funny?"

Jessie had the strong impression that Micah was losing what little interest he'd had in the pictures, so she cut to the chase. "Micah. You said you first saw Keith before you were a baby, remember?"

He lifted his eyes to hers but said nothing. She tried again.

"Before you were a baby. Remember, you told the professor that you knew Keith from before you were born?"

Micah's stare was blank, his eyes drooping. It was getting very close to bedtime, but she'd hoped that in this serene, almost meditative state, he might be more in touch with—with . . . whatever mystery was out there. In desperation, Jessie blurted out: "Did you—did you ever see these people, Micah? My mommy and daddy? In the before-time?" She held up the pictures again, positioning all three of them in front of Micah's face. "Look, Micah! Were they there? Did you see them?"

"Mama, I'm tired."

Jessie's hands dropped to her lap. She felt defeated but did her best to hide her disappointment, forcing a smile.

"Of course, baby. It's bedtime for you."

She rose from his bed as he slid down and rested his head on the pillow. Setting aside the board book on the nightstand, Jessie pulled up his covers, placed Dot close beside him, and kissed him good night. Maybe she lingered a little longer than usual. "Goodnight, Micah."

"Night, Mama."

"I love you."

"Love you."

Next, Jessie went in to check on Eli. To her surprise, except for the pale glow of the stars on the navy-blue ceiling of his outer space-themed room, it was totally dark. Eli was in bed with the rocket-ship blanket drawn up around his neck, his back to the doorway. Getting him ready for bed usually involved a series of negotiations that included a chapter —or several—of his latest book, a request for water, a last trip to the bathroom, and the special thirty-second "Great Big Hug" reserved for nighttime.

"No story tonight, Eli?" There was no reply. She knew his body language well enough to know that he wasn't asleep. "Don't you want to know what happens to Charlie now that he has the Golden Ticket to the chocolate factory?"

Eli did not bother to turn around. "No."

"How about a Great Big Hug?"

"No."

"Can I kiss you goodnight?"

"No."

Oh. Jessie didn't remember Eli ever turning her away so abruptly and completely. It was painful. Was this the way it would be from now on? "All right, honey. Have a good night. I love you."

There was no reply.

When Jessie returned to their bedroom, Cassandra was still in the bath. She could hear the faint music of Cass's playlist and the occasional badly sung lyric. It was still early and there was plenty of time before they, too, would retire for the night. She dropped down onto the bed, and, resting her chin in her hand, studied the photos minutely: her parents' clothes, their body language, their mood. She could practically feel the warmth of their entwined hands, hear her mother muttering out of the side of her mouth in good humor, "Why don't they take the picture already?"

"It's so unfair," she said aloud, knowing full well that she sounded more like Eli than his mother. How could they be getting this tantalizing glimpse into the greatest unknown of life and yet still be unable to answer the question of what happens after we die? Why couldn't Micah give them more details? What if he'd interacted with her parents but couldn't remember? It was agony.

While it hadn't been her intent, she was still in the same position when Cassandra came out of the bathroom in her pajamas. "Hey, babe. Whatcha up to?"

"What?" Jessie was startled out of her reverie. She had intended to put the photos away before Cass came back into the room.

Tilting her head to the side, Cassandra took a closer look and said, "Your parents, huh?"

"Yeah. I was, um"—flustered, Jessie couldn't come up with any plausible explanation—"reminiscing."

"Were you?" Cassandra looked at her through lowered lids, assessing. "Oh, no. Tell me you didn't."

"Didn't what?"

"Show these pictures to Micah to see if he met your parents in the afterlife."

Damn. "What makes you think—"

"Hah, I know you too well. That's what you've been after ever since we figured out who Keith was."

Jessie leapt up and set the anniversary photo back on her dresser before shoving the other two into her sock drawer. She turned around, leaning against the dresser as she folded her arms across her chest. "Well, maybe I was. So what?"

Cassandra reached out and took Jessie gently by the wrist. Drawing her to their bed, she encouraged Jessie to sit beside her on the fluffy, blue-and-white duvet. With the only sound the gurgle of the water draining from the tub, she took Jessie's hand in her own and touched her cheek with the other.

"Jess. You have to accept that you're never going to get the answer you want. I get it: Now that you know it *can* happen, you want it to happen for these specific people. But life doesn't work that way; death sure as hell doesn't work that way.

"Your parents, they're not coming back, and they're not going to use Micah to send you a message from the Great Beyond."

That's all it took for Jessie's tears to start flowing. She leaned away and grabbed a tissue from the nightstand. "You don't know that. You *couldn't* know that."

"No, but I can make a really good guess. I think it's possible that this—thing—with Micah and even the other recorded cases are likely just a drop in the bucket in the history of humanity. A glitch, not the norm. Why it happens, well, I'll leave that for people smarter than me."

"You mean Dr. Abernathy," Jessie said, scowling. "He said almost the same thing."

"And who am I to argue with an expert? Maybe there's a handful of cases when the trauma of death was so great that the . . . energy can't settle. Or something. Whatever. Otherwise, the world would be filled with . . . recycled souls.

"I mean, there are so many more people alive today than ever before. Are some of them new souls, and some of them old? Who gets to decide? Do you see how insanely confusing that could be?" She shook her head. "I can't get behind that."

"Well, I can." *And so could millions of Hindus, Buddhists, and Sikhs around the world,* but Jessie did not say as much, because it was clear that Cass didn't want to hear it.

Cassandra grimaced. "Not everyone would want to come back, anyway."

"What do you mean? Of course they would!" Jessie flung her arms out, barely missing Cassandra's face. "Who wouldn't want another go-round at *life*?"

"Maybe someone who had a shitty go the first time around?" Jessie stared at her. "Maybe for some, even once is too much."

"That's . . . dark."

"Tell me about it."

As she had many times since they'd met, Jessie wished her wife would open up more about her life at home. How bad had it gotten that *this* was her view of the world? Jessie would have suggested therapy if Cassandra hadn't shot down that particular idea years ago. Maybe there would be another time in the future; it was never too late.

"That's reality, though," Cass continued. "Look, babe, I know where you're coming from. When you've been lucky in life, it's normal to want it to continue forever. But not everyone is so fortunate, and to some people it would be their worst nightmare to have to go through it all over again. Everything ends, Jessie. Don't set yourself up for disappointment expecting otherwise.

"And, not for nothing, but you don't want to be putting more pressure on Micah. That's plain selfish."

Jessie flinched. Micah had been taking these extraordinary events so well, with no complaint and no real interruption to his daily routine—and certainly more smoothly than Eli—that she hadn't considered he might be feeling stressed. If he didn't articulate it, was it because he didn't feel it, or because he didn't have the words? Jessie was aghast that she might be adding another layer of convolution to her baby's already confounding life.

"I-I'm sorry," she said. "You're right. I shouldn't pressure him. It's not good for him, and that's not what my parents would have wanted."

"Well, you would know. OK, so no more 'reminiscing' with Micah?"

"No, I promise."

"Good. Now, how about you get ready for bed?"

Looking at the clock, Jessie was startled at how late it was getting.

She stood up and headed into the bathroom. "Thanks for the reality check, honey," she said.

"Anytime," Cassandra replied. "But one more thing . . ."

Jessie turned around, exhausted from the discussion, wondering what more Cass could possibly add. "What?"

"Don't let me catch you with a Ouija board."

Cass dodged as the hurled roll of toilet paper whizzed past her ear.

FOURTEEN

By Monday, the excitement in the household over Dr. Abernathy's visit had already faded. As they didn't expect another visit any time soon—if at all—Jessie and Cassandra did their best to keep the boys focused on school and their friends. Jessie needed additional discipline to concentrate on work because the temptation to continue her past-life research was distracting her from her duties.

So, she was already exhausted and ready to call it a night when the phone call came.

"Oh, hey, Angela. What's up?" Cassandra furrowed her brow as she paced past Jessie with her phone plastered to her ear. It was late—Jessie squinted at her phone—nearly 10:15 on a school night, nearly bedtime. Why was Angela Barlow calling at this hour? "Sure, we're here. See you in ten."

"What was that about?" Jessie was stretched out on the sofa in their tiny formal living room. It was stiff and tweedy and not nearly as comfortable as the one in the den, but the boys had been letting off steam by flinging Legos at each other after school, and since it was the first time she'd seen Eli smile in days, she hadn't had the heart to scold them or the patience to supervise a cleanup. It was a minefield in there.

"Angela is stopping by. She said she's on her way back from the inaugural PPAW meeting and wanted to give us the lowdown." Cassandra looked down at Jessie. "Oh, I'm sorry, babe. I should have asked. Are you feeling up for that?"

"Not really." Jessie rubbed her eyes and for good measure scrubbed her cheeks as well, leaving her hands covering her face.

"Should I call her back and tell her not to come?"

"No, no. That's OK." She sat up. "I'd rather know what we're facing so we're not taken by surprise. Or—maybe more accurately when it comes to PPAW—ambushed."

When Angela arrived, they all decided that the kitchen was a far more comfortable place to sit than the formal living room.

"Wine?" Jessie offered.

"Beer?" Cassandra offered.

Predictably, Cass knew her friend better and opened a bottle of beer each for Angela and herself. Jessie poured herself a glass of merlot.

"OK, Ange, what can you tell us?" Cassandra said, sitting down across from her.

Angela took a sip from her bottle. She was a stay-at-home mom, a sturdy, blonde woman with a ready laugh and a practical, no-nonsense attitude about her three kids and life in general that Jessie admired. Her husband, Pete, was one of Cassandra's best friends at the station, and their family attended the same church. And now that Eli was in Mrs. Donohue's class, their eldest, Oliver, was his classmate again, as he'd been in first grade. From what little she'd managed to pry out of Eli these days, it was clear that Oliver was remaining steadfast in his friendship, and Jessie was grateful for the instruction Angela's son had obviously received from his parents.

"Well," Angela said, "the bad news is that the meeting was pretty well attended. I'd say there were about fifty, maybe sixty people there.

Mostly the usual suspects, if you know what I mean: the Meyers, the Paulsons, the Craigs. Chuck Lebow, Mickie Taylor. I was kind of surprised to see the Duke and Diana Hadlin there, but maybe they were there for the same reason I was. The Marshall adults, junior and senior, were there, of course, front and center. Dean sat with the PPAW organizers, a married couple with strong southern accents. They introduced themselves as Christopher and Heather Greer."

"And Trish?" Jessie still hadn't seen or heard from Trish since Dean's call. Unexpectedly, she missed her. She told herself it was because of Eli's heartbreak, or the comfort of the familiar, but the strange reality was that Trish was a source of relentless energy and positivity that had been lacking in their lives recently. More than once since the whole Quentin debacle, she wondered what would happen if she texted Trish, asked to meet. But she was afraid to put herself out there, dreading the kind of bigoted pushback from Trish that they'd already seen from her husband. At least this way, she could imagine that Trish was better than that.

"Well, she was in the front row, next to Dean's parents. Looked a little uncomfortable, if you ask me. But that could just be because she was sitting with her in-laws." She downed some more of her beer. "I would have been, too, frankly."

"And what did the Greers have to say?" Cassandra asked.

"They talked a bit about the organization, which they founded in Texas nine years ago. They claimed they now have over 175 chapters in eight states, with over ten thousand members, and they've had great success in—and I'm quoting here—'saving our children from the woke agenda and bringing them closer to God.'"

"Did they define said 'woke agenda'?" Jessie asked.

"Naturally. Anything that doesn't align with their worldview: straight, white, Christian. Or their brand of Christian anyway. 'Ungodly' things like—"

"Being gay?" Cassandra interjected.

"Yes, or being an atheist, or someone who believes in nontraditional gender roles. Or equality for minorities. Evolution. There's nothing new about any of that. But you know what else they said? Another excuse they're using? Oh, this kills me: They don't want to make their children *feel bad about themselves.* They don't want their kids to be *uncomfortable.* So anything that might make their child question what their parents or church leaders have taught them—say, um, that slavery was a totally immoral shitshow that benefited generations of White people—is out of bounds. Oh, no, we wouldn't want little Logan feeling guilty for hundreds of years of oppression! It might put him off his dessert.

"Who are the fucking snowflakes now?" Angela took a long drink from her bottle, draining it. She patted her lips dry with the back of her hand and slid the empty bottle away from her. "So, they'd rather teach their children to hate strangers."

"Or people in their own community," Jessie said with a sigh. Cassandra slung a comforting arm around her shoulders and gave her a squeeze.

Angela pulled a folded sheet of paper out of her purse and flattened it onto the table. "They gave out this list of book titles they wanted to see removed from our schools and our library. But I guess you've seen it already?"

A quick glance at the page was enough for Jessie. It looked identical —within a volume or two at least—to the one Allison had provided. "Yes."

"Most of these make no sense at all to me." She ran her finger down the list. "I mean, from the distorted Pee-Paw point of view I get that they want all these LGBTQ-sympathetic titles gone, but what's so bad about—"

"Talking animals," Jessie said with a grimace when she saw where Angela was pointing.

"Are you kidding me?"

"Demonic, or something. Witchcraft, maybe. Don't go looking for logic from these people."

"Welcome to the Dark Ages 2.0." Angela murmured. "Anyway, toward the end they talked about running candidates in the next school board election and passed around a clipboard for anyone who thinks they might want to take a stab at it. There were a few takers. Thank God we have another year before the next election."

"You said the attendance was the bad news," Cassandra said. "Is there any good news?"

"Well, it seems to me that most of the people there were on the older side, I mean like past school-parent age. There were a handful of teens there too, but it looked to me as if their parents had dragged them there; some of them, anyway. They did *not* look inspired to be leading the charge to make their town less 'woke,' by the way. Alanna Marshall in particular looked *pissed*, though that could just be the seriously uncool nature of the whole gathering."

"That is good news, I guess." Jessie looked at Cassandra, who nodded.

"There is one more thing, though, Jessie."

"What's that?"

"Your name came up. I guess in most of the districts that PPAW's invaded, they don't have a convenient scapegoat, but in Hadlinsburg, tag—you're it."

"Oh." The word escaped Jessie like air from a deflating balloon. She slumped in her chair, rubbing her forehead.

"Dean made sure to remind the crowd that their very own town had a 'woke librarian' in its midst. A scary lesbian to boot."

"Fucking great." Cassandra slammed her hand on the table, making Jessie jump. "Fucking Dean."

An alarming thought occurred to Jessie. "Our kids! What if they go after the boys?"

"Now, hold on," Angela responded. "There was some mumbling in the audience, but they're not out there suggesting that you—or the boys—should be chased out of town."

"Not yet," Cassandra said, both hands now clenched in fists, her knuckles white.

"My take is that Pee-Paw is going to find Hadlinsburg a harder sell than they think. We've got some good people here." Angela gave a half-smile, leaning back in her chair and stretching out her legs. "I will have to say, though, I understand that stuff that's going on with Micah is some crazy shit."

Jessie sat up. "Wait, what exactly do you know about what's going on with Micah?"

"Um, you know, *Keith* and all. The Towers. Dr. Abernathy. I think it's fascinating." Angela exchanged a quizzical look with Cassandra. "Wait. Was I . . . not supposed to know about it?"

"You *told* her about that?" Jessie could feel her face growing hot. "All of it?"

"Why, was it supposed to be a secret?" Cassandra, obviously caught off guard, frowned. "I had to talk to *someone* about it, Jessie, and Pete was willing to listen."

"And Pete told me." Angela looked chagrined. "Hey, I'm really sorry."

"It's not that you told Pete, or that Pete told Angela," Jessie said to Cass, "it's that . . . aren't we having a hard enough time right now without the whole town thinking we're genuinely insane?"

"It's hardly the whole town, hon—"

"And we don't think you're insane. Pete hasn't told anyone else," Angela said. "I promise I won't, either. Swear to God." She looked from one woman to the other and stood up. "Guess I'd better be going."

Cassandra saw her to the door while Jessie sat at the table, finishing her wine and feeling stunned. Shaking her head, she rose and walked to the sink, washed out the glass, and set it on the dish drain.

"I'm sorry about Angela. How was I supposed to know you'd mind?" Cassandra said after Angela had made her hasty retreat. She rinsed out the beer bottles and dropped them with twin clanks into the recycling bin. "You never said not to; you never said anything! You mean to tell me that you haven't been spilling your guts to any of your friends?"

As she got up to sponge down the table, Jessie was still feeling agitated and wished she'd had another glass of wine. The PPAW news from Angela, coupled with finding out that Micah's past-life memories were now known outside their family, would make it hard to sleep tonight. She was unhappy with Cass and wanted her wife to know it. "I've danced around it a little bit, told them that Micah is going through a difficult stage, hinted at a conflict with Eli's friend's family, but have I actually *told* any of my girlfriends what we're going through? No."

"Why not?"

"I don't know, other than the obvious? I guess whenever we talk, it seems like an awkward thing to bring up. You know, in between the vacation plans and home improvements and—It would be like, 'Hey, love your new kitchen! Great backsplash! And by the way, Micah's been channeling a dead FDNY firefighter. How are *your* kids?'

"Besides that, there are too many chances for people to take it the wrong way, to make assumptions, to let their imaginations run wild."

With a nod, Cassandra acknowledged the difficulty of explaining the situation to people who hadn't even met Micah.

"So you'll have to excuse me," Jessie said, "if I'm a little salty that you've been talking to people about Micah."

"I *said* I'm sorry. And Pete isn't *people*; he's someone I trust with my life."

"And *he* told Angela. Who knows who else he told. And who else she'll tell!"

"No one. You heard Angela: He told no one else. And she won't either."

Jessie wished she could be as sure.

"I trust them," Cass insisted. "But then how are you dealing with . . . the situation?"

"Oh, you mean besides the extra glass of wine I occasionally have these days?" She shut off the kitchen lights and headed up the stairs with

Cassandra close behind, listening. "I'm reading. Researching. I'm trying to convince myself that if all these other kids have made it through this weirdness in a few years, Micah will too. I just hope that he doesn't make too many waves along the way."

And I hope we survive it.

Fifteen

A week and a half later, Jessie was enjoying some rare peace and quiet while Micah napped in his room and Eli played a game on the tablet. She looked up from her book with a smile when Cassandra came in from the supermarket, where she had gone to pick up some emergency groceries between major shopping trips.

What Cass brought back, though, was only a couple of magazines and a sour look.

"What are you doing with that trash?" Jessie asked, her grin dropping at the sight of the tabloid in Cassandra's hand. Cassandra was no intellectual, but she was a confirmed skeptic who didn't look to supermarket tabloids for answers. And certainly never bought them.

Cassandra, silent, flipped a few pages of the publication and held up a page in front of her face. There was a dramatic photo of the Twin Towers burning, and a bold headline reading: *Lesbian Family's Toddler Claims to Be Reincarnation of Gay 9/11 Firefighter*. "What a crock," Cassandra snorted. "I mean, Micah doesn't 'claim' anything."

"Oh, for ffff—"

"Nice that they led with *Lesbian Family*, too, isn't it? And threw in *Gay Firefighter* for good measure? A shocker. Leanne Olivetti, remember her? We met her during Eli's first tee-ball season? I'd barely gotten through the door of the store when she cornered me to ask me if I'd seen the article. Of course, I had no idea what she was talking about. So she grabbed my hand and dragged me over to the magazine rack at checkout. I swear, the woman was downright gleeful; I guess she's the kind of person who actually reads that garbage.

"They've got all the details there, too: the town; our first initials; Keith and Joey's full names. At least they didn't mention our last name, for what that's worth. As if there's more than one lesbian couple in Hadlinsburg, Ohio, with a son whose name begins with M."

"Here's another one." She opened the paper to show Jessie the article, headlined: *Reincarnation or Hoax? A Child's Astonishing "Memories."* "At least *this one* didn't mention any names. They both claim to have made attempts to contact us, but, well, you know: 'the family was unavailable for comment.'"

Of course no attempt of the sort had been made.

"But you'd better believe there's a juicy quote from the Pee-Paw people, those Greers, in both articles," Cass continued, "about how this is the sort of thing they 'fight to protect children against.' About how kids should be allowed to grow up without, in their exact words, 'being forced by their parents to mimic abnormal gender roles.'"

Jessie groaned, covering her face with her hands.

"I'll spare you the rest of what they say but suffice it to say that the articles are every bit as unflattering and sensationalistic as you'd expect."

"So how did they find out?" It came out in a hoarse whisper. Jessie scanned the article in a blink—a librarian superpower—and recited aloud, "*According to a neighbor who prefers to remain anonymous.*" She glared at Cassandra.

"No," Cass insisted, "it is most definitely *not* Pete or Angela. I've already spoken to them, and they're as shocked as we are. Professor Abernathy?"

Jessie shook her head. "I will *not* believe there's a leak in the research team. I actually trust the prof and his assistant. They have reputations to maintain, and they can't risk that by leaking information like this to a tabloid. It's like—"

Jessie felt Cassandra's hand seize hers, and she looked up at her. Cassandra's head tilted to the side, and her eyes slid over to the same angle. Following that glance with her own, Jessie's eyes alit on Eli.

He had put down the tablet and was looking uncomfortable, twisting his fingers. It was his tell. If a toy ended up broken, if there was a mess in the kitchen, if the toilet was clogged up, chances were that Eli would be standing apart from the chaos, trying to act as if he didn't care, but entwining his fingers. This time they were red from the intensity of it.

"Hey, buddy," Jessie said, laying a gentle hand on his shoulder, "is there anything you want to tell us?"

Looking down at the floor, Eli hunched his shoulders almost to his ears and frowned. He ran a hand back and forth under his nose. "Maybe," he replied.

In situations like this, Jessie and Cassandra had discovered that Eli would eventually reveal his role in the mischief if left by the two of them for a time to stew in his discomfort.

It didn't take long, and it came out in a rush.

"It wasn't my *fault*! Quentin's dad said if I told him if anything cool or weird happened in the house, I could play with him at recess again."

Cassandra facepalmed.

"It's not my fault, Mommy! I missed Quentin so much, an' Mr. Marshall promised that it would be OK with you, 'cause we're all friends an' all.

"So, I talked to Quentin while we were on the swings an' told him all about the professor from Orgon, an' Keith having a father, and the big buildings falling down. But now Mr. Marshall says it's enough an' he changed his mind an' Quentin still isn't allowed to play. I don't understand; I did what he asked. *He promised*." He looked up at his mothers with filled eyes. "Please don't be mad."

Jessie could feel the blood rising to her face, making her feel as if she had a fever. The family had been betrayed from the *inside*. But this was their boy Eli, and he wasn't after money or notoriety, just the company of his best friend.

And he'd been manipulated by Dean Marshall, that son of a bitch.

"We're not mad at you," she said in careful tones, while inside her head she was shrieking in frustration, "but you don't understand how difficult this is going to make life for us. Not just for Micah, but for all of us." Of course he could have no idea of the ramifications, now that the cat was out of the bag.

Eli nodded vigorously, his eyes squeezed shut. He burst into tears.

"I'm sorry, Mama!" he said through his sobs. "I thought you wouldn't mind if it was just Quentin."

And it might not have been a disaster had it remained "just Quentin." But Quentin was not as circumspect as Pete and Angela. He told his father, who told the folks in PPAW, who called the tabloids. And who knows what else was to come, for God's sake. Thank goodness they no longer had a landline: A public listing would have the phone ringing off the hook.

"From now on," Cassandra stepped in, "can we agree that what happens inside our house stays here, Eli?" She glanced at Jessie, who nodded her acknowledgment. The irony was not lost on her. "Micah is going through some things. Our business is private, and nobody needs to know."

"And 'nobody' includes Quentin too," Jessie added. "I'm sorry, Eli, sweetheart, but I think at this point we know that you and Quentin won't be playing together at all, at least for the time being."

This caused a fresh round of sobbing from Eli, and Cassandra picked him up in her arms, resting his head against her shoulder and rocking and shushing him the way she did when he was a baby.

"What do we do now?" she whispered to Jessie. "Do we ignore the stories and hope it all dies down? Do we get ourselves a lawyer? Practice saying *no comment*? Or what?"

"No idea. Maybe it won't be so bad. I mean, who's actually reading these things? This is new territory for all of—oh, what now?"

At that moment Jessie's phone rang, and with trepidation she glanced at it.

Dr. Abernathy.

"Hello?"

"Jessie, it's Vince Abernathy," came the kind voice. "I wanted to make you aware of an unpleasant new development."

"If you're talking about the tabloid articles, Professor, Cassandra just informed me."

There was a sigh on the line. "You should know that my team is still committed to your case and to your privacy. My assistant, Lorraine, informs me that the tabloids had emailed our office to confirm the story, but naturally, she told them that per departmental policy we couldn't and wouldn't give out any information on any of our cases, even to confirm or deny their existence. My guess is that they decided to run with it, anyway, knowing that you likely wouldn't want to call more attention to it by filing suit."

Unfortunately, he was right. And their family didn't have the deep pockets they'd need to do battle, either. "If you do in fact want to go more public, my office can advise you on the best way to do that, with reliable news outlets, podcasts, etc. If not, my advice to you and Cassandra would be to decline to speak with anyone, no matter how apparently well-meaning. Don't answer unknown numbers on your phone, don't talk to any stranger who might approach you on the street." He paused. "I will understand completely if you don't want to proceed with us."

"No, Professor, we don't hold any of this against you and Savannah. We absolutely want you to continue with your research."

"I appreciate that. In the meantime, we can hope that this will all die down on its own."

Jessie hoped it would. The optimist in her thought, *How many people are still reading tabloids, anyway?* But the pessimist in her was doubtful.

Several days passed, and if anything, the situation had deteriorated. Jessie had had no idea that supermarket tabloids were so popular in Hadlinsburg. Well, to be fair, it was more likely that it wasn't that the tabloids were so popular, but that gossip certainly was. Leanne, who was part of Trish's MLM circle, certainly must have done her share.

Some library patrons were either staring at Jessie with a combination of open curiosity and hostility or avoiding her, steering their children away from her in favor of trying to find their selections themselves. *Maybe I'm just being paranoid*, she thought, trying to be optimistic. But her fears were confirmed in other ways. Several parents had begun carrying preprinted lists, which Jessie could only surmise contained "PPAW-approved" reading material. Her suspicions were proven correct when one of the parents left their list behind, and Jessie could only shake her head at the contents: bland, "safe," poorly written, and often religion based. There was nothing in the least bit challenging or thought-provoking on offer. Traffic in general in the children's and youth section was down, but according to Allison, online submissions to the Material Request Form—for new books and movies—had skyrocketed. All the new requests had come directly from the PPAW mold, but because of the volume of forms they received, Allison told the staff that she was forced to take them seriously.

That same week, when Jessie went to pick Micah up from preschool, the director took her aside. Rubbing her hands together in a fit of nerves, she told Jessie that two families had already pulled their children from Micah's class, not—as they assured her—because they thought he posed any danger to their kids but because they didn't want to appear to be "condoning his lifestyle."

"For God's sake!" Jessie snapped at her incredulously. "A three-year-old doesn't have a 'lifestyle.' He's just a little boy who—who . . ." She was at a loss to describe exactly what Micah was going through, but her point was taken.

"Oh, *I* know that," the director said with an anxious smile, the kind of grin a dog makes when it's afraid of being hit, "but these are PPAW families, you understand. I was able to move them into the other class, but that one's full now. So if anyone else complains . . ." She gave a helpless little shrug.

PPAW families. As if they'd found a new religion, and in some ways they had. Jessie could only stare at the director in frustration and disbelief. "I can't believe that you could accept such a ludicrous argument anywhere, much less in a *preschool*. Aren't the children supposed to be learning to accept each other's differences and play nicely together?"

"Of course! But Jessie, I want to assure you that *I* don't agree with them at all, and I would never insult you or Cassandra in any way." The owner of the preschool had no doubt instructed the director on how to cover her ass in the event of a bias-related lawsuit. Jessie was not impressed.

As Jessie fumed her way back to the car with an oblivious Micah, she thought with some dismay about her lack of alternatives should he be asked to withdraw from school. What's more, poor Eli continued to come home from school morose and argumentative. He had begun to pick at his meals and ask to be excused before dessert. He did his homework, but only after a great deal of prodding and complaint. Two scraped elbows prompted a call to Mrs. Donohue, who confirmed that some children in his class had started making fun of him, and one had even tripped him on the playground. While Jessie was grateful that Mrs. Donohue exercised a genuine zero-tolerance policy for bullying— further confirming that her choice of class was the right one for Eli— even the most dedicated teacher couldn't catch every incident every time. Worse, Jessie suspected, the adults at home were no doubt excusing or even encouraging this behavior in their children. Punitive visits to Ms. Campbell's office would have no effect on complicit parents.

She wondered whether she would have to quit her job to home-school her own children. The whole idea was abhorrent to her, as she believed firmly in the power of public education and the necessity of children socializing with others to create functioning members of society, an area where she suspected a lot of PPAW supporters had gone wrong. She loved her job, she really did, despite its frequent headaches. Never mind that she and Cass needed both incomes if they were to keep their house and plan for the boys' education and their eventual retirement.

More than that, though, Jessie felt that the worst thing she could do would be to let the zealots win. She thought about how Cassandra had been literally chased from her own home at seventeen into the armed forces so she would have an income and a place to live. That move had presented its own hardships, of course, since homophobes and misogynists exist everywhere, but once Cass had become part of the squadron, there was nothing they wouldn't do for each other. If you asked Cass, an already determined and iron-willed woman, she'd tell you that she had come out stronger for it.

Back at work, an email Jessie received from the library board confirmed that PPAW had sent them the same list of book challenges that had been sent in East Daniston, with a couple of the additions Jessie had spotted on Angela's list. As in the nearby town, the leadership of the Hadlinsburg schools and library declared publicly that they wouldn't bow to pressure from PPAW or any other group. Cassandra had pointed to this promise as evidence that they wouldn't cave, but Jessie countered that the mayor, who had won his three terms on a very conservative platform, could be expected to put pressure on both boards. To Cass's point that the boards were independent, non-partisan, and free from local government oversight, Jessie could only roll her eyes at Cass's naiveté. "Supposed to be, babe," she'd said to Cassandra. "*Supposed* to be."

Removing books from a public library. Like looking directly at the sun, the very thought of confronting such an objectionable idea head-on was too much for Jessie. So, in her mind, she was already trying to calculate the amount of time it would take to remove the "offending" titles from the shelves. Time that would take away from the real work she already had to do, and for what? To appease a group of people with metaphorical torches and pitchforks?

She slumped back into her chair. *Done, I'm so done*, she thought, rubbing her eyes. Stacking the books that needed review in front of her, she felt rather than heard the presence of someone standing by the desk. She suppressed a sigh. *Just don't bring me any more drama, please!*

It was Tyler Curtis, the reference librarian. The only male among half a dozen women, he was also younger than the others. At twenty-seven, he was recently married and expecting his first child in January. At the moment, he had his long, lanky back to the room and was leaning down on Jessie's desk, propping himself on both elbows.

"Don't look now," he whispered, a fringe of reddish-brown hair falling across his forehead, "but there's a man in one of the armchairs who's been watching you. He's been here at least two hours, and he's barely read anything in the book he picked out from Philosophy. Something by Kant, I think. Maybe he should have picked up something less challenging for a weekday afternoon. Anyway, mostly he pretends to be reading while you're dealing with patrons, but when you go back to your desk or you're shelving books, he's been staring at you."

He leaned closer. "He's not, let's say, our usual kind of patron."

Tyler shifted his position slightly so Jessie could see the man without looking directly at him.

The man seemed out of place in their library—hell, in their *town*; in fact, some of the regular patrons glanced at him with unabashed curiosity. His hair, pure white, flowed down his shoulders, and he had a long, unruly white beard. He wore tinted glasses, even here inside the building, and several necklaces, the most prominent of which was a large silver cross dangling from a piece of black rawhide to just below the tip of his beard. In one hand he held a book; his other hand lay atop a woven white hat which was resting on his knee. He was also sporting several bracelets, and nearly every finger had a large silver ring on it.

His overall look said "aging rock musician," a type not generally seen in Hadlinsburg. Almost as if Tyler could read her thoughts, he added, with a crooked smile, "He smells like weed."

"And he's been watching me?" Jessie murmured back.

"Yup."

"Please tell me he hasn't been wandering into the children's area or staring at any of the kids." In her current mood, Jessie was more than ready to have the man ejected or, even better, to call the police on him.

"No, nothing like that. He only seems interested in you. Thought you should know." Tyler glanced at the analog clock on the wall behind Jessie's desk. "It's almost quitting time. Do you want me to walk you to your car?"

But before Jessie could respond, the man in question stood up, left his book on the table beside the chair, set his hat on his head, and walked out of the library without a glance in her direction.

"I don't think that will be necessary, Tyler, but if you wouldn't mind having a look to see whether he's left the parking lot, I'd appreciate it."

"On it."

"I might have a stalker."

It was late, and Jessie and Cassandra were getting ready for bed. Although they had already discussed the other stressful events of the day, Cassandra clearly had not anticipated such a remark and stopped brushing her teeth with a foamy mouthful of toothpaste.

"Wha?"

Dabbing her face dry, Jessie smoothed on a little of the sample of nighttime moisturizer Trish had given Cassandra. "Suitable" for her skin type or not, she wasn't about to let the expensive product go to waste. It smelled good, and as long as it didn't make her break out she was going to make the most of it. Her pricey hand cream would wait, however. One last indulgence before bed. "I said, I might have a stalker."

Cassandra spit forcefully into the sink. "What happened?"

"There was a man at the library. I'd say early seventies. Ish. Caucasian, long white hair, white beard . . ."

"You're being stalked by Santa Claus?"

Jessie snorted a laugh. "No, he's thinner than Santa. And not exactly dressed for the part."

"And he's stalking you?"

"Tyler told me he was pretending to read but was actually watching me. For a good couple of hours."

"Huh." Cassandra rinsed her toothbrush. "Is this someone you've seen before?"

"Uh-uh. Total stranger. Tyler said he's pretty sure the guy isn't one of our patrons. Said he looked like he might be from out of town. And smelled of weed. Which would bolster that argument."

"I wonder if he came to gawk at you because of the articles. That would be too weird." Her toothbrush set aside in the holder, Cass ran the water in the sink, aiming for the ideal temperature to wash her face. "Does anyone even read the tabloids anymore?"

"Maybe not on paper, but they all have an online presence, so who knows?" Though she wouldn't say, Jessie *did* actually have an idea of the print circulation of the tabloids, which had dropped in recent years. (She couldn't help herself; she'd *had* to look it up.) But she wasn't sure how far their reach extended online; they did have an awful lot of followers on social media. In any case, she suspected that most of the trouble was coming from PPAW.

It was clear Cass was agitated, even spoiling for a fight. Jessie could tell by the aggressive way she scrubbed her face and splashed the cleanser away. "Do we need to make a report to the police?" she asked from behind her towel.

All Jessie had to do was say the word, but now, in the safety of her own home, she was hesitant. "I don't think so? I mean, it was only one day. Before I jump to any conclusions, I want to see if he shows up again. He didn't approach me—or, God forbid, any of the kids—or even ask anyone else about me. I can't explain it, but he didn't *feel* threatening."

"I hope you're right. But if he approaches you, I'll want to know about it. Call me, OK?"

"OK."

"Promise?"

"Promise."

Sixteen

"Should we speak with the *Hadlinsburg Herald*?" Cassandra was making coffee while Eli was presumably getting himself dressed upstairs. Micah was at the table eating a tube full of yogurt and somehow getting much of it on his face and hands. And hair.

"Why do you ask?" Jessie tried using a damp washcloth to clean up Micah, but he wouldn't sit still. "Could you let me do this, please, baby?"

"I mean, maybe it's time for us to take the bull by the horns to nip this thing in the bud."

Jessie chuckled a little. "I love it when you mix your metaphors."

"I'm serious. Do you think we should do an interview with the *Herald*? Get ahead of more serious repercussions in town? Quote Dr. Abernathy, explain the weirdness going on, and how it doesn't change the fact that we have an otherwise normal little boy?"

"I don't know. What do you think *normal* looks like to the Pee-Paws, though, Cass?" She walked over to Cassandra with her back to Micah, leaned in close, and said in a tense whisper, "Is it two women married to each other? Two children born to two different mothers via a sperm donor?" She shook her head slowly. "How about a little boy who is likely the reincarnation of a gay firefighter killed along with his boyfriend on 9/11? Is *that* their idea of normal? Anyone's idea of normal, for that matter? I mean, the articles were incendiary but not inaccurate.

"What could *we* possibly say to a group of ignorant people who are calling for *book banning* that could make them change their minds?" She backed up and looked at Micah, who was now occupied with squishing the gooey remnants of his bright pink yogurt between his fingers. Rubbing her forehead with her thumb, she went back to Micah, washcloth in hand, and gave him a thorough cleansing while he shrieked in protest. "Besides, the *Herald* has its own biases, and lately it's only been useful for high school sports and finding plumbers and landscapers."

"OK, fine. Sorry I asked." Cassandra leaned against the counter, her arms folded across her chest. "Then what do *you* recommend we do?"

"I have no idea. I'll think about it. In the meantime, it's time for me to get Micah dressed. See if you can work some magic on Eli, or he's going to be late for the bus."

The more Jessie considered it as she drove Micah to preschool, the firmer she was in her belief that approaching the *Herald* was the wrong move. True, Micah's memories and the visit by Dr. Abernathy could be the most newsworthy things to happen in the area in years—at least since that day when the F2 tornado touched down just outside of town, knocking down wires and flattening an empty warehouse. But she knew, as Cassandra didn't, that the biweekly was no longer a true local paper with neighborhood roots, and she didn't trust the corporation that owned it and a dozen other small newspapers in the area to be open-minded, particularly about a story as potentially politically charged as this one. She'd seen too many instances of remarks taken out of context and misquoted statements that changed the entire intent of the story, and it would be so easy for a writer or editor with an agenda to skew the entire narrative . . . with PPAW waiting in the wings to take advantage.

And did anyone still read it for news, or were they getting all their information online from even more questionable sources?

Still, she regretted snapping at her wife. So when she got back into the car after dropping Micah, she sent a text to Cass: *I'm sorry. Will try to think of something.*

But she was immediately distracted when the bearded stranger strolled into the library, tucked his hat under his arm, and headed for Fiction. While he perused the shelves, Tyler told her that the man had come in the day before, too, but left almost immediately, presumably when he saw that Jessie's desk was empty, her computer off. Then with a nod at Jessie, Tyler—bless him—followed the man into the stacks. The conversation was too muted for Jessie to hear, but later Tyler told her that he had offered the stranger assistance in locating something but was assured that he had found what he was looking for: Charles Bukowski's *Ham on Rye.*

First Kant and now Bukowski. "Well, isn't he the eclectic one?" Jessie mused.

"Assuming he's actually reading it," Tyler responded. Skepticism was his default position, which Jessie supposed went along with his research specialty.

Jessie went about the rest of her morning, acutely aware of the presence of this man. For once she was grateful for having very little downtime, because she knew she would have spent it fretting. When she did look up at him at random times during the day, he did appear to be engrossed in the book. Since he wasn't disturbing anyone, and in fact was doing exactly what any patron of a public library was welcome to do during operating hours, she had no excuse to approach him. He left shortly before noon and didn't return for the rest of the day. Nor did he return the next day, and since he hadn't attempted to take any books out, Jessie hoped that he had only been passing through town and that she—already on high alert—had been alarmed for nothing.

With the stranger gone, Jessie was able to turn her attention back to the issue of the chatter circulating in town. After days of mulling it over, she thought she had the solution. As they prepared dinner, she suggested to Cassandra that instead of approaching the *Herald*, they take advantage of Jessie's friendly relationship with the faculty adviser, Carla Linden, to get a student interview with the high school newspaper, the *Hadlinsburg Hawkeye*.

"See, that way, we know that we have someone on our side, who can assign a sympathetic student to interview us—and what are you laughing at?"

"Let's look at this objectively," Cass said, trying without success to stifle her laughter. "You're being accused by Pee-Paw of using your position at the library to influence the children of Hadlinsburg. So you want to clear up that misunderstanding by—do I have this right?—telling your story to *a minor* in the hopes that they will write something favorable about us?"

Jessie scowled. "Well, when you put it that way . . ."

"Sorry to burst your bubble, Jess, but I think the best option open to us right now is to hunker down and hope that people move on to the next shiny object."

While she still believed that if only people had access to the details, they'd be more supportive, Jessie had to agree with Cassandra. Like it or not, gossip had more power than news; the truth had to do battle with "alternative facts" and all too frequently lost.

Dinner was a largely silent affair as everyone grappled with their own thoughts. Jessie considered without satisfaction how little she'd been eating lately and the pounds she'd dropped. Even the usually chatty Micah had gone quiet, and Jessie wondered whether their three-year-old was having an internal conversation with Keith or merely tired from an active day at preschool. In a well-meaning attempt to liven up the evening and distract them all, Cassandra brought up what she must have considered to be a sure-fire topic of conversation.

"Hey, Eli! Your birthday's coming soon, bud! Ooh, presents! Have you thought about what you want?"

Still frowning, Eli didn't even look at his mother. "Nothing."

"Aw, that can't be true, big guy," Jessie said. "Isn't there anything?" She racked her brain for whatever was the current favorite toy among second graders, but she came up empty. They all seemed to want to play video games on tablets, and she was far better at recommending books. Instead, she asked, "How about a party? What kind of party do you want? I know: How about we bring some friends to Fabulous Felix's House of Fun?" It was an expensive arcade that would blow their budget for the month, but Jessie would be willing to do it for Eli, if only this once. "Huh? What do you think? And how about cake? What kind of cake do you want?" She knew all his favorites; which would it be? "Let's see, last year wasn't it . . . a carrot cake with cream cheese frosting?"

"I don't *want* a party, and I don't want a cake," Eli finally said. "There's only one thing I want."

That was a relief. Given the current environment, Jessie was terrified that none of his classmates would show up to a party anyway. "What's that?"

Now Eli looked directly at Jessie, challenging. "I want to play with Quentin. I want him to be my friend again."

Her heart sank. It was like that old joke, using a genie to wish for peace in the Middle East. An impossible task.

Getting no response from the expectant look he sent Jessie, Eli pushed himself back from the table and slid off his chair, clomping up the stairs and slamming his door. Cassandra and Jessie looked at each other over Micah's head.

"What do we do now?"

Cassandra shrugged. "I think we let him be sad and angry for a while. I'll go up and check on him in ten minutes."

But Jessie wasn't willing to accept the situation as it was. Eli had been depressed for weeks, and there was no end in sight, not even his birthday to look forward to. She thought about it as she watched Micah finish his dinner, as she cleared the table, as she put the plates in the dishwasher. She could hear Cassandra trying to reason with Eli upstairs and Eli's shouted replies. It frustrated her that there was nothing she could do.

Until she was finishing her bedtime routine and decided that there *was* something. Something that might help their situation in town as well.

Unlocking her phone, Jessie looked at the last text that Trish had sent her: *I'm sorry.*

Let's see how sorry she is, Jessie thought. She typed out a text and sent it.

SEVENTEEN

As Jessie had expected, Trish couldn't resist a request for a refill on her hand cream. But she wouldn't let Trish cop out by sending the product through a third party. She insisted that they meet in person, giving her the option of getting together in East Daniston—or even as far as Cincinnati—if she felt uncomfortable being seen with Jessie in Hadlinsburg.

That was how the two women ended up meeting at a café Jessie had never been to on a quiet side street of the neighboring town. Even so, Jessie almost laughed out loud at the sight of Trish waiting for her in oversized sunglasses and a dark-green silk scarf covering her hair, her cup of coffee already set in front of her. She looked like an amateur spy from a 1960s-era film, the kind Jessie's mother had enjoyed.

Beside the coffee was one of Trish's ubiquitous little white plastic bags containing Jessie's hand cream.

"Thanks for coming," Jessie said as she sat down.

"Well, I couldn't very well let you go without our special hand cream, could I?" Trish was a lower-key version of her usual self. "I wouldn't want to be responsible for the consequences."

"My hands and I appreciate that." Jessie withdrew cash from her wallet, handing it over to Trish, who pushed the white bag toward her. After giving her latte order to the server who appeared at the table, she tucked the bag into her purse.

"So," Trish said, stirring cream into her coffee and trying to act casual, a behavior that she no doubt also learned from those 1960s-era spy flicks, "does Cassandra know you're here?"

"No." There was no reason to ask if Dean knew.

"Mm. And how are the boys?"

"Micah is fine. Still, um . . . revisiting the past, as it were."

"I see."

Jessie wondered if Trish could ever really see or was beyond seeing. Well, maybe it was time to try. The server appeared at this moment with Jessie's latte, giving her a moment to collect her thoughts. She sipped from her cup even though it was still too hot, burning her tongue. The sting stiffened her resolve and propelled her to action.

"I want to tell you about it, Trish, and I'd like you to listen without judging. It's equal parts fascinating and heartbreaking. I'm going to start from the beginning, when we first realized that Micah wasn't just making things up."

Over the course of the next ten minutes, Jessie told Trish about the things her friend already knew—Micah's obsession with firefighters, his nightmares, and his tendency to talk to himself as he played alone—and how they dovetailed with the astonishing things that they had only recently learned about their son's inner life. She told Trish about their earth-shattering conversation on 9/11, about discovering that Keith was a real person, about *Keith me*. And to top it off, about *'fore I am a baby*.

"I had no idea," Trish said with her eyebrows arched high.

"Well, the tabloids could only drum up a frenzy with the information they had. Without our cooperation, or data from Dr. Abernathy's team, all they had was what a six-year-old could tell them." *Via your husband, of course.* But Jessie decided not to provoke Trish by mentioning Dean. Not yet. "And what we told Eli was only what we thought he needed to know, in terms he might be able to understand.

"Now, Eli . . . That's the real reason I asked to meet you. I mean, yes, I do need the hand cream. But I'm not going to lie to you: Eli's hurt, Trish. Badly. He doesn't have many friends in his new class, and certainly not any he likes as much as Quentin. He asks about him all the time, and he told me the only thing—the *only* thing—he wants for his seventh birthday is to play with his best friend again.

"So, what I want to know is: Does Quentin also miss Eli, and if he does, what can we do to give Eli the single birthday gift he wants?"

"To be honest"—Trish leaned back in her chair and took off her sunglasses, pinching the bridge of her nose. Even her expertly applied makeup couldn't disguise how uncharacteristically weary she looked— "Quentin has been impossible. He's acting out in school, picking fights, and refusing to do his homework. And you know how little homework we're talking about. He's also been rude to Dean, blaming him for the situation, and in return Dean has been taking away privileges and toys. Which starts the whole cycle over again." She pulled her coffee closer to her but didn't pick it up. "He's so unhappy, and the whole family is suffering for it.

"And Alanna! She's at a difficult age as it is, and she has been *impossible*. I'm trying to plan her big Sweet Sixteen party, but she's refusing to participate, or even cooperate. She's taken Eli's side—calling us bigots, can you imagine!—and it's gotten pretty loud in the house."

Well, you are *bigots, or at least Dean is, and hooray for Alanna!* "OK, we agree that we have two broken-hearted children who are making the rest of the family miserable. What are we going to do about it?"

Jessie believed the answer was a simple one, but she had to let Trish get there on her own. After all, it was *her* husband who had started the rubbish about Micah and who had sealed the deal with his abusive language and support of PPAW, not to mention leaking the information to the tabloids and the general public. So, while Jessie ached for poor Quentin, who was as much an innocent victim as Eli, she had no sympathy for Dean's receiving the brunt of his son's temper. He deserved that, and more.

Watching her friend in silence as they drank their coffee, Jessie considered as she never had before what life might be like for Trish at home. She rarely interacted with Dean and Trish as a couple—and then only at social events outside the house—and what little she knew about him wasn't flattering. He was more like his parents, she felt, than his spouse: loud, overbearing, and intolerant. They had married so young, right out of high school; Jessie wondered if Trish ever regretted it.

Or . . . maybe the couple had more in common with each other than Jessie had been seeing? She watched the play of emotions on Trish's face as she tried to decide what to say. It shouldn't have been that hard. It should have been easy, unless . . .

"Unless you agree with Dean, of course. That Quentin needs to be 'protected' from Eli and my family?" Jessie put her coffee cup down with a clatter. "That's it, isn't it? You haven't said anything, you haven't pushed back, because *you agree with him!*"

"No. No, that's not it at all." Taking the scarf off her head, Trish ran her hand through her hair. "It's just that . . . you've met his parents, so you know how he grew up. Dean has some very strong opinions . . ."

"Bullshit!"

Though she had surprised herself as well with her outburst, Jessie was proud to have shocked Trish. She'd told Cass once that the benefit of not using profanity in everyday life was its effectiveness on the rare occasions when it was deployed. She'd never been one to make a scene in public, but in this case, well, if she had to, she would. While Trish, wide-eyed, was still absorbing this, Jessie leaned toward her.

"You forget, Trish, that *Cassandra* grew up with parents like Dean's. Can you imagine what that did to her? And what her town's embrace of PPAW is doing to her now?

"Is this what you want your children to believe? That my family is a mistake, an abomination? That the little boy who is Quentin's best friend in the whole world is somehow unsafe because he has two mothers? Your silence is complicity, Trish. You and Dean are teaching Quentin and your other kids that it's OK to hate, that it's OK to reject other people who are different from you. And it's fine, because that's what Daddy was taught, and it's all just a matter of *opinion* anyway. Right? I'd say that runs counter to pretty much everything the two of you like to claim you believe in, what your kids are supposed to be learning in church.

"I'd also say you deserve what you get, but your own little boy is an innocent victim here."

She pushed her chair back and stood up. With her purse on the table and her hands trembling, she pulled out her wallet and counted out some bills. "That's for the latte," she said as she tossed them down. Spotting the white bag with the hand cream inside her purse, she yanked it out and dropped it onto the table, where it landed next to Trish's cup with a muted *smack*. "You can keep this too."

"Jessie, sit down." Trish reached for her hand. "Please."

After taking a moment to assess Trish's sincerity, Jessie acquiesced. She took her seat and waited for Trish to say something. Instead, she pushed the white bag back toward Jessie.

"First of all, take the cream, for heaven's sake. Your hands will be dry as the Sahara within two days. Second of all, I never said that I agree with Dean. I heard how he spoke to you, and I'm embarrassed."

"At his language or at his 'strong opinion'?"

"Both. He doesn't speak for both of us . . ."

"And yet, since you didn't push back *at all*, Trish, I would say he does. I'd be willing to give you the benefit of the doubt if you did anything at all to earn it. But I've yet to see any evidence."

"What makes you think I didn't push back? God, Jessie, don't be thick! Dean made the decision without asking me and then insisted that we all join PPAW. We had a fight about it, a big one."

"But I heard you were there at the PPAW meeting, along with Dean's parents, and so was Alanna."

"Dean demanded it." Jessie rolled her eyes. "Look, don't *you* ever do something because Cassandra insists on it?"

"Yeah, I've sat out in the hot sun at her softball games and gone out to dinner with her friends from the station. Sometimes I'm bored to tears, and at worst I've wasted an evening. But otherwise *no harm done*." She leaned back in her chair, folding her arms across her chest. "You can't say the same. So if that's your argument, it's worthless, and I'm not interested."

Trish slumped back in her chair with an air of defeat. It was a look Jessie had never seen on her.

"So, what do you want me to do?"

"Well, for one thing, you can start speaking up in public about what's going on with Micah when someone mentions it. You're pretty influential in town, Trish. Your family's been here for generations, and you've got so many friends, customers . . . People will listen to you in a way they won't listen to Cassandra and me. Go ahead and tell them Micah's story if they really want to know the truth. Tell them we're not a—a danger to anyone, for God's sake.

"*And* you can do something for the boys. Fix this problem Dean created. I know it's a lot, but you need to at least try, or you're no better than him."

"OK." Trish cleared her throat. "OK, I'll think of something."

Eighteen

"Why do I have to go to the park with you and Micah?" Eli was sulking again, cross-legged in the middle of his bed. "Why can't I stay home with Mommy?"

"Because it's a beautiful sunshiny fall day, and you haven't been outside in ages. Plus Mommy has errands to run, and she—"

"Then I can go outside with *her*. I'll go to the store, or whatever. I don't want to go to the stupid playground." He plopped back against his pillow and turned over with his face in his pillow. "And I'm *not* going," his muffled voice said.

"Come on, Eli," Jessie said, checking the time on her phone. "It's time to leave. Get your sneakers on." She walked out of the room and nodded at Cassandra, who went inside in her place.

Jessie walked Micah downstairs. "Ready to go, honey?" She popped on his sneakers and secured the Velcro closures. "Let's leave Dot at home today, OK?" Without protest, Micah dropped the Dalmatian onto a kitchen chair.

"All set," Cassandra announced as she appeared in the doorway with a sullen Eli at her side.

Jessie wasn't sure what Cass had done or said to get Eli moving, but she was grateful. "Thanks, babe. Catch you in a bit," she said as she hustled the boys out the door.

Whether it was due to the bright sunshine or the intense fall colors or the cheerful cacophony of the playground, Eli's mood had improved somewhat by the time they got out of the car eight minutes later. This particular park was one of their favorite places in Hadlinsburg: kid friendly, dog friendly, clean, and well maintained. There was a good variety of modern playground equipment and enough benches for weary parents. Its proximity to their neighborhood was one of the reasons they had chosen their house when they'd first moved to town, and it was one of the many things that kept them there whenever they felt out of place.

"We're gonna have a good time, right, boys?" Taking each son by the hand, Jessie scanned the park. "Ooh, I know!" she said. "Let's go climbing!"

"But I wanna go on the swings, Mama!" Eli said, trying to tug her in the opposite direction. Jessie, however, kept walking as if she hadn't heard him, pulling him and Micah along at a rapid clip. His whining accompanied them all the way across the play area.

"Eli!" a jubilant voice squealed out as they approached the climbing structure. Eli turned to look for the source and was nearly tackled when Quentin flew out from behind the red and yellow tower and flung himself at his friend. As the boys reacquainted themselves at the kind of high decibel levels only acceptable at a playground, Jessie and Micah walked over to Alanna, who was standing beside the structure in a T-shirt and jeans, a canvas tote bag slung over her shoulder. She wore a pair of oversized sunglasses similar to the ones her mother had worn at the coffee shop, but they were clearly for style rather than disguise and genuinely suited her.

"I appreciate this more than you know, Alanna," Jessie murmured. "Thank you. I hope you don't get in trouble with your father."

"Well, Mom set it up, right?" Alanna shrugged, grinning. There was a glint in her eye. "*And* dropped us off. Besides, I can't help it if we happened to be at the same playground at the same time, can I? It's a public place."

"It certainly is. All right, we have an hour. We won't be far. Give a shout if you need me."

After about ten minutes of going down three different slides (short, long, and circular), Micah switched to the swings, and Jessie was happy to push him robotically while her mind—for the moment freed from all worries of past lives and present threats—was allowed to wander. If she looked to her right, she could see Quentin chasing Eli, and then Eli chasing Quentin, and their unabashed joy at being together again made Jessie more relaxed than she'd felt in weeks.

It didn't last long. She realized with a start that the stranger from the library was sitting on a bench across the park. She had no way of knowing whether he'd been there prior to their arrival or if she had been followed. Her throat tightened. He wasn't staring directly at them, but this time he was also not reading anything, nor looking at his phone. The breeze gently lifted and dropped the ends of his hair and beard. Wearing a pair of jeans and a white, short-sleeved guayabera shirt, he lounged with his left ankle slung across his right knee, his elbows hanging over the back of the bench where a lightweight jacket, unneeded, was draped. He appeared very relaxed; Jessie was not. She considered telling Micah that it was time to leave, but the limited time Eli had with Quentin was precious. So she refused to glance the man's way. Instead, she focused on directing her son's attention anywhere else: pointing out a couple of noisy bluejays, marveling over the slightly older boys reaching dangerous heights on the swings, asking him to go down the slide a few more times so she could video him.

As he was scrambling up the spiderweb-shaped climbing equipment, Jessie spotted two women—one of whom she recognized as a frequent library patron whose son, Liam, was in Miss Walberg's class—enter the park with their dogs and sit down on a bench at the far end from the stranger. Eli had gone through a dog-breed obsession when he was Micah's age, so she was able to say to tell him, "Look, honey!

There's Mrs. Kirby with her Bernese Mountain Dog, and a friend with her Vizsla! You don't see those kinds of dogs every day. Aren't they cute? Why don't we go see if they'll let us pet them?

"Remember, you never go near a dog you don't know without asking permission." She lifted Micah off the equipment and, taking his hand, guided him to the women. Standing a respectful distance away, she asked, "Hi, Samantha. Can we say hello to the dogs?"

To Micah's delight, they assented immediately. "This is Rupert," said Samantha Kirby.

"And this is Gwyneth," her friend, who was at least a decade older, said.

"Hi, Rupert, hi, Gwyneff," Micah said, enchanted.

"Gentle," his mother reminded him. She crouched down to his level and, with one hand on Rupert's soft fur, encouraged Micah to reach out.

Micah extended his hand to Rupert and squealed in glee as the dog coated it with an enthusiastic tongue. Gwyneth, meanwhile, poked her nose into his ear, and he screamed out a laugh. Jessie's heart swelled at the sight of her son doing something so wholesome and ordinary. She wished she could get the boys a dog, or maybe even a cat, but it never seemed to be the right time. And the chaos they were currently going through ensured it wouldn't be anytime soon.

"You're our librarian, Jessie Wilton, right?" the Vizsla owner asked. "And so is this . . . ?" She indicated Micah with a discreetly pointed finger.

Her entire body tensing, Jessie nodded. She hoped the woman wouldn't make a fuss in front of Micah. Or worse, storm off in a flurry of slurs.

Instead, she extended her hand, and Jessie shook it with relief. "I'm Joyce Marvella. I don't have kids in the district anymore, but I don't approve of censorship." She sniffed. "Seems to me we've been through this song and dance before. People don't learn."

"Thank you," Jessie said. Their support was heartening; it had been a difficult time, and she said as much. "It's nice to know that there's someone on our side. We're trying to keep everything as normal as possible for Micah and his brother, but you can imagine how—

"Hey, what's he up to now? Micah? Hey, Micah!"

In the few seconds while Jessie was engaging with the other mothers, Micah had scampered away from the dogs and dashed over to the bench where the stranger with the white hair and sunglasses sat in the shade.

"Micah!" Jessie yelled in panic, jumping to her feet. Micah had clambered up onto the bench and was staring at the man. He stretched a tiny hand out to touch his beard.

Winded from her sprint across the playground, Jessie arrived at the bench and reached out, grabbing Micah by the arm.

"I'm *so* sorry," she said to the man. Between the sunglasses, the woven hat that covered most of his forehead, and the strobe-like flickering of the shadows and sunlight through the trees, it was impossible to read his expression and know how he felt about this intrusion. "I'll bet it's the beard. He probably thought you were," and here she whispered, "*Santa*." Even as she said it, she knew it was a lie. Despite Cassandra's joke, aside from the beard the slender stranger bore no resemblance at all to Santa Claus—certainly a lot less than Mr. Marshall and look at how Micah had rejected *him*. Still, Jessie was at a loss to explain otherwise.

The man chuckled and opened his mouth to reply. But before he could speak, Micah piped up, his voice full of awe.

"Dad."

Nineteen

Micah had said it, clear as day, so there was no excusing it as the incoherent mumblings of a three-year-old.

"Oh, no, honey. No, no, no," Jessie said, trying to be calm as she attempted to lift Micah away, but he had gripped the stranger's left index finger and was holding on with the single-mindedness only a preschooler could muster. She had been afraid this day would come eventually, but she'd hoped it wouldn't be in public. Without a father figure in the house, and without an age-appropriate understanding of what it meant to have "two mommies," it seemed as if Micah had chosen his own daddy at random on their local playground. "That's not—"

"Dad!" Micah exclaimed, louder. Jessie could feel the eyes of the other parents and babysitters on the playground on them. It would only be a matter of moments before some "concerned" individual decided to start filming the interaction or call the police. In a town already on edge, and with Jessie and Micah at the center of it, the last thing she wanted was more attention on her unusual little family.

So she switched tack, sitting down beside Micah on the bench with a smile plastered on her lips and slinging her arm around her son's shoulders even as he clutched the man's finger, hoping she appeared more relaxed than she felt, hoping that their trio would now look to the others as if they were having a casual chat under an oak tree rather than an existential crisis.

"I really am sorry," she said, having for the moment given up trying to pry Micah away from the man who, she hoped, was just a traveler taking a break as he was passing through town and not some pervert shopping around for a guileless child. To her distress, he covered Micah's tiny hand with his own, and the boy rested his head against the man's arm. They looked very comfortable together, and she was grateful at least that Micah wasn't frightened. There would be time later, at home, to discuss personal boundaries and approaching strangers. "He doesn't have a dad—I'm married to a woman—and I don't think he really gets the concept that he doesn't get to find one on his own."

The man cocked his head to the side and removed his hat with his free hand. He drew his fingers through his hair, the silver rings a stark contrast against the white, and shook his head.

He set the hat back on his head. "I wouldn't be so sure of that, Ms. Wilton," he said, his soft voice at odds with his appearance.

He knows my name, Jessie thought with some panic. He had been stalking her, after all. They were in a public place though, right? She reminded herself that he couldn't pull anything without alerting the whole playground and, by extension, the whole town. Samantha and Joyce were still on the bench across the way, glancing at them from time to time. She could always call out to them; they would run over with their dogs, and Micah would still be safe . . .

This time the man moved his free hand under his sunglasses, pinching the bridge of his nose, and swiped a finger underneath his eyes. What? *Was he . . . crying?* "I'm Bill Weyerhauser," he said, smiling down at Micah. "Keith's father."

. . .

"Dad," Micah said again, almost sighing, as he stared up at Weyerhauser, and the purity of the smile on his face damped the fears that were causing Jessie's stomach to twist.

"I'm sorry to take you by surprise like this, Ms. Wilton," Weyerhauser said. "I know it seems like I've been stalking you, and it was never my intent to make you nervous." He gave an amused snort. "I've been a nervous wreck myself. That I was here in the park today was a coincidence; I needed some fresh air."

Jessie tried to summon words, but the shock had caused them all to disappear down her throat when she needed them the most. Her mouth gaped open, useless, and it took conscious effort to close it.

"I got a letter—overnighted—from Dr. Abernathy at Salem State," he continued, "and I'm not going to lie to you, it threw me for a loop. I spent a bit of time mulling it over, passed a couple of sleepless nights, wondering if I had the stomach for it. But then an acquaintance—an old coworker of mine—called me. He used to be an account exec. for one of the tabloids and still likes to leaf through them at checkout to see what bonkers things they're talking about this week. He saw the story about Micah and Keith. Once I read it, I knew I'd have to come by and meet Micah. I didn't have your last name or address to work with, but frankly, there was enough information in the article to figure out how to find you. Thank the internet, for better or worse.

"At that point, I didn't even bother to think; I didn't even respond to Abernathy. I threw some stuff into a bag, hopped into the car and drove here from New York. The past couple of days I've been trying to work up the courage to speak to you."

"You're . . . Keith's father?" When the words finally came out, they seemed inadequate.

"Yes. Call me Bill."

"I . . ." But the words refused to come. Why had she not anticipated that something like this might happen? "I'm glad to meet you," Jessie finally managed. "Your timing could have been a little better, though," she added, feeling short of breath. "Micah being Micah has, well, upset the balance around here."

"So I've heard since I've been in town. What a crock of horse—droppings these Pee-Paw people are trying to sell."

"That's one way to put it." Jessie chewed her lip. Her eyes kept drifting over to where Eli and Quentin were shrieking with laughter. She wanted to make sure that Alanna was keeping watch over them and not staring at her phone. From what Jessie could see, the girl was doing her job. With three younger siblings, she was probably used to it at home.

"One of those yours too?"

"Yes, Eli, over by the climbing equipment. The one in the striped shirt." She nodded in Eli's direction and smiled. "It's a bit much to go into right now, but he's being allowed to play with his best friend for the first time in weeks, and he has"—she checked the time on her phone—"another fifteen minutes of playtime."

"Oh, was he grounded?" His face said that he thought it a questionable punishment for a six-year-old.

"No." Jessie blew out a breath. "But the friend's father is one of the Pee-Paw instigators and, well . . ."

"Oh, ouch. Say no more. He sure looks happy now, though."

"He is," she said, "and I'm going to be the bad guy when I break it up." She inclined her head at Bill as Micah played with the rings on his fingers. "How am I going to explain you to Cassandra?"

"In private, I'd imagine," he replied with a glance around the playground, and Jessie, seeing the same curious looks directed at them, agreed. "It will look too weird if I go in your car with you. Best if you give me your address and I follow after a few minutes."

"If you could give me at least a half hour head start, I'd appreciate it. I have to extricate Eli from his playdate, but I want to give him the full time."

Bill withdrew his hand from Micah's grasp so he and Jessie could exchange phone numbers, and she texted him their address.

"All right, big guy," Weyerhauser said to Micah, getting to his feet and lifting Micah off the bench, "I've gotta go."

"Wanna go wif you, Dad!" Micah, so content a moment before, seemed on the verge of tears.

Bill bent down to the boy's ear and said in a low voice. "I don't have the right seat in my car for you, sport. Go play on the swings for a bit and be good for your mom, OK? Will you do that for me? When Eli's done with his playdate, I promise I'll see you back at your house, and you can show me all your toys. How's that?"

Micah looked reluctant, but said, "Uh-huh." He kept glancing back at Bill as he and Jessie walked over to the swings. The time passed agonizingly slowly for Jessie, who wanted to dash back home to give Cassandra the unexpected news. For Eli's sake, though, she pushed the swing again and again and again until it was time to collect her elder son.

"Noooo!" yowled Eli the moment he saw her. "I don't wanna leave! We're having fun!"

This time Alanna stepped in; Jessie was happy to let her play the villain. "Sorry, guys," the girl said as she crouched between the two friends, who were both moaning their dismay. "Quentin and I gotta go home.

"But there's one more thing." Alanna opened the large tote bag she had dangling from her shoulder and withdrew an expertly wrapped box. From the precision of the creases, Jessie could tell that Trish had wrapped the gift. She smiled.

Alanna handed the box to Eli and said, "Happy birthday, Eli. Hope you like it. Quentin picked it out himself. *But*"—she draped her arms over their shoulders—"remember: This is our little secret, OK? Pinky swear?"

The boys gave their solemn promise, which Jessie had little hope of either of them being able to keep for very long. After thanking Alanna again and prying Eli away from Quentin, she ushered her boys to the car.

Jessie was amazed that she made it home without incident; she drove more on muscle memory than anything else, her head filled with the surprise appearance of Keith Weyerhauser's father and Eli's illicit playdate. She was relieved that neither child spoke on the ride home. Eli didn't even open the present but turned it over and over again in his hands. Both boys looked out their respective windows, deep in thought.

But once they reached the house, the floodgates opened.

Because Eli could release himself from his car seat without assistance, he was the first to make it into the house. "Mommy! I saw Quentin at the playground! He gave me a birthday present!" Micah followed close behind and also started yelling the minute he got inside: "Mommy! Mommy! I found Dad!"

"What's that, now?" Cassandra said, her eyes wide, walking into the foyer, the boys' barrage of words overwhelming her. She knew about Eli's playdate, of course, but Micah's information was news to her.

"My dad. I found him! In de park!"

"Your dad?" Eli's excited rant about Quentin ended abruptly as he stared at his brother. "Does that mean he's my dad too? Where is he?" Eli wanted to know. He started to jump up and down, chanting, "Dad, dad, daddy, dad!"

Micah and Eli did, in fact, share a sperm donor. When Eli had first asked about his father about two years ago, Jessie and Cassandra had given him a very simple answer about how his father had made a generous contribution that helped bring him and Micah into the world, but he wouldn't be part of their lives. Though it had been sufficient at the time, Jessie could now see that the time would soon arrive for greater clarity.

"Hold on there, Eli." Cassandra looked alarmed. They had specifically chosen to keep their donor anonymous and had legal protection against him showing up, at least until the boys turned eighteen. "You, too, Micah. Back up a minute." She scratched her head in apparent confusion. "Jess?"

Jessie, finally able to get a word in, shook her head. "Cassandra, we only have a couple of minutes until he gets here. But what Micah means is that we met *Keith's* father at the park. Sorry, Eli. Mr. Weyerhauser isn't your dad, and he's not really Micah's either."

Cassandra looked at Jessie in shock. "Are you effing kidding me?"

"I kinda wish I were."

"Oh." Eli's face fell. "Keith again." He turned around and shuffled off to the den, no longer interested and disappointed that his own news had gone uncelebrated. But then he remembered the present he was still holding in his hand, and from the other room the women could hear the ripping of paper and a delighted, "Oh, cool!"

Jessie didn't have the chance to see what the Marshalls had bought for Eli, as they had barely finished the conversation when the doorbell rang. Since she had been right inside the front door, all Jessie had to do was pivot around and open it to let the man in.

"Cassandra, this is Keith's father, Bill Weyerhauser. Bill, my wife, Cassandra."

They solemnly shook hands, and Micah took Bill by the sleeve. "Come see my firetruck, Dad."

As Micah led Bill away, the women followed. Cassandra squinted at Jessie, whispering, "This dude looks a lot like the stalker you described from the library."

"Yup, same guy. He's been scoping me out for a few days."

"So, how do you know he's legit?"

"Because Micah approached *him* and called him dad."

When they reached the den, Eli was reading the instructions on his gift and pointedly ignoring Bill, who sat down on the couch with his forearms on his thighs, looking far more at ease in the situation than he had any right to be. Micah ran back and forth from the couch to the mat where he played with his cars, bringing over his favorites.

"See, dis is Keef's," he said, waving a white one in one hand, then picking up a blue one, "and dis is mine."

"He's right, you know." Bill raised his eyes to Micah's mothers. "Keith drove a white Chevy."

"That could be just a good guess," Cassandra said, her arms folded across her chest, her mouth tight. "White is the most popular car color in the country." Jessie nodded. She had a point.

"And dat's mine too!" Micah lunged into Bill's chest and grabbed the silver cross that was dangling around his neck.

"Micah, no!" Jessie scolded.

He kept yanking on it until Bill lifted the cord over his head and handed it to Micah, who slipped it on without any of the clumsiness he usually displayed when he tried to dress himself.

"Mine," he said with satisfaction, patting the cross where it landed, almost down to his thighs.

Jessie made a move to intervene, but Bill stretched out an arm to stop her. "It's OK," he said, a thin line of tears streaming down his bearded cheeks from bright blue eyes. "That cross was Keith's; he wore it constantly when he was off duty. I found it in his apartment when I— when I cleaned it out."

Once she recovered from her astonishment, Cassandra said to Jessie in a low voice, "I think we need to have Dr. Abernathy come back. This changes everything."

"I agree." Jessie was watching Bill sitting on the couch between Micah and his brother. Eli had given up the pretense of disinterest and was now trying to engage Keith's father in conversation by showing him his new outer space-themed activity kit. The noise level increased substantially, and while the Wilton family was used to it, Jessie thought Bill's patience was remarkable—though no doubt the idea of suddenly getting his deceased son back had done wonders for his mood.

Bill looked up at the women and smiled. They had to smile back. Such pure love, such relief. "I have some photos here that I'd like to show Micah, if that's OK with you."

"Uh-uh." Cassandra shook her head. "Not yet. We need to wait," she said. "The research team will want to record Micah's reaction to the pictures in real time."

"That's right," Jessie agreed. That thought hadn't occurred to her, and she was pleased at how seriously Cassandra was taking the professor's work. "It strengthens their case if Micah can identify other people in the photos without prompting. I'm going to contact Dr. Abernathy."

Leaving Cassandra to keep an eye on Bill and the boys, Jessie went into the kitchen to send a text to Dr. Abernathy.

The phone pinged with a response before she even made it back to the den: *I can be there on Wednesday. Can Mr. Weyerhauser wait that long?*

"Bill, can you stay in town a few more days? We'd like you to meet Dr. Abernathy and his assistant. I know they'd appreciate the opportunity to interview you and to see you and Micah interacting."

"I'm retired now," he said with a smile. "I've got nothing but time, and frankly, there's no place I'd rather be at the moment. I have a suite at the extended-stay place just off the highway, and I'll stay as long as it takes."

"How about at least staying for dinner?" Cassandra asked. Jessie turned to her in surprise. "What? Isn't that what you were going to say?"

"Yes, but . . ." Jessie would have said something about it being too soon, about not wanting Micah to be overwhelmed, to get attached and possibly be disappointed. But the invitation had been extended, and she didn't want to be seen as inhospitable. Particularly by Keith's father, who had already been through so much.

Dinner ended up being pizza, as there wasn't enough meat on their small roasted chicken to feed an extra adult. She found herself apologizing for the quality, as she figured a New Yorker would no doubt find small-town-Ohio pizza lacking. She and Cass certainly had, at first. But Bill ate without complaint, though Jessie suspected his enjoyment of the meal had more to do with Micah's enthusiasm than anything else.

Micah insisted on having Bill tuck him into bed, and Cassandra and

Jessie couldn't find a reason to deny him. They watched Bill's face as he walked into Micah's room, noting all the firehouse décor with a smile that seemed very close to tears. He read the book Micah handed him—twice—and kissed his forehead as he said goodnight, leaving the bedside lamp on, of course.

Jessie had a strong feeling that there would be no nightmares, no night terrors, tonight.

Twenty

After the boys had fallen asleep, the adults sat in the kitchen for a cup of tea. "I realized that we don't really know anything about you, Bill, other than, well, the obvious," Jessie said. "I made a point of not diving too deeply into Keith's life so as not to influence Micah."

Toying with his mug, Bill said, "There's not an awful lot to tell. I grew up in Queens, not far from where I live now, son of a housewife and an aluminum-siding salesman." He paused for a self-conscious laugh. "Does anyone today even know what aluminum siding was? Anyway, married my high school sweetheart, Janine, when we turned twenty-one. I wasn't much of a student . . . well, a pretty lousy student to be honest, but I managed to graduate from Queens College in Flushing. I wanted to major in art, but you couldn't really make a living that way back then . . . Heh. I suppose that's still true now. Anyway, after a few false starts, I had a nice career as an advertising account executive. Keith was our only child, and though Janine had a secure position as an administrative assistant to an insurance executive, she chose to stay home with him, which is what she wanted. She lived for him." He paused and sipped his tea, then placed it on the table slowly and deliberately. "I was at work at my firm in Midtown Manhattan on 9/11."

This wasn't the direction Jessie thought the conversation would take. She wasn't ready to hear it. Beneath the table, her hand groped for Cassandra's. She felt a reassuring squeeze, and Cassandra continued holding her hand through what came next.

"Although we didn't have the resources we have now—remember the iPhone didn't come around till much later—at an ad agency, there were TVs everywhere. We saw the whole thing, starting with the news reports after the first plane hit. When the second one hit, we all packed up and left the building. Our office was far enough uptown that we weren't directly affected, but it was a high-rise, and no one wanted to be up there, in case . . . Well, in case. I was reluctant to leave because I knew that Keith was on duty that day, and I was hoping that he would call. But Janine insisted that I should try to get home. You can't imagine what it was like—the crowds, the smoke, the panic."

Jessie started, thinking of the nights Micah woke up screaming about darkness and smoke. Bill's son had lived through it and died from it. *A traumatic death*, and her poor boy was reliving it. Her lips trembling, she held her breath, willing herself not to cry. A tear escaped her eye anyway. With her free hand, Cassandra passed her a napkin.

"It took me all day to make it back to Queens, sharing a car with a bunch of strangers. Janine had spent the day glued to the TV with one hand on the phone. Other people called us, but we never got the call we wanted the most. We held out hope as long as we could: phoning the hospitals, putting up flyers. Like everyone else. But. Well, as you know, it was a lost cause.

"Janine died two years ago of breast cancer, but she was never the same after we lost Keith. She suffered from depression, lost all her joy in life. We couldn't even have a funeral for him. I wish . . ." Bill dropped his chin to his chest, his breathing uneven. "I wish . . . that she could have met Micah." The strained words had barely left his lips before he held his head in his hands and sobbed.

Jessie's heart broke for this man, and she gave up trying to withhold her own tears, letting them flow freely. Even the usually stoic Cassandra sat with her lips trembling. Bill had suffered so much loss. And what could she possibly say to him? Micah was her son, not his. Could what little of Keith that remained in Micah really provide a balm to his pain?

"I'm sorry," Bill said, collecting himself. Cassandra had risen from the table and returned with a box of tissues. Bill took one with a nod of thanks, and Jessie did as well.

She shook her head. "No, don't ever apologize. We couldn't possibly know what you went through."

"I didn't really anticipate spilling my guts on the first day. I know how hard it is to hear."

"It's OK, really," Cassandra said.

They took a few moments to recover in silence, which was finally broken when Bill asked, his voice raw, "How about you tell me about you two?"

Cassandra and Jessie looked at each other with affection. "I grew up on Staten Island, and Jessie in Jersey," Cassandra said. "And we met online. Such a Millennial thing to do, isn't it?"

"Oh, you're both East Coasters too? So how did you end up in Ohio?"

"Once I interviewed for a library position in Hadlinsburg, we found out they had a job opening at the firehouse as well," Jessie said. "And the cost of living made the decision even easier. Our jobs, this beautiful old house . . ." She gestured around.

"Jessie had always wanted a Victorian, and at that price . . ." In a stage whisper, Cassandra told Bill what they'd paid for their home, and he whistled in admiration. "I know, right?"

"Added to that," Jessie went on, "what we thought at the time were the pleasures of living in a small town. Seemed like a no-brainer back then." Tapping her fingers on the kitchen table, she said in a lower voice, "I'm afraid we were so enamored with the charming small-town vibe that we forgot the reason why so many gay people leave for the city when they get the chance.

"Anyway, my parents are both gone; they died years ago. So there was less reason to stay in Jersey. Cassandra's are, well . . ." Her voice trailed off as she gestured dismissively.

"Assuming they're still alive, I'm guessing that mine are still the narrow-minded assholes they've always been," Cassandra said with a shrug. Bill displayed no surprise and in fact nodded as if he understood. "Pardon my French. We haven't spoken since I enlisted in the Air Force at seventeen."

She acted nonchalant, but Jessie knew the pain behind it. Being rejected by your family is no small thing, and it angered her to think how Cassandra had been treated by her own flesh and blood.

"I see," Bill said, his voice full of sympathy.

"Well, forget them," Jessie said, dismissing the people who didn't deserve her wonderful Cass. "We decided to create our own family, and we moved to Hadlinsburg when Eli was three. Micah was an infant.

"It was a good life, and it will be again."

Though even as she said it with all the conviction she could muster, she wondered if it would ever be true.

To Micah's disappointment, Jessie insisted that the boys stick to their schedules until Dr. Abernathy's return. That meant that he still went to preschool in the morning and Eli went to school as usual, when all that both boys wanted to do was to spend time with Bill. "It's only for a couple of days," she promised, "and then we'll have more time to get to know Mr. Weyerhauser."

Jessie did take the precaution of sending a note into preschool with Micah, warning that he might start talking about "his dad." Already uneasy from the warning—or, calling it what it was, the *threat*—from the director, she explained it away as wishful thinking on Micah's part, stemming from an encounter in the park with a pleasant, grandfatherly gentleman. She also had to remind Eli not to discuss his playdate with Quentin or his present, instructing him to pretend to be a spy on a secret mission. That seemed to be exactly the right thing to say to him, as he accepted the role with perhaps too much enthusiasm.

"I hate this, you know," she said to Cassandra as they headed off to work. "These lies. It's not exactly the kind of storytelling I'd planned to teach my children."

"Desperate times, et cetera," Cass replied. "Someday we'll look back on the absurdity of our lives right now and laugh."

There was no guarantee any of it would work, either, and Jessie fully expected word to get back to Dean eventually. But she was hoping she could buy them a few days of peace. And at least—for once—Secret Agent Eli didn't fight going to school and Mrs. Donohue's class.

Dr. Abernathy could barely contain his excitement while shaking hands with Bill. As they sat down at the dining room table, he went through the same opening explanation that he had given the Wilton family and set up the camera.

"Your name and age, please?"

"Bill Weyerhauser. I'm seventy-five years old."

"And what is your profession?"

"I'm retired from a career in advertising. I dabble in art now for fun and therapy."

"What is your marital status?"

"I'm a widower."

"Your wife's name?"

"Janine."

"When did she pass?"

"May fifteenth, two years ago."

"Are you related to Keith Weyerhauser?"

"I'm his father."

Jessie noted that he did not say *I was*. She tried to imagine the horror of losing a child, no matter what their age, and knew that she would have always answered the same way: in the present tense. *I am.*

Always.

"How long have you known Micah Wilton?"

"I didn't know him until this week. We met in the park on Saturday."

"Which park?"

Jessie piped up to provide the name, and Abernathy nodded his thanks.

"How did that encounter go?"

"I was on a park bench, and Micah came up to me. He sat down beside me, and . . . he called me Dad."

The last word came out as a croak. Jessie replayed the moment in her mind and shook her head at the wonder of it all. Despite all that he'd seen and heard in his career, the professor, too, looked affected.

Abernathy opened his folder and withdrew a photograph of the firefighters. "Do you recognize anyone in this photo?"

Bill reached into his shirt pocket and pulled out a pair of reading glasses. Once the photo came into focus, it didn't take him long to conclude, "I have this same photo hanging in my den." He smiled and put his finger on Keith's handsome face. "My son, Keith."

"This picture was taken months before 9/11. Is this a good representation of what Keith looked like? Is there anything about Keith that would have changed had it been taken right before he died?"

Leaning in to look more closely at the photo, Bill nodded slowly. "About a month after this picture was taken, Keith broke his nose in an accident at the station house. He got smacked in the face by a piece of equipment. They told him he couldn't work until it was completely healed, because firefighters have to be able to wear a full respirator mask. So he was out of work for about five weeks, and he *hated* it. It healed

OK, but he ended up with a bump right here," he gestured to the bridge of his own nose, slightly to the right of center. "I told him we could get him a little plastic surgery to fix him right up. But he said, nah, he liked it. Gave him character. Or made him look tougher, or something." He chuckled. "But I think it was because his boyfriend claimed he liked it."

"And his boyfriend's name?"

"Joey—that is, Joseph Killigrew." Jessie saw Savannah take note: They now had independent verification of Joey's name. Another box ticked off.

"Micah said that the picture showed his 'old nose,'" Jessie said. "Do you think that's what he's talking about?"

"Very likely," responded Abernathy. "That's what I was after with that prompt."

Bill opened his soft-sided briefcase and shuffled through some photographs. He drew one out: It was a candid of Keith looking at the camera with what could be described as fond annoyance. "He didn't know I was going to take a picture; he wasn't ready, he said. I thought he looked great." His brow furrowed; his voice came out thin and hoarse. "I took it the week before he died."

Cassandra and Jessie moved in for a closer look.

Abernathy addressed both of them. "Do you happen to notice anything interesting about the site of Keith's injury? The area that's slightly reddened and scarred?"

"That's . . ." Jessie and Cassandra started as one; Jessie finished the thought. "Exactly where Micah's birthmark is."

"That's crazy." Cassandra was shaking her head.

"Actually, it's not uncommon for a child to have a birthmark or even what looks like a scar at the same location as a mark on the previous personality's body," Abernathy said as Savannah typed notes, nodding along. "We've had many cases where marks correspond to bullet holes or stab wounds. But it doesn't necessarily relate to cause of death, and it almost always fades as the child gets older.

"So, Mr. Weyerhauser," the professor continued, "where did Keith meet Joseph Killigrew?"

"They were both firefighters in Manhattan, though with different companies. Met through mutual friends at some sort of event, maybe a barbecue. They'd been dating for about six months before Joey transferred into Keith's firehouse." Bill bit his lip. "They moved in together two months before 9/11."

Jessie listened with fascination, wondering how the couple dealt with being gay in such a macho profession. She'd heard stories about the off-color jokes, the omnipresent porn. Even Cassandra had to tough her way through a hostile atmosphere until she was accepted, although she'd learned some coping skills during her time in the Air Force. Did they face discrimination? Hazing? Or was the brotherhood of the calling enough to insulate them? Bill wasn't volunteering that information, and Jessie felt it would be rude to ask. Maybe someday, when they knew each other better.

As if sensing the painful turn the conversation was taking, Dr. Abernathy deftly pivoted to another topic. "All right, let's talk about Keith's youth. Can you give me a few details? Childhood pets, favorite school subject, hobbies, special friends? Please be as specific as you can, because we'll be asking Micah the same questions and comparing the answers. The more information you two agree on, the better our data will be."

Bill leaned back in his seat, looking at the ceiling, remembering. After about a half hour of reminiscences, Dr. Abernathy said, "I think we're ready to bring Micah in."

Cassandra got up and grabbed her purse. "I'll pick him up from preschool. Be right back."

After she was gone, Abernathy addressed Bill. "We're going to ask Micah some questions about the photos you brought with you. It's very important that you do not prompt or coach him in any way or try to provide answers for him. We don't want to influence the results. Do you think you can sit silently and respond only when asked a direct question?"

"Absolutely," Bill replied without hesitation.

"Then you may stay in the room." Turning to Jessie, he said, "That still applies to you and Cassandra, no matter what you hear from Micah, right?"

Jessie nodded, wondering what Abernathy's concern might be. She would find out soon enough.

TWENTY-ONE

When Micah came home, he made a beeline for the dining room. "Hi, Dad!" he chirped, climbing into Bill's lap. Dr. Abernathy nodded to Savannah, who made a note.

"Micah, do you know this man?" he said, pointing at Bill.

"Yeah! Dis my dad!" He turned to smile at Bill, who grinned back. Jessie's chest clenched a little.

"Oh, this man here is Micah's father?" Abernathy continued.

"No! Dis *Keef's* dad, Mr. Where-house."

"I see. Did Mr. Weyerhauser come here to your house to visit you?"

"I met him at the park. But Keith knows him always." There was that switch in pronunciation again.

"And Keith knew when you saw his father at the park?"

"Uh-huh."

But how, Jessie wished she could ask, *how did Keith tell you? How did you know?*

"And what happened then?"

"I seed him an' sat with him."

"Tell me, Micah, did Keith have any pets when he was a child?"

Micah swung his legs forward and back as he thought, and Jessie winced as she considered how uncomfortable Bill must be, repeatedly getting kicked in the shins. But even that failed to dampen the serene look on his face.

"Cat. Keith was little, he had a cat. Black an' white, an' his name's . . . Cookie?" He shook his head vigorously. "Oreo. Cookie. But I'm 'lergic." Micah sniffed. "I sneezed. A lot. My eyes hurt. I want a dog, but Dad says no. Says I'm prolly 'lergic to dogs too. Made me sad. I want a dog sometime."

This was precisely what Bill had related to Dr. Abernathy earlier. He had said they'd only kept Oreo for a week before rehoming him, and that disagreement had been a source of irritation to Keith for years. Jessie thought how sad it was that Keith never got to have his dog and wondered if that explained Micah's attachment to his stuffed Dalmatian. She was also both amazed and concerned by how mixed up together the personalities of Keith and Micah seemed to be in Micah's mind.

"I see. And what did Keith and his father do for fun together?"

Giggling, Micah turned halfway around to face Bill. Curling his hands into fists and raising his arms, he exclaimed, "Let's go Mets! Let's go Mets!"

The adults in the room laughed. "What does that mean, Micah?" the professor asked.

"Mets baseball. We go to see the Mets. All the games at Shea." Season tickets, as Bill had explained. "Ag-ba-yani, Alfonzo, Ventura, Pizza."

"What are those words?"

"The lineup." From 2001, as they had discovered. "Mets lineup."

"Did Keith enjoy going to the games?"

"Uh-huh."

"What was the best part?" Bill had mentioned that their favorite tradition was going for a beer and a couple of hot dogs with all the trimmings during the seventh-inning stretch. "What did Keith like the most about going to the baseball games?"

Micah's little hand patted Bill's much larger one, which was resting on the table beside him. "Being with Dad."

Bill's eyes filled with tears, and he sniffed in deeply through his nose, but his grin was broad and genuine. Jessie could feel the love radiating from him.

"Micah, we're going to show you some pictures again. Do you think you can tell us if you recognize anyone?"

Nodding vigorously, Micah turned back, shuffling himself to the edge of Bill's knees, and tapped his fingertips on the table in anticipation.

Abernathy pulled out the photographs Bill had provided and identified, laying the first one in front of Micah. "Do you know this person?"

It was the photo of Keith from the week before he died.

Micah giggled. "That's me! Keith me!" He touched the picture with his index finger. "With my *new* nose!"

"What do you mean your 'new nose'?"

Scrunching his nose, Micah pointed directly at his birthmark. "It got broke. Here. It's all bumpy now."

Jessie shared a glance with Cassandra. She could tell they were thinking the same thing: *amazing*.

"What happened to your nose?"

"Got hit."

"With what? What hit Keith's nose?"

"A . . . a halgan."

"A halgan? What's that?"

"A stick . . . big . . . heavy . . . that . . . "

As he struggled to describe it using his hands, it became obvious that Micah lacked either the vocabulary or an accurate memory to explain the source of Keith's injury. Since he was growing frustrated, Dr. Abernathy looked to Bill for an explanation.

"A Halligan bar," Bill said. "It's kind of an all-purpose tool firefighters use for prying open doors or car hoods, things like that."

"I see," the professor said. "And is that an accurate assessment of how Keith's nose was broken?"

"It is."

"Well, very good, Micah! What do you think of your bumpy nose?"

"I like it. Joey likes it. Says I look like a tough guy."

"OK, excellent." Abernathy removed the photo and put another down in its place. "Do you know anyone in this picture?"

The photo was of a party of some sort, full of young people. There must have been at least fifteen people crowded around, laughing, smiling, holding drinks and plates of food. Bill had explained that it was from Keith's high school graduation and filled with recognizable faces.

Micah's brow furrowed in concentration. "I dunno." Jessie couldn't remember seeing Micah focus so single-mindedly on a photograph. His eyes flicked from face to face. But ultimately he said, "No."

"That's fine." Switching out the photo for another, the professor said, "Do you know these people?"

The change in Micah's attitude was immediate. He beamed. "Mommy! That's my mother! And little me."

Jessie could feel Cassandra, who was seated next to her at the table, tense up. *Mommy* was the boys' name for *her*, and it must have been difficult to hear Micah call a stranger by her beloved title. She glanced at the photo of a pretty young woman in a brown winter coat and a yellow-and-white hand-knitted scarf, holding a toddler in a bright blue snowsuit. Keith's mother.

Mommy.

Micah twisted his body to face Bill. "Where's Mommy?" he asked, his expression eager. "Dad, did you bring her?" When Bill, his face showing strain, didn't respond, Micah repeated, "Where's Mommy?"

Bill looked helplessly at Professor Abernathy. "What do I do?" he whispered. "What do I tell him?"

"I called her," Micah said, becoming agitated. As Cassandra and Jessie looked on in horror, he added: "When I died. I called her."

"Oh, God!" Jessie burst into tears.

She felt a maternal anguish well up from deep inside her, more painful even than childbirth: In his last moments—in the dark and the heat and the choking smoke, with the certain knowledge that he would die as the building collapsed around him—*Keith had called out for his mother*. She'd never known the man, but she knew the heartache of love and loss, recognized it on a visceral level. Cassandra put her arms around Jessie and held her like a vise. Her own eyes were filling, but Cass wouldn't let Jessie go.

Bill covered his face with his hands. The tears ran between his fingers and his shoulders shook. A keening noise that he failed to suppress issued from him.

Micah didn't notice the effect his words had had. "Mommy!" he shouted, pounding his little fists on the table and thrashing on Bill's lap. "I want Mommy! Where is she? Where's Mommy?" He had collapsed into a full-fledged meltdown, and his screaming was ear-piercing.

Jessie tried to get up to go to him, but Cassandra held her back. "We have to leave him be," she said to Jessie in a low voice, "and remember he's not calling for us."

"It *hurts*."

"I know."

Throughout the turmoil, Abernathy and his assistant appeared unfazed. Jessie wondered how they could deal with such emotional chaos day after day.

"Would you like to see another photo, Micah?" Dr. Abernathy asked, his voice neutral and pleasant.

"NO! I want *Mommy*!" Micah sobbed. "MOMMY!"

"Have a look," Abernathy coaxed, a photo in his hand. "I promise you'll like this one."

He turned the picture toward Micah. At first, he refused to look at it, closing his eyes and turning his head away the way he used to when Jessie first tried to feed him broccoli. But shortly he began to run out of steam, and, sniffling, he finally opened his eyes.

"Who's this?" Abernathy asked.

"Joey!" Micah sighed. "Lemme see Joey." He tried to grab the picture from Abernathy, but the professor said, "Let's get you cleaned up," and indicated that one of his mothers should wipe his runny nose and soiled fingers first. Cassandra rose. Jessie, reading her pained expression, could tell that she desperately wanted to say, "Mommy's here, baby. Mommy's here." But she kept their promise to the team and remained silent, though she did kiss Micah's head as she withdrew to get a wet washrag and, presumably, to dry her own unshed tears.

Bill, too, left the room and came back with the edges of his hair and beard surrounding his face damp from the powder room faucet. He cleared his throat twice as he sat down.

After Micah had been cleaned and calmed, Abernathy laid the picture in front of him.

"Now, tell me, Micah. You know these people?" he asked.

"Dat's me and Joey. In my backyard." His voice had returned to his normal, babyish sound, and Jessie relaxed a little. The two men stood in a tiny, narrow yard, not much bigger than the Wilton's driveway. Dressed in T-shirts and shorts, they had their arms slung around each other's waists, their heads inclined so Keith's forehead was pressed to Joey's bangs. Both wore huge grins, and each held a bottle of beer. Though she should have expected it, Jessie was still startled to see Bill's silver cross hanging around Keith's neck.

Micah pointed to the barbecue behind Keith. "We ate hamburgers. Dey're burnded, but we don't care."

"Very good. Where's this backyard? Do you mean here in Hadlinsburg?"

"In Queens. Keef me lived in Queens."

"Where is Queens?"

"In New York, silly! Ever'body knows dat!"

Bill, Cassandra, and Jessie all burst out with a laugh, a much-needed break in the tension.

"Oh, of course, New York. All right. How about you hold onto that picture for a bit"—Abernathy could tell that Micah wouldn't give up the photo without a fight—"and we'll look at a couple of others."

The distraction had done the trick. Micah examined the next two pictures, correctly identifying his house in Queens among other very similar-looking ones and picking out his own (white) car on the street.

Wisely, Dr. Abernathy ended the session soon afterward, congratulating Micah. "You did awesome today, Micah. We're all proud of you. But your moms tell me that it's time for Eli to come home from school, and it's time for Savannah and me to go back to our hotel and get some rest. OK?"

Taking out a clean tissue, Bill blew his nose. Again he cleared his throat. With a significant look at Jessie and Cassandra, he gestured toward Micah. Understanding what he wanted to do, Jessie nodded her permission.

"C'mon, buddy," Bill said, lifting Micah off his lap and taking his hand. "Let's go get you properly cleaned up, OK?" Jessie could hear them talking as they went off to the powder room, Bill's voice fading as he asked Micah, "Do you want to go potty first?"

She turned to Dr. Abernathy when they were out of earshot. "I'm so sorry about my reaction. I couldn't help myself. It was—it . . ."

Abernathy waved it off. "Don't worry about it. As you've discovered, these sessions can be very harrowing at times."

"Why was he so upset about his mother and not about Joey?" Cassandra asked, her own voice husky from emotion. She took a gulp of her tea, but finding it cold and unpalatable, she made a face and pushed it aside. She coughed a little. "I mean, he loved them both. I would think he'd be livid that he didn't get to see Joey."

"My guess," responded the professor as Savannah packed up their gear, "it's because he already knows that Joey is dead. Remember, he acknowledged that they died together in the Towers. There's been closure; he doesn't expect to see Joey walk through the door. But as far as Keith knows, his mother is still around, he still loves her, and we are the bad guys for not bringing her to see him."

"Oh, my God, our poor baby!" Jessie said, tears threatening to start anew. She was grateful to be seated as she was unsure whether her legs would hold her. "Are we—are we going to have to tell him at some point that his—uh, I mean Keith's—mother is dead?"

"I don't think that will be necessary. Now that we know that Micah recognizes Janine Weyerhauser as Keith's mother, there's no need to ever bring her up again."

"I can't imagine what Micah is going through," Cassandra said. "Aren't we re-traumatizing him with all these questions?"

"Not at all. He's a young child, and his memories of these sessions will most likely fade in time as will the memories of his past life and even his early life as Micah. Most of us adults can't remember much at all from this age; it's called 'infantile amnesia.' I won't go into the details, but it's a well-recognized phenomenon, and you can research it if you like." Dr. Abernathy smiled. "Think about it: What do *you* recall from when *you* were three?"

Jessie couldn't speak for Cass, but her own answer was *nothing*. Her earliest memory was a fragment of a day in preschool when she was four, and then most of her more vivid memories started when she was in kindergarten.

"Besides, Micah is not always in 'Keith mode,' if you will. You'll notice that he'll go back and forth with what he remembers, and how much of it he remembers. There were people in the photos that Micah couldn't identify at all, and Bill has assured me that there were friends and relatives whom Keith would have definitely known: a beloved first cousin, the pack of friends he hung around with in school. You've noticed that even his speech patterns will change minute to minute."

"Yeah, what's that about?" Jessie asked.

"We have no way of predicting exactly when it will happen, but we've found that some children will speak in more mature ways and even produce a more advanced vocabulary while discussing their past lives. It's another proof of the validity of the phenomenon."

"All set, Dr. Abernathy," Savannah said. "I'll head out to the car. Thanks again for your time, folks." Cassandra saw her to the door.

Abernathy continued speaking to Jessie. "I realize this has been a difficult day for everyone. I'd like to assure you that we've been through the worst of it, and in fact it's very clear to me that this case can be considered solved. I don't mind telling you that, even before today, the information you and Micah provided alone would have been sufficient. But the inclusion of Mr. Weyerhauser and the details Micah added in his presence were invaluable. I don't think anyone can witness the interaction between the two of them and still doubt that your son is experiencing the echoes of Keith's past life. I find it . . . very moving. And I never get tired of it.

"So. I'm thinking this might be our last session. As fascinating as this case is, I don't see a need to continue to disrupt your family's lives. Savannah and I will probably leave earlier than planned, perhaps tomorrow evening or the day after. If anything else occurs to you, please give us a call or drop us an email.

"When the details have been logged and the case written up, I'll email you a link so you can read our assessment."

As he shook their hands, Micah, clean and calm, walked back into the dining room followed by Bill. Dr. Abernathy crouched down and took the boy's hand.

"Micah, you have been very helpful, and very brave. Keith would be proud of you. I know your moms and Mr. Weyerhauser are."

Bill smiled and nodded. Micah dropped the professor's hand and ran to hide behind Bill, hugging his legs with both arms and peeking out shyly.

Returning with ease to an upright position, the professor said, "Thank you, Bill," extending his hand. Bill shook it, remaining stiffly in place so as not to disturb Micah. "I can't imagine how hard it must be to relive the most traumatic events of your life in this way. But I appreciate your contribution to this case, particularly the photographs. With your permission, we'll scan those and have the originals returned to you."

"Of course, take whatever you need."

"We wish you all the best."

"Thank you, Professor," Bill replied, adding his left hand atop the one Abernathy was holding.

"Are you OK?" Jessie asked Bill once the door had closed behind the professor and Micah had left his hiding place in favor of the den and a book.

Bill dipped his head and thought for a moment, then he replied. "I don't mind telling you that this was one of the hardest things I've been through since Janine died.

"But at the same time, I feel . . . more at peace now. It's like—like a door that's been ajar for over twenty years. I couldn't shut it, no matter how hard I tried, and there was a cold wind blowing through the opening all year 'round. And there was that feeling that if I could just see what was happening beyond that door, I could move on. But it was always there, slightly open. Today the door was flung open for a second, and I saw the most brutal, awful, heartbreaking thing but also great beauty and love. And now, finally, it closed completely. I can't reopen it, but I don't have to. I can be warm again.

"You know . . ." He looked up at the ceiling, blinking, in an effort to keep the tears in his eyes from spilling yet again. "Keith told us through Micah that his favorite part of our trips to Shea Stadium was being with me. I thought he was a big baseball fan, but it turns out that he just wanted to spend time with me." Giving up, Bill looked at Jessie and Cassandra, letting some drops slip. He brushed them away with his fingertips and smiled weakly. "I can live with that."

Jessie nodded. "I think we need some tea."

"I think we need something stronger," Bill replied, "but it's probably best if we left it for later."

TWENTY-TWO

"So, what are you going to do next?" Cassandra asked. Micah was napping upstairs, and the adults needed to decompress. They sat at the kitchen table as their tea cooled.

Bill smiled. "Well, that's the sixty-four thousand-dollar question, isn't it?" At their blank look, he explained, "An old game show. God, I'm ancient." He stretched his legs out under the table and as if to prove his point, his back gave a loud *pop*. "But yes, if you remember, I didn't even give a whole lot of thought to what I'd do once I'd arrived here; I'm pretty sure I should have brought more clean shirts and socks at the very least, and I need to do a little shopping. All I knew was that I had to meet you and Micah; and believe me when I say that in my wildest dreams, I couldn't have imagined these past few days, and the things Micah would say. Now that I've had this experience—this *life-changing* experience—I don't know how I could go right back to Queens and pretend as if it never happened.

"I've never been to the Midwest before, though. Flown over it, of course, lots of times. Driven through it on my way to somewhere else." He laughed a little. "Damn, but Ohio takes a long time to get through."

"That it does," agreed Jessie with a slight grin.

"Anyway, I figured I'd tour around a little. See the sights. Seems like a good time to do it. The weather's nice . . ."

"Fall is a wonderful time for a visit. You're just in time for leaf peeping, if that's your thing," Jessie said. "Head a little north and you're almost at peak color. We can recommend a few things to see and do."

"Sounds like exactly what I need right now."

"Hang on a sec," Cassandra said, and left the table. She came back with a fat folder, which she set in front of Bill. "A lot of these places are for parents traveling with young kids, but I think you'll find plenty of stuff to do. Museums, zoos, cider mills . . ."

Bill shuffled through the brochures and printouts, scanning through one and then another. "Yes, I think I can find enough to keep me occupied for a week or so."

"The boys will be disappointed that they can't come with you," Jessie said, but she wasn't only thinking of the boys. As she imagined what it would be like for them to have a grandfather to travel with, to share new experiences with, it filled a hole that had been growing larger as their children grew older.

"Maybe someday we'll be able to do that," he said.

In the meantime, he promised he wouldn't leave without saying goodbye to Micah and Eli. After a dinner of spaghetti and meatballs, which resulted in a soon-to-be cherished photo of the boys—and Bill, who was a good sport—with generous helpings of sauce on their grinning faces, he left with an assurance that he would be back in a week. Cassandra marked the date on the kitchen calendar and declared that she would help the boys with counting down the days.

They would all need something to look forward to.

"Oh, hey, Allison is looking for you," Tyler, his arms loaded with books, said the minute Jessie walked through the library entrance. "She's waiting in her office."

This couldn't be good. Allison, who trusted her employees to do their jobs with a minimum of correction, didn't often call them into her office. A quick, casual conversation in the stacks was sufficient for most concerns.

"Have a seat, Jessie," Allison said, moving her cane aside. Jessie sat, eyeing her boss as she did so. Allison fussed with papers on her desk, refusing to meet Jessie's gaze as her anxiety worsened.

"I suppose you've heard," Allison started, glancing Jessie's way before looking down at her desk again, "about the demands being made by PPAW's new Hadlinsburg chapter."

Clearing her throat in an attempt to steady her words, Jessie replied, "Yes, I have heard."

"It's the usual complaints about the usual books, of course. Identical to the ones attacked in East Daniston. So obvious that it's almost laughable. They have a group of a few dozen people churning out challenges as if they were gumballs: over five hundred 'Request for Removal' forms, all made out by the same people, who you *know* haven't read any of the books, or maybe even seen them on the shelves. Under any other circumstances, I wouldn't worry about them at all. For now, I believe they're a small, fringe group being controlled by wealthy outside agitators, not a majority of the people of our town by any stretch."

It certainly doesn't feel that way to me, Jessie thought. She hadn't mentioned to Allison Micah's and Eli's troubles at school nor her own perception of the frostiness directed her way.

"I think we have enough support here to head them off," Allison continued, "and we have already reached out to PEN America, just as East Daniston did. But that's not what concerns me at the moment. They have another demand, one that doesn't match up to their crusade in East Daniston."

Jessie wiped sweaty palms on her cream slacks, hoping they wouldn't leave a stain.

"They want you gone, Jessie," Allison said, finally looking straight at her. The bluntness of her declaration hit Jessie like a slap in the face. "They said that you're 'grooming' your children to be gay like you, and that they can't trust you to make recommendations for books for their own children."

Her mouth dry, Jessie tried to respond, but the words stuck to her tongue. "I . . . what even . . . how . . ."

"I know you're going through a lot with Micah right now; the whole town is talking about it. I can't pretend to understand it all." She paused, scratching her nose. "Or any of it, to be frank."

"Do you want me to tell you the whole story?" By now, Jessie was ready to give the details to anyone who would listen. At Allison's nod, she launched into an abbreviated version of what she'd told Trish. Her supervisor took it all in, engrossed. When she reached the end, Jessie added, "So you see, Micah wasn't—he wasn't talking about himself. But even if he were, what would be so wrong with that? Doesn't it happen all the time, toddlers and preschoolers and elementary school kids claiming they have a boyfriend or a girlfriend? I see it all the time, and most of the time the reaction from parents is, *Aw, isn't that adorable?* They take pictures of the kids holding hands and joke about planning weddings twenty years down the road. Why should this be any different?"

Collecting herself after Jessie's astonishing story, Allison cleared her throat and said, "Come on, Jessie, you know why. Of course you and I don't have any problem with it. But you can understand why *this* particular group has their knickers in a twist about it. And unfortunately, it's given them ammunition for their specious arguments against LGBTQ books and, well, you."

"So, what are we going to do?"

Allison let out a loud breath. "I'm sorry to say that there's going to be an emergency meeting of the library board on October third. As much as we despise it, we're obligated to take their issues seriously before they can turn the whole town against the very idea of a public library."

Dumbfounded, Jessie stared at her boss. "So that's it? A handful of people make an unfounded accusation, and my career depends on a half-dozen board members not bowing to their pressure?"

"That's how it works, Jessie. We're all at the mercy of the board for funding and everything else. We're waiting to hear when the community hearing will be scheduled. You'll have an opportunity, if you want it, to defend yourself—"

"*Defend* myself? As if *I've* done something wrong?" Jessie looked wildly around the room as if in search of sanity that was lacking in this conversation. She did not find it. "This is craziness!"

"I agree with you. Which is why in the meantime I've refused to suspend you. You keep doing your job right up until the time the board makes their decision. If they do decide to act, we can call on PEN America or even the ACLU to make an appeal.

"I'm really sorry things have turned out this way. These groups have been popping up around the country doing a lot of damage to schools and libraries. The only thing we can do is muster support from the community and make them irrelevant."

Jessie shuffled back to her desk in a daze, a headache building behind her eyes. The morning was only starting, but the news had taken the wind out of her, and she couldn't imagine how she was going to make it through the day. Tears sprang to her eyes. It was bad enough that patrons were avoiding her. For every person who approached her, requesting her help, or smiled fondly as they passed by, there were at least two others who glanced at her and then turned away. But to have to fight for her job! It was unnerving not only how quickly word had gotten around, but how willing people were to believe the worst.

Sunday morning, Jessie was still in her pajamas, cleaning up from the pancakes she'd made the family as Eli bounded around the house pretending to be an airplane. Cassandra, back from an early run, coaxed a still-sleepy Micah to finish his last pancake, drowned in too much syrup. Jessie loved the mornings when neither she nor Cassandra had to go to work, and they could enjoy breakfast as a family. Particularly now, with their lives topsy-turvy, a little normalcy went a long way.

"Mama, what does o-p-e-d mean?" Eli asked as he zoomed back into the kitchen, his arms extended at his sides. In the division of labor in their household, questions about word meanings usually went to Jessie. But this time she and Cassandra looked at each other, puzzled. What an odd word to ask out of the blue.

"That's an interesting question, honey," Jessie said. "An op-ed is a newspaper column that gives the opinion of the writer—what they think about some subject—rather than simply stating what happened, the way a regular news story would." She paused for a tick. "Why would you ask?"

"'Cause someone wrote it big on our driveway."

Her brow furrowed, Cassandra leapt to her feet. She charged to the front window and looked outside. When she came back, her face was white. "Eli, can you stay in the kitchen for a minute while I show Mama something?"

"Are you gonna show her the op-ed? I wanna come too!"

"Nope, buddy. Hang out here for a moment. I promise we'll be right back."

"What's wrong?" Jessie asked as she followed Cassandra to the window. In answer, Cassandra simply pointed.

There, on the driveway, in red spray paint, were three-foot-tall letters spelling out the word which Eli had reported. But he—and they—saw it upside down, because it was meant to be read from the street.

Pedo.

Twenty-Three

"What do we do now?" Jessie gasped, her hand covering her mouth in horror.

"First, I'm going to go get a tarp out of the garage to cover the damn thing," Cassandra said, putting on her shoes. "I'd like you to call the police. Use the non-emergency number."

Nodding, Jessie pulled her cellphone from her pocket and with shaking hands found the number among her contacts.

"We're going to file a report," Cassandra continued as she walked out the door. "I want it on record as a hate crime. If I ever find the sonofabitch who did this . . ."

The squad car arrived fifteen minutes later. It was an officer whom Cassandra knew well—Steven something, a youngish cop with whose family they'd socialized at softball games and holiday events—and Jessie, now fully dressed and on high alert, stayed inside with the children as he took pictures and Cassandra's statement. Afterward, as Jessie peeked out the window from behind the now-drawn curtains, it seemed as if they were discussing the best method for removing the paint. Cassandra, her face grim, stood with her arms tightly folded across her chest. Finally, the officer helped her drag the canvas tarp back over the graffiti, securing it with bricks, and shook her hand.

Stepping back into the foyer, Cassandra said, "I'm gonna run to the hardware store to get something for the paint." She peered at Jessie, holding her face in her hands. "You OK?"

"Not really." Her voice squeaked as she whispered, "Cass, our neighbors think that we're pedophiles!" After a thought, she amended, "Or at least, that I am. As if that's any better! Oh, my God!" Her eyes filled with tears.

Cassandra sighed and shook her head. "Keep the kids busy and the door locked. I'll be back in half an hour."

Jessie nodded, and Cassandra kissed her cheek before heading back outside. As instructed, she locked the door behind Cass. A few deep, calming breaths and a dab at her eyes later, Jessie walked into the den.

"OK, who's going to color with me?" she announced to the children with feigned enthusiasm. She was grateful that they were too young to recognize the forced brightness. "Ooh, look: I've got a brand-new box of ninety-six crayons and two new books!" They were from her emergency stash, and this certainly qualified as an emergency.

"Me!" said Eli.

"Me!" echoed Micah.

As Jessie sat on the floor with her boys at the coffee table in the den, she hoped she could keep them distracted and not asking questions until Cassandra got back. Keeping herself distracted, well, that was a bigger assignment.

When Cassandra returned with an armload of cleaning solution and brushes, she put a call into Jeremy and Nicholas, who came back early from their Sunday morning bike ride to join her on the driveway. They had a handful of other friends, of course, but Cass decided that the people most likely to help them through this were those who were equally likely to be targeted. Jessie made sure that the boys stayed away from the windows as her wife and their two friends—three slender figures, two short with dark hair and the other tall and balding—labored over the graffiti.

After they'd finished the cleanup and had a couple of beers, Cassandra thanked their friends and saw them out. She immediately sat down at the kitchen table, picking up her tablet.

"What are you doing now?"

"Ordering a few security cameras. Overnight shipping. I'll install them tomorrow."

Jessie stared in surprise. "You always hated the idea of cameras. You said you didn't want to feel like you were living in some kind of police state, and that they didn't go with the aesthetic of the Victorian."

"I've changed my mind."

There was no persuading Cass otherwise when she'd set her mind to something, but this time Jessie wasn't inclined to argue. She hated not feeling safe in her own home.

Once the cameras were installed, Cassandra showed Jessie how to work the app. "OK, look: You can see video and everything. And it will send a notification when someone enters the perimeter, in this case, our driveway. Or the sides or back of the house. Of course the downside is that every time a squirrel runs across the yard, you'll get a notification, and I've heard that it can get to be a bit much after a while."

Jessie quickly found out what "a bit much" was as soon as the cameras were active. An energetic bird, a squirrel, the UPS driver delivering a package, all set off the motion detector, and the *ping* of the app's notifications soon became the background noise of her day whether she was driving to work, getting ready for story hour, cooking dinner, or reading to the boys.

While she didn't expect the police report to turn up a suspect, as the days passed she and Cassandra found it increasingly hard to proceed with "business as usual." Conversations in public places would stop as they passed by, and occasionally they were subjected to the kind of offensive terms they hadn't heard since their move to Hadlinsburg.

After a couple of decades of this sort of thing, they mostly knew how to let it slide off their backs by considering the source. So Jessie wasn't expecting anything unusual when she sent Cassandra off to work an evening shift Tuesday night.

"Oh, there you are, Cass," Jessie said, squinting into the shadows of the den, where the lights were off. It was well after midnight, and she had expected Cassandra back in the house by eleven. She pulled her robe more tightly around herself. "When did you get home? It's late! And why are you sitting in the dark?"

As she got closer, the smell hit her almost immediately. "Cassandra. Have you been . . . smoking again?"

But it couldn't be. Though Cassandra had started smoking at sixteen, she had never been a heavy smoker, and she had sworn it off entirely the minute she had found out she was pregnant with Eli. As far as Jessie knew, she had gone cold turkey and not had a single cigarette since.

"Just a little," Cass mumbled. "Just today."

"Why?" Jessie sat down next to her and put a hand on her shoulder. She knew Cass wouldn't smoke in the house; they'd both agreed on a smoke-free environment for the children. It must have been at work, but recently. The odor was still fresh on her clothes. "What happened?"

Cassandra shook her head. In the dim light emanating from the hallway, Jessie could see her staring at the floor.

"Cass, tell me," she urged. "It had to have been something pretty bad."

A slight nod was all she received in return.

"Did you . . . lose a patient?" That was the most distressing thing Jessie could conceive of for an EMT.

Cassandra snorted her reply. "Hah. Close enough."

"I don't understand. Help me out?"

After a pause, Cassandra responded. "We received a call today from an elderly couple. I can't give you names—privacy laws and all that crap —but let's say it's someone we know, someone we've seen at church.

Someone we've spoken to a dozen times and who's always been nice to the boys.

"Anyway, possible cardiac event in the elderly male. I go in there with Ben and Warren and all our equipment. And it's clear the guy is suffering from something, white as a sheet and nearly crying from the pain, and I go to take his vitals. And this woman—his wife—stops in the middle of the explanation she's giving Ben and says to me . . . I mean, she points at me and says"—Cass's voice was shaking, and Jessie could feel her body stiffen—"she points at me and yells, 'Not her! Don't let that *pervert* touch him!'"

"My God." Jessie's hand tightened on Cassandra's shoulder. She reminded herself to take long, deep breaths, because she felt perilously close to a cardiac event herself.

"Told me I'd burn in hell, too, for good measure. I never, *ever* thought . . ." Cassandra said, her head shaking slowly, emphatically. "She's always been so *nice* . . ."

"Oh, babe."

She gave a humorless laugh. "So, if I had a cigarette, or maybe two, maybe you can understand."

"Of course, of course."

The two sat in the dark, the silence thick and suffocating.

"It was like this with my parents, you know," Cassandra said after a long while.

Jessie stilled. She knew the barest outlines of Cass's break with her strict, religious parents, but she never asked for details, aware that it was Cassandra's story to tell, whenever she was ready to tell it. Up until now, she had been very stingy with specifics.

The biggest fight they'd ever had, one that had almost ended their relationship before it had really taken hold, had happened when Jessie had innocently asked about Cass's parents. The explanation Cassandra gave then in a clipped voice, shorter and less detailed even than the one she'd given Bill, was meant to be sufficient: "We're not in contact. Turns out they didn't count on their daughter being a lesbian." She hadn't realized at the time that when Cass had given her those two sentences, it was all she could manage through her bitterness and heartache. But Jessie, trying to be a supportive girlfriend, had said, "Oh, I understand. My friends got really weirded out when I told them too. A couple of them stopped talking to me."

It had been absolutely the wrong thing to say. "You *understand*?" Cassandra had shouted. She had never raised her voice to Jessie before and hadn't since. "What could *you* possibly understand! So you lost a couple of friends, did you? Boo-hoo! What about your *parents*—didn't you tell me they didn't mind when you came out? Actually embraced you for it? So spare me your sympathy, Jessie. You don't understand *shit*."

Cassandra later apologized, and Jessie never raised the topic again. It was true: Her own mother and father had been a dream; they had coddled her, cuddled her, and made sure she always felt wanted, adjusting quickly to their new reality. She'd never had the people she depended on—the ones who were supposed to love her unconditionally—reject her. While she had been exposed to some of the same discrimination Cass had, it had been mild: some bad jokes, some disapproving stares. The occasional insult from the usual suspects. Nothing in her life had been as devastating as Cass's experience. That was why she had been so shocked at the reaction of her Hadlinsburg neighbors upon the arrival of PPAW, and also why this situation was hitting Cassandra differently.

"I knew who my parents were, of course. Heard them laugh and talk shit about *the fags* and *the queers* and all from the time I was old enough to understand it . . . and learn to hate myself in the process without knowing it. Dad was vocal about his views, but Mom didn't push back. She let him take the lead in everything. She voted how he told her to vote, parroted all the things he said. I don't think she had an original thought in her head her whole life.

"We didn't have a particularly warm relationship—they weren't like that—but they gave me what I needed . . . as long as I conformed to their expectations. And I tried. It worked while I was younger, maybe till around the time my father realized that I wasn't going to keep on being Daddy's Little Girl in the scratchy lace dresses and shiny shoes they had me wear. Even then, for a while he was happy to teach me how to throw and catch and fish alongside my brother. I thought we were good.

"But from the time I came out, when I was around fifteen, right up until the day I enlisted," Cassandra was now saying, her forehead puckered, "my folks, they attacked me with . . . well, pretty much all the same shit that old lady threw at me. The names, the slurs. The threats of hell and damnation. I thought they'd make an exception for me: their daughter. They loved me, right? Well, I was wrong. We must've had a different definition of 'love.'

"Oh, and the icing on the cake? They told me they were *ashamed* that I was part of their family. It was a huge shitshow, and my brother, John, took their side. I wasn't surprised at *them* so much, but John . . . well. That was a surprise in the worst possible way. The worst. He'd always protected me, taken my side, and I thought we were buds. 'Ride or die,' y'know? Guess I was wrong there too.

"I had about six months before I started basic training. I crashed on a friend's couch, worked out every day like a maniac so I was in the kind of fighting shape the force recommended. But it wasn't only about being in shape; I used my time in the gym to work off my anger and grief. I did my stint in the service, and by the time I got out, I pretty much was over the rage—or at least knew how to manage it—and was ready to move on.

"Then I met you, and we had our family, and life was all sunshine and rainbows, pretty much." She reached out a hand and lightly touched Jessie's. Before she could react, though, Cassandra withdrew her fingers, returning them to her lap. "I could deal with assholes like Dean by just avoiding them. But this . . . in a life-or-death situation? God, this brings it all back." Jessie couldn't see if she were crying, but she could feel Cass's body shaking from the tension of holding it all in. She wished she would let herself cry it out. She deserved that much.

Barring that, Jessie suspected that the best thing she could do for Cassandra at the moment was to let her say her piece and simply be there to absorb it. What Cass had told her years ago was still true: Jessie *didn't* understand. Couldn't understand.

Not at all.

Twenty-Four

Assigned an overnight shift on the Saturday night before the board meeting, Cassandra on Thursday declared her intention to decline it. "I don't want to leave you alone."

Jessie shook her head. "Look. Realistically, I don't know how long I'll be employed at the library; they could pull the plug on me any time after Monday night. Not to put too fine a point on it, but we could use the money. Not only in case I find myself unemployed but also in case we—we decide we need to move on. So I think it's important that you take whatever shifts you can right now."

Cassandra drummed her fingers on the kitchen counter; it was clear she was nervous and undecided. "Are you sure you'll be OK here alone all night with the boys?"

"I'll be fine." Jessie laughed a little. "I probably won't be able to sleep anyway."

"That's not a good thing, you know. Should we ask someone to come over? To keep you company? I could ask Jeremy and Nicholas. Or, hey, Bill is supposed to be coming back on Saturday to make it to the meeting. *That's* an idea; we could ask him to stay over." She drew out her phone. "Should I text him?"

"Put your phone away. That is *so* unnecessary." It wasn't that Jessie didn't like having Bill around; he was excellent company. Or even Jeremy and Nicholas. But she hated the idea that a woman needed a man to feel safe, that her boys would see her depending on someone with a tenuous relationship to their own family to protect them. Their mother was a capable, educated adult, and *she* would be enough—would *have to* be enough—to keep her children from harm.

Potential harm, she reminded herself. Not that anything would go wrong. "Cass, Bill's an old man; he's going to need some rest after his trip, and I'm not going to ask him to crash on the sleeper-sofa."

Cassandra *tsked* but tucked her phone into her pocket. "Are you sure?"

"I'm sure. Take the shift, and I'll give you a full report the next morning."

Micah and Eli knew nothing of the meeting Monday night, but they could tell that their mothers were growing increasingly uneasy. Without being able to understand what was happening, they defaulted to being cooperative and quiet. Besides, Eli had been much happier since their day at the park, and though he hadn't said anything, she suspected he was enjoying Quentin's company at recess again. Jessie was grateful to Trish for this small grace. The evening passed uneventfully, and the boys settled into bed with stories and kisses without complaint. Jessie decided to take the opportunity to retire early. Despite her joke to Cassandra, she was exhausted; the emotional work of the past few weeks—dealing with the surreal drama with Micah, managing Eli's devastation, defending their family from unjustified accusations—was weighing on her. After going through her nightly routine, she got into bed and read as much of one novel as she could manage and then switched to another. She had returned her tablet to the top of the stack of books and papers on her nightstand and reached to shut off the bedside lamp, when the security camera app pinged. As a reflex, she picked it up immediately and smiled at the chubby raccoon waddling its way across the driveway. With a relieved sigh she put down the phone and turned off the light.

The minute she pulled up the covers and lay down, though, the phone pinged again. With a grunt, she reached out a hand and tapped on the phone to make the raccoon go away, but she missed the Dismiss button. Annoyed, she picked up the phone to silence it but stopped mid-tap. The hair on the back of her neck stood up.

Walking onto her driveway were three hooded figures. And each one of them held something, long and rigid, either in their hand or tucked under one arm.

"Oh, shit! Oh, shit!"

With her heart pounding in her ears, Jessie pushed back the covers and set unsteady feet on the floor. Once there, however, she froze in place. Her thoughts came in wild, rapid succession. What exactly was she thinking of doing? Confronting the intruders? She'd have to get dressed first. Did she have anything that could pass as a weapon? A knife, a softball bat? But there were three of them and only one of her.

Should she call Cassandra? Or 911? It would be embarrassing if she overreacted. What if it were just some lost partygoers, and—knowing that her indecision had reached peak absurdity, she grabbed her phone again to look at the camera feed and, if necessary, to call the police. The trio was still there, but to her shock, they were now seated at the foot of the driveway facing the street.

The objects they'd been carrying were now, it was obvious, folding camp chairs.

Staring at the screen, Jessie puzzled over this development as her heartrate struggled to return to normal. It looked as if the three were relaxed and chatting amongst themselves, glancing at their phones. They made no move to approach the house and in fact didn't so much as turn to look at it. Still, feeling vulnerable in her bedroom in her nightgown, she threw on the clothes she'd worn that day and tiptoed down the hall, pausing to listen at the doors to the boys' rooms to make sure that they were both, in fact, asleep.

Her phone clutched in her hand, with 911 on the screen and ready to be called, she made her way downstairs in the dark, not wanting to turn on the lights to alert the intruders that she was onto them. Jessie felt along the familiar walls until she reached the window that faced the front of the house. Keeping her body well back, she peered through the curtains. What she saw in person differed from the security footage only in degree of resolution. There were three people in matching dark-green hoodies and jeans sitting with their chairs spread at equal distances across her driveway, right off the sidewalk. A backpack lay at their feet. While she couldn't make out what they were saying, they made no attempt to keep their voices down and sounded downright cheerful.

And young.

This is ridiculous, Jessie thought. She shoved her feet into the first pair of shoes she came across, which were Cassandra's lawn-mowing sneakers and a half-size too big, grabbed a jacket from the hooks by the front door, and ventured onto the porch.

When the front door opened, all three figures turned her way.

Was that . . . "Alanna? Is that you?"

"Oh, hi, Ms. Wilton," Alanna Marshall, seated on the left, said. She pulled down the hood of her Hadlinsburg Hawks sweatshirt and ran her hand through her blond hair, like her mother's but a shade or two darker. "I hope we didn't wake you."

"No, I was—But what are you *doing* here? And"—Jessie squinted at the other faces, which became recognizable the closer she got to them—"Ryan Lebow? Gabe Henry?"

"Hey, Ms. Wilton," the boys said in unison, taking down their own hoods. Gabe gave a little wave. All three were juniors at Hadlinsburg High, kids whom Jessie knew well as regular visitors to the library. The tension drained from her body, leaving her shaking. She rubbed a hand over her face.

"What are you all doing here at"—Jessie looked at her phone—"ten thirty at night?"

"Well," Alanna said, smiling at the boys, "we came here from the fall dance, and our parents think we're out at the after-party at Waffle House."

"Yeah, our curfew is midnight," Ryan said. He was a tall, dark-haired boy whose slender build was largely due to running long-distance for the track team. Jessie knew his literary tastes ran to sword-and-sorcery epics and always kept him informed of the latest acquisitions. "So we're taking the first shift."

"First shift?"

"Making sure nobody messes with you," Gabe said, leaning back in his chair with his arms folded across his chest. He was on the wrestling team, known to be wiry and fearless.

"Why would someone be messing with us?" Jessie was startled: the graffiti incident had happened in the dead of night a few days ago and had yet to make it to even the *Herald*'s "Police Blotter" column.

Gabe looked embarrassed. "My uncle is a lieutenant with the Hadlinsburg police. We know about the graffiti, Ms. Wilton."

"Oh."

"So we're gonna hang out to, y'know, discourage anyone who wants to pull any kind of crap. And when we go home," Ryan continued, "the seniors will come take the next shift. *They* can stay till two."

"Next shift?" Jessie was flummoxed. "That's—that's all very nice, guys, but really. It's not necessary, and your parents would never approve."

"Mine know," Gabe said, his foot jiggling where his ankle rested across his knee, "and they're chill with it."

"And we've got another two shifts set up for tomorrow night," Ryan added. Jessie noticed that he did not mention *his* parents; according to Angela, his father had been at the PPAW meeting. "We've got you covered until the meeting."

"You won't tell my dad, though, will you?" Alanna asked, her eyes wide. But she was smiling.

Jessie's mouth curved up in response. She pictured Trish sending

Alanna off her with her blessing, behind Dean's back. "I can't imagine why I would, Alanna."

"As long as I'm back by curfew, he won't mind." She spoke with great confidence—and apparent indifference to the consequences, should her father find out—and again Jessie was reminded of her resemblance to her mother.

"Why don't you go back inside, Ms. Wilton?" Gabe said. "We've got this. If anything happens, we can call the cops." He waggled his phone at her. "Otherwise, we've just wasted a few hours of our own time. No biggie."

Jessie shook her head. They weren't her children, so there was no punishment she could threaten that would have any teeth. She could, of course, order them off her property and have them charged with trespassing. But she would *never*; that was far too severe a consequence for well-meaning kids. Besides, she was tired, and stressed, and all she wanted was to go to sleep.

"All right. I'm going back to bed, and I'm going to pretend that I didn't see *any* of you here."

While she wasn't fond of their secrecy—or the fact that she hadn't been informed and nearly had a heart attack over it—Jessie had to admit that she was proud of the children: for their initiative in creating their own little Neighborhood Watch, and particularly for their defense of her family. As she moved quietly back up the stairs and changed back into her nightgown, she was heartened by the thought that at least some of the PPAW parents had failed in their battle against woke.

The next day, Jessie told Cassandra about their visitors, whom she laughingly referred to as their "guard dogs." Cass was both amused and deeply moved, and despite declaring her exhaustion, she decided to stay up long enough to greet the Sunday night shift. So while Jessie got ready for bed early, Cassandra went outside with some soda and snacks and spent an hour or so chatting with the students sitting on the driveway.

"Nice bunch of kids," she said as she returned to the bedroom, finding Jessie reading in bed, propped up against the headboard. Jessie had switched from her tablet to a physical book, one of several from her nightstand stack.

"They are." She stuck a bookmark in her place and closed the volume. "Recognize anyone?"

"No, that's really more your department. From the conversation I gather they're seniors, though."

"Likely." Jessie added the book back onto the stack, taking time to align the edges of the pile so she didn't have to look at Cassandra as she asked the next question. "I don't suppose your cop friends have made any progress on the graffiti?"

Even before Cassandra spoke, Jessie could tell from her sigh that the answer was negative. "They've got nothing." Jessie pulled her feet in, and Cass sat down on the bed beside her, draping her arm across Jessie's knees. "From what I understand, they spent some time knocking on doors in the neighborhood, seeing if anyone caught anything on their doorbell cameras. Not too many folks around us have that kind of technology, though, and since it happened overnight, they would have had to review a dozen hours of footage from each."

"So, correct me if I'm wrong, but what it sounds like you're telling me is, they have no leads and they're not trying particularly hard, either."

"That's about the size of it." She rested her chin on her forearm. "Jess, as supportive as the guys in my station are, I think you'll find that the Hadlinsburg police are . . . not. At least, not as much."

"What do you mean?"

"I mean, they've got some good guys like Steve in there who really care about us and our problems, but there are also a few who . . . let's say they went full Pee-Paw before it was even a thing."

Choosing her words carefully, Jessie said, "In other words, you mean there are some officers who don't mind what the vandals did."

"In other words, I mean there are a few who might well have done it themselves." At Jessie's distressed cry, Cassandra moved up to take her in her arms, brushing her hair off her face. "I'm so sorry. I wish I had better news. But let's face it: We're all we've got."

"Well, us and the kids on the driveway," she said, resting her head on Cassandra's shoulder. "If only that were enough."

"I wasn't going to mention this, but I think it's time to bring it up."

"What's that?" Jessie asked, lifting her head.

Keeping Jessie wrapped up close, Cassandra took her time responding. "Something Bill said to me when I told him about the graffiti."

"Wait, when was that?"

"I called him right after it happened, while I was at work. He basically threatened to drop everything and rush back to Hadlinsburg right away, but I told him it wasn't necessary, there was nothing he could do, and that he should continue on his trip for now."

"And he said . . . ?"

"He said, if there's ever a time when we feel as if we don't belong here, we're welcome to come live with him."

"In Queens?"

"Yeah, in Queens. In . . . the house where Keith grew up."

For an instant, Jessie imagined Micah playing in Keith's room, Bill looking on with a benevolent smile; or going to baseball games, the two of them yelling "Let's go Mets." She blinked away tears and gazed at Cass. "What did you say?"

"I said thank you, we'll consider it if it ever comes down to it."

After a beat of silence, Jessie said, "It's tempting, isn't it?"

"In some ways, for sure. But this is our home, right?" *Was Cassandra trying to persuade Jessie, or herself?* "And we're OK for now?"

Thinking of the meeting looming over her, Jessie put her head back down on Cass's shoulder and sighed. "For now."

Twenty-Five

When the next day arrived, and with it the knowledge that the emergency library board meeting would begin within hours, what little bravado Jessie had been displaying faltered. With encouragement from Allison, she'd taken the day off from work. She hadn't wanted to; she didn't want the PPAW people to think they'd already achieved their aim. But as she moved around the house, jumping from one task to the next without accomplishing much, Jessie saw the wisdom in it. Once they both were home from school, the boys provided a welcome distraction, and the normalcy of their weekday routine helped her move from afternoon into evening. They enjoyed "breakfast for dinner," as the novelty of chocolate-chip banana pancakes on a school night helped brighten the mood.

"Do I have to go?" Jessie said in a half-whisper, half-whine. It was time to attend the meeting and suffer through the "public comments" period. She feared that "public humiliation" would be more accurate. Her fate was hanging in the balance, and there was no way to know how sentiment in the town would turn: for her or against her. Wearing her most conservative outfit, a modest skirt suit of a subtle black-and-white herringbone paired with a pale-blue blouse, Jessie sat on the couch in the den, her hands covering her face.

Cassandra slung an arm around her shoulders. "Yes, babe, you do have to go. You have done nothing wrong, and you need to be there to make those bastards look the innocent woman they're smearing in the eye." She licked her lips and asked quietly, "Are you sure you don't want to speak? You might feel better."

"Positive. We've been through so much in the past few months, Cass, and it's going to be brutal. Listening to these people we've lived with and served for the past four years trying to get me fired. Trying to make our family into the 'other.' How could I possibly get up to speak? I don't even know how I'm going to sit there and take it!" A headache was starting to form between her eyes, and Jessie was wondering if it could get serious enough to beg off from the meeting. The idiocy of wishing a debilitating migraine on herself did not escape her. "It's awful."

"Well, look at it this way: The board will make its decision one way or another based on what they hear from the community tonight. After that, our lives will either go back to normal, or we'll start looking for another place to live."

"Wouldn't that mean they've won?"

"Temporarily. But it's more important that Eli and Micah grow up where they're accepted, where they can be happy. We'll make that happen, one way or another, in Queens with Bill or someplace else."

Jessie was still casting about for an excuse to avoid the meeting when the doorbell rang. Their babysitter, a high school senior named Madison, had arrived. She was one of a handful of sitters they could always count on for the occasional dinner out. The fact that she had accepted the job after all the town had heard about them cheered Jessie; she tallied one more "friend" in her column. The little voice inside her head, however—which sounded suspiciously like Cassandra—reminded her that the approval of a bookish seventeen-year-old whose mother and father worked as a professor at the local community college and an attorney, respectively, wasn't representative of the town as a whole, so she shouldn't try to extrapolate the mood.

Jessie had never seen the high school auditorium so full for a board meeting of any kind. A long table had been set up on the stage for the library board, four men and three women, all of whom Jessie knew—if not well, then at least casually. Her interactions with them had always been pleasant, but it was impossible to know what side they'd fall on. They all looked nervous and uncomfortable. A library board meeting, while always open to the public, usually generated a handful of observers, if that. More often than not, the board members conducted their business in one of the library's public rooms in the absence of anyone at all from outside. If there was something urgent on the agenda, like a new budget item, there might be a dozen people, tops. But tonight, there were easily over two hundred people from all demographic segments of the community sitting in the blue tweed, folding theater seats, the kind of crowd the school usually only got for their big end-of-year musical performances. A podium with microphone had been set up at the base of the stage, which was flanked by an American flag on one side and the state flag on the other. Although they'd been among the first to arrive, Jessie had refused to sit in the front row where she would feel as if she were on trial, knowing that everyone was staring at her, and instead told Cassandra that they would be sitting several rows back. Near the aisle, in case she felt the sudden need to escape.

Bill came in shortly before the meeting was called to order and sat down next to Cassandra in the seat they'd saved for him. In a nod to the importance of the occasion, Jessie noticed that he was not wearing the casual gear in which she'd grown accustomed to seeing him, opting instead for a pair of pressed khakis and a long-sleeved button-down shirt, new clothes he must have bought during his trip. He'd also left his rings, sunglasses, and hat behind, and it looked as if his hair and beard had been recently trimmed. Jessie hadn't realized until that moment how much she'd missed him and gave him a hug that lasted a couple of beats longer than it might have in other circumstances. To her surprise,

Cassandra, too, embraced him warmly; she was not usually that demonstrative in public.

Promptly at seven p.m., everyone was asked to stand for the Pledge of Allegiance. Like the rest of those assembled, Jessie and Cassandra put their hands over their hearts, but Jessie didn't feel certain enough of the strength of her voice and only mouthed the familiar words. She wondered with some despair whether "liberty and justice for all" still applied. If it ever did.

"Ladies and gentlemen, thank you for coming tonight to this emergency meeting of the library board, as we discuss the continued employment of Youth Librarian Jessie Wilton." The speaker was longtime board member Victor Horace. He was a round-faced, round-bodied sixty-something man who was respected in town for his ownership of two local car dealerships and his charitable giving, and he was comfortable speaking in public. "We have thirty-two people registered for public comments tonight, and everyone who signed up will have an opportunity to speak. It is going to be a long and possibly tense night, folks. Please keep your remarks brief and, above all, civil. I'll repeat: *civil*. Your comments will be kept to a limit of three minutes each, and we will permit no foul language or personal attacks."

The first name on the list was Crystal Hutchinson: a member of the PTA and one of Trish's oldest friends from elementary school as well as an early adopter of her MLM team. Standing before the microphone in the same red, white, and blue PPAW shirt the rest of her group was wearing, she said in a solemn, whispery voice, "I'd like to begin our meeting with a prayer."

Around Jessie and Cassandra, many bowed their heads. "Dear Lord," Crystal said, her tone still hushed, "guide the fine people of our library board in their decision-making, and may they see fit to protect the innocent minds of our precious children from the forces that would warp them. In Jesus's name, amen." A handful of people echoed *amen*; to Jessie it appeared that they were mostly PPAW members.

"I'm Crystal Hutchinson, a mama bear to two wonderful kiddos,

Colin and Maggie, ages eight and ten. I want you all to know that I have nothing against Jessie Wilton personally, and I've been nothing but kind to her and her little family, *unusual* as it is. But in light of the shocking reports about her son, I think it's only reasonable that we ask her to step down. It has become clear to me now that she is a Marxist groomer who has manipulated her own child into thinking that he's a homosexual, and it's only a matter of time before she indoctrinates other children in town. I pray that she gets the help she clearly needs for her psychiatric problems and, above all, finds Jesus. In the meantime, she doesn't belong in a position of influence around our vulnerable children.

"Thank you."

"I guess that's what Crystal calls *civil*," Cassandra said in a barely lowered voice. She reached over to hold Jessie's hand. Jessie squeezed it to keep from crying.

So, that's what Crystal had to say "in Jesus's name," Jessie thought with dismay. She had believed that their attempts to control what others read was the single most offensive thing about the PPAW members, but now she was reassessing. Jessie was an irregular churchgoer, but she was devoted to the Beatitudes. The message of the Jesus *she* knew was one of compassion, tolerance, and love. What the PPAW people were offering was the opposite of that. Talk about "the forces that would warp them"! She couldn't believe how quickly the rhetoric had escalated. How was she supposed to sit through an hour and a half of these attacks?

Dean was next to speak. Instead of a PPAW shirt, he was wearing a somber dark blue suit and a red tie, with an American flag pinned to his lapel. He looked as if he were running for office, and in Jessie's mind there was a distinct possibility that this meeting might be his way of testing the waters. Dean walked up to the podium with an air of righteous indignation, a couple of index cards in his hand. Once in front, he gazed out at the audience as if he were about to give a valedictory address but refused to look at Jessie and Cassandra.

"Good evening, Hadlinsburg. My name is Dean Marshall, and you all know me as a husband, father of four, businessman, and civic leader."

Jessie's eyes slid over to Trish, sitting at the end of the second row, knowing that Dean was expecting to speak for them both. From this angle it was impossible to know how she was reacting, although Jessie saw with relief that she was not wearing a PPAW shirt, but instead a soft, lightweight pink sweater. She imagined Trish giving Dean some excuse about "her company" or "her image," a small assertion of her independence and exactly the sort of thing he would be likely to accept from her. "My six-year-old Quentin has been friends with Jessie Wilton's son Eli since preschool, when they were both three. Even though as a Christian I didn't approve of Jessie and Cassandra's lifestyle, I like to live by the motto, 'Hate the sin, love the sinner.' I thought, as long as they kept their lifestyle to themselves and out of public view, well, that's between them and God. So, until recently, I didn't think there was any reason to deny my son the opportunity to play with one of his favorite little friends, and Eli *seems* perfectly normal.

"But that all changed when Quentin told me that Eli's younger brother, Micah, had started acting very strangely. Quentin came home from their house one day, very confused, saying that Micah claimed that he had a boyfriend. Of all things! Now, of course at that age, we know he was making things up—children have such amazing imaginations. But it wasn't a one-time thing, and Micah talked about it on more than one occasion, apparently even making up physical attributes for this imaginary boyfriend.

"Now, let me ask you: Where would a three-year-old *boy* come up with the idea that it's OK for him to pretend to have a *boyfriend*? I put the blame squarely on his—his *mothers*. Poor little Micah, so impressionable. Like any child, he looks to his parents for his moral code. But in this case, he had the misfortune of being born into an abnormal family without the strong guidance of a male hand."

"I'm going to kill him," Cassandra, her forehead pressed up against Jessie's temple, whispered to her.

"I'll help you hide the body," Jessie whispered back, her throat tight.

"Naturally, I was horrified. I brought this shocking news to the attention of our new local chapter of Patriot Parents Against Woke, which had the good sense to demand Jessie's resignation. It. Is. Not. Right," he added, emphasizing his point by hitting the podium with the flat of his hand with every word, "that a person who would groom *her own child* to believe he is homosexual have an opportunity to do the same to the other innocent children in this town. I regret to say that Jessie Wilton must resign, or the board must fire her, for the good of the community.

"Thank you."

Three high school students, all seniors, followed Dean. Jessie wondered if any of them had participated in the ad hoc Community Watch that had appeared on their driveway, but she had been asleep for the later shifts and figured everyone would be better off if she didn't know. Though equally passionate, their testimony was very unlike Dean's and Crystal's. They spoke of the help Jessie had given them during difficult times in high school and the respect their younger siblings had for her. Jessie felt tears of a different sort well up, and she nodded her thanks as the students returned to their seats.

A dozen or so other citizens followed and made their statements, some in favor of Jessie and some insisting that she be let go. Then her coworkers came up as a group—Allison, limping, though without her cane; Tyler; adult librarians Suzanne and Marie—allowing Allison to speak for them, about how qualified and kind and well-liked Jessie was. The minister of their Unitarian church, Reverend Breuer, made an impassioned speech about loving the stranger, but Jessie doubted that the ears it was intended to reach were open to the message. Jessie knew she would always remember the names and faces of the people who had turned against her, people she might not have agreed with but whom she had always treated with respect. That they wouldn't do the same for her wounded her deeply.

When Cassandra's name was finally called, Jessie reluctantly let go of her hand and watched as she walked up to the podium.

"My name is Cassandra Wilton, and I have been married to Jessie for ten years. For four of those years, we've lived in Hadlinsburg happily and without a single issue, without receiving so much as a parking ticket. We've made a life; we have friends of all kinds. We have two young sons: Eli, who's almost seven, and Micah, who is three years old.

"Micah is a little boy with his own thoughts and ideas, and we allow him to explore the world in a safe, healthy way. Other than making sure that he's truthful, treats people well, and knows to share with others, we don't tell him what to think or to be. I grant you that something unusual—OK, let's say *inexplicable,* is going on with Micah, and I'm as confused as anyone. But we're handling it as rationally as parents can under these very strange circumstances. We even have respected scientists working with us, and I have documentation on every word. Now that you know about it, you could ask us about it directly, if you cared to, and we'd give you the whole story. Yes, it *is* weird, but it isn't scary or dangerous in any way, and it affects literally no one else in this town, *no one*, and I can't see how it's anyone's business but ours."

Cassandra stood up straighter, in what Jessie called her "military stance" but was more accurately parade rest—feet exactly twelve inches apart, hands clasped behind her back—and continued, "I served my country in the US Air Force, received an honorable discharge, and now I'm serving my community as an EMT. I find the bigoted persecution of my wife and me not only insulting but un-American.

"Jessie provides guidance at the library for children who ask for it. Their parents always have the final say over what they can read—always —and she respects that. Not a word comes out of her mouth that's meant to make these kids into something they're not. And just like you, we parent our own kids the way *we* choose to, but we don't try to make *our* kids into something they're not, either.

"I hope the board, and the people of Hadlinsburg, realize what they're doing and come to their senses immediately. If you're so concerned about the children of this town, you should really stop and think about what this is teaching them. This whole ugly situation says more about you all than it does about us.

"And what it tells me is that you should be ashamed of yourselves."

Amid the loud whispers as Cassandra returned to her seat and kissed Jessie on the lips for good measure, Charlie Duquesne was called up. The Duke, clad in a red-and-blue flannel shirt and jeans with suspenders, secured his favorite black "Korean War Veteran" cap atop his remaining wisps of white hair and made his way from his seat leaning on his cane. When he reached the podium, he rested his cane against it, coughed twice and cleared his throat, the wet, phlegmy sound making Jessie flinch. Then, using his hands to support him, he dipped his head toward the microphone and paused, his rheumy-eyed gaze taking in the room. The audience waited in respectful silence for their war hero to speak. When he finally did, he said, in a voice rough from age:

"You Pee-Paw folks need to read some goddamn history."

A scattering of hooting and laughter from the high school students and some teachers greeted this declaration, and Cassandra stood up and clapped slowly. The Duke tipped his hat in her direction, then hobbled back to his seat.

Thus, the audience was already in an uproar when Bill's name was called. Although he was a stranger to most in the room, by now almost everyone in town knew the bare bones of the story about Micah and Keith. Bill stopped for a moment before he spoke, looking down at his feet to collect himself. But then he hit the ground running, and his voice was strong and sure.

"My name is Bill Weyerhauser, and no, I'm not from Hadlinsburg. I live in Astoria, Queens, New York. But I've asked to speak tonight because I have some important perspective to add to this conversation.

"My son Keith was a firefighter with the FDNY. He died in the Twin Towers on September 11th, 2001, at the age of twenty-eight, running into the buildings while everyone else was running away. He was an honest-to-God *hero*, and I will *fight* anyone who says otherwise.

"You might have heard that Jessie's son Micah has been saying a lot of things that no three-year-old could possibly know about. Now, if you refuse to accept that Micah Wilton could be Keith reincarnated—or maybe is 'channeling' Keith—and would rather believe that a preschooler is somehow pulling off an elaborate and convincing hoax under the guidance of his mothers to advance some sort of bizarre gay agenda, well, that's on you and your frankly ludicrous prejudices.

"What I will tell you is that my son—my sweet boy, my only child, the apple of his mother's eye—and yes, his *boyfriend*, another of New York's Bravest, Joseph Killigrew, gave up their lives to rescue innocent people from an attack perpetrated by a group of religious extremists." He paused, rapping his knuckles on the podium. "I'm going to repeat that: Religious. Extremists. The terrorists who brought down the Towers and murdered three thousand people there and in D.C. and Pennsylvania did it in the name of their religious and political ideology. Stop and think about that for a second, if you can wrap your heads around it: This astroturf organization, this Pee-Paw," he said with a dismissive movement of his hand toward the group in matching tee shirts, "that's been brought into your community, has more in common with murderous thugs than the fine people you are vilifying.

"Yes, that's right: They are acting just like the Taliban and Al-Qaeda terrorists."

Several people in the PPAW section grumbled, and one older man, wearing a bright yellow Gadsden flag "Don't Tread on Me" T-shirt yelled out, "How dare you!" The board president called for silence from the audience.

Bill put his hands on his hips and spoke over them as the din grew louder despite Victor's request. "Oh, what's the matter, don't like the comparison? Do you think it's different because they claim they're doing it in the name of Christianity rather than Islam? Stop kidding yourselves. Pee-Paw wants you to do exactly what the terrorists did: impose *your* religious and ethical values on folks who don't share them.

"People, *don't* let them convince you to call for the removal of a fine and well-respected librarian because she doesn't fit the picture you have in your head of the little old spinster lady who lives with eight cats.

Don't let them tell the parents of this town what their children can and cannot read. *You parents* make that decision for *your* families, not a bunch of uptight, sexually repressed reactionaries who live in fear and whose default position on anything they don't understand or approve of is to ban it."

"Mr. Weyerhauser," Victor interjected, his amplified voice cutting through the noise, "I will remind you that we are to keep our remarks *civil.*"

"I believe, Mr. Horace," Bill said without missing a beat, "that I've been at least as civil as Mr. Marshall or Mrs. Hutchinson were."

"Oh, burn!" Cassandra whispered in admiration.

"And by the way," Bill added, leaning closer to the microphone so his voice came out deeper and more resonant, "cut out the 'Patriot Parents' crap—those folks are not *patriots*," he added, nearly spitting out the words. "Jessie's wife, Cassandra, *she's* a patriot. Charlie Duquesne, God bless him, is a patriot. And *my son* was a patriot. Pee-Paw appropriated the term for their own purposes; they don't even know the meaning of the word."

Twenty-Six

It took several minutes for the furor to die down after Bill returned to his seat. Another dozen people were called up to voice their opinions, including members of the clergy—the opinions of whom were split along fairly obvious lines depending on their denomination. A couple of them used words like *sinning. Damnation. Satanic.* Several speakers, obviously echoing language that PPAW had specifically instructed them to use, accused Jessie, Cassandra, and their supporters of being "pedophiles and groomers." It was hard for Jessie to listen to; she felt on the verge of a panic attack. As for Cassandra, well, Jessie had been afraid to look her way, wondering if she were being gutted again by the kind of words that had shattered her family life.

When the Reverend Harold Robinson's name was called, Jessie braced for more of the same. She and Cassandra had met him a few times when they were new to the town; their interactions with him, always chilly, had left her wary. Known for his oratory and often fervent, revival-style sermons, he was not recognized as a friend to the small gay community.

The reverend strode down the aisle, a worn brown leather portfolio tucked beneath his arm. Although he was lean and of average height, the energy he projected, and his ramrod-straight posture, made him seem much larger, more imposing, and younger than his seventy-one years. He wore wire-rimmed glasses, and his closely trimmed gray Afro and beard were one shade lighter than his sharply tailored charcoal-gray suit. A gold cross was pinned to his lapel.

Setting the portfolio atop the podium, he began, "Friends and neighbors, brothers and sisters," his voice sonorous and pleasing, the mark of a man accustomed to speaking in front of a crowd. "I am the Reverend Harold Robinson of the First Baptist Church of Hadlinsburg, a congregation of 239 fine Christian souls.

"I have been in Hadlinsburg since birth, and in the pulpit for thirty-seven years, since the passing of my father, may he rest in glory. I am, as you know, a traditionalist; no one will ever mistake me for a *progressive* thinker." Smiling, he bowed his head slightly with this admission. "So, when I met Ms. Wilton and her wife several years ago, I immediately rejected their relationship as contrary to Scripture. I still do find it . . . problematic."

Here it comes, thought Jessie with a frown.

"However!" the reverend said, with both an index finger and his voice raised. "I am not here today to discuss the home life of two women who are, to all appearances, otherwise clean-living Christians, devoted wives, loving mothers, and productive members of our town. I would rather focus on a different kind of threat to Hadlinsburg, not a perceived one from a respected librarian, but a real one from a group of people who have decided to challenge and censure what our children are reading and learning."

From his portfolio, he withdrew two paperbacks, which Jessie recognized as middle-school chapter books about the Black experience during slavery and Reconstruction. Both were historically accurate, brilliantly written, often disturbing.

And on the PPAW removal list.

He held them aloft, turning his body right and left to make sure everyone saw. "There are those among our own community who would like to hide the truth from our children, the truth of our shared and devastating history. They want books such as these to be banned from our schools, from our public library. They want to tell us, 'No, you may not tell stories of your people's involuntary servitude and oppression, of discrimination and death; you may not tell the next generation of your suffering and our shame, so as not to offend the delicate sensibilities of those who did not suffer the same.'

"Now, folks," he continued, lowering the books, "I recently had an epiphany—yes, my friends, even this old dog can learn new tricks!—when I realized that we needed to push back on this proposed erasure of our history, of topics some may find unpleasant, I prayed on it for days, asking Jesus for guidance. And do you know what I concluded with his help? That the stories of *others'* struggles and trials should not be similarly erased. Not the Holocaust, certainly, and not even—and I confess I surprise myself by saying it—the tribulations experienced by our homosexual neighbors. I still do not agree with all of it, and I could be going down the wrong path—the Lord Himself alone will judge me. But today I would rather err on the side of freedom and knowledge. That is the least we owe our ancestors.

"We are all sinners, my friends. But let us not compound our other sins by allowing a handful of people to whitewash history and deprive an innocent woman of her livelihood. I have seen no evidence that Ms. Wilton has had any undue influence over the children of my congregation nor, indeed, elsewhere in our town." He paused, his eyes narrowed. "And I doubt that anyone of you here have, either.

"So should these Pee-Paw folks succeed, and you have trouble finding these titles, I say, reach out to me. I will personally purchase one for your child, so that they may know the truth."

There was scattered applause, and one woman shouted, "Amen!" Jessie noticed that the PPAW crowd, while stewing in their seats, was uncharacteristically silent at the dig the reverend had made at them, and she smirked. No doubt they were unwilling to speak up and be thought racist, publicly. She recalled what Allison had said about the demographics of Hadlinsburg and hoped that PPAW had indeed miscalculated. Being on the receiving end of discrimination had a way of creating strange bedfellows.

The last person scheduled to speak was Ms. Hadlin. Or rather, she had insisted on going last, sitting at the board table listening intently through the other comments, her face impassive, unreadable. She was dressed in a slim, navy-blue pantsuit with a soft white blouse and walked with steady, even steps down to the microphone in immaculate high-heeled pumps.

"I'd like to thank you all for attending tonight and for presenting your points of view," Ms. Hadlin began.

"Most of you know me." Even after years of retirement, she still could command the attention and respect of a crowd with only her voice. "I'm Diana Hadlin, and I taught social studies at Hadlinsburg High School for forty years. I was honored to be Ohio's Teacher of the Year in 1992."

There was some scattered clapping. Trish yelled, "God bless you, Ms. Hadlin!"

Hadlin acknowledged the applause with a smile. "Oh, and here's a fun fact: My great-great-great grandfather Christopher Hadlin founded our beautiful town in 1823."

Several in the audience laughed. No one who had lived in Hadlinsburg for any length of time was unaware of the history of the town. The Founder's Day celebration still took place on May ninth every year, with Ms. Hadlin taking over as the mistress of ceremonies at the parade and subsequent festival following the death of her father. And the historical society was still housed in the 1897 Victorian the founder's grandson, Henry, had later built.

"But who here has been in my classes?"

Dozens of hands shot up.

"Or maybe your parents or your kids?"

Other hands went up as well.

"So, you know me fairly well, I think. Now, who remembers Mr. Jansen? We called him Mr. J, who taught trigonometry, AP calculus, and the other advanced math classes back in the '80s?"

There was an approving murmur from the crowd and nodding heads.

"Besides being a wonderful teacher—he was, wasn't he?" she added after a few older people applauded. "Besides being a wonderful teacher, he was a damn good-looking man."

Laughter.

"Oh, yes, don't think I didn't notice how all those happily married class mothers made eyes at him," she added, shaking a scolding finger. More laughter.

"Well, Mr. J left Hadlinsburg High before the start of the 1987 school year. Who knows why?" Silence. "No one? Let's see." She squinted, searching the room and finally settling on a robust-looking woman in her late fifties. "Cicely Peterson, *you* had us both on your schedule. And if I recall, you were pretty tapped into the local gossip. What did you hear?"

Heads turned to look at Cicely, who was blushing the same deep red as the "Mr. Lincoln" tea roses she was known for, straight up to the roots of her gray-streaked blond hair. "I heard that you two were, um, close."

"Go ahead, don't be shy: You heard that we were having an affair, right?"

Cicely cleared her throat. "Well, yes."

"I was certainly flattered by the rumors. I mean, as we've already established, he was a damn attractive man, and I was a woman in my prime. We were both unattached. And we did spend an awful lot of time together.

"*But*. I'm sorry for the lengthy delay in telling you all, but there was no basis in fact at all for that rumor. None. His departure had nothing whatsoever to do with me." Her face was now devoid of the good humor that she had worn since she started talking. She put her elbows down, grasping the front of the podium, and leaned forward.

"Mr. J left Hadlinsburg High because he was in love." There was a collective intake of breath from the crowd. "But not with me. Bradley Jansen was in love with another man."

Several people from the older generations gasped and shrieked. Many started talking, but Ms. Hadlin's voice rose above the din. "And the reason Mr. J and I were spending so much time together was that he had no one else he could trust to talk through his decision. To help him decide whether to stay here and live a lie, alone, or to leave for New York and live as his authentic self with his chosen partner. I told him to go for it.

"And he did. Good for him."

Now the audience erupted. Jessie and Cassandra looked at each other, wide-eyed. "Well, well," Jessie murmured, "an ally indeed."

Ms. Hadlin stood calmly at the front of the room, leaning a hip against the podium with her arms folded across her chest, the very picture of a veteran teacher facing an unruly class. Victor, looking increasingly discomfited, called for order again and again. The poor man had started to sweat. Clearly this was not the meeting he had envisioned leading.

When the noise had finally died down, she continued. "You're all pretty surprised, aren't you? No one guessed. No one had any inkling that one of your favorite teachers was gay. During that time he had to hide, suppress who he was. All for the same *stupid* reasons that *some* of you are spouting now.

"Maybe you liked it that way, hm? Maybe you preferred that gay people stay in the closet so you could pretend you didn't know anyone who wasn't just like you.

"But guess what? *You* had him as a teacher and somehow didn't turn gay. And I taught you about the Stonewall riots and the history of gay rights, and still, somehow you managed to grow up straight. Could it be . . . *could it be* because being gay or straight is actually part of *who you are*, not what you read or who teaches you?"

Her eyes scanned the crowd. "I'm looking at *you*, Dean Marshall," she said, flicking her fingers at him, "and the rest of the PPAW brigade." All eyes turned Dean's way; he frowned and glared. "You were in my class, and your parents were in Mr. J's class as well as mine. Yet here you all are today, living your heterosexual lives, completely unaffected by your teachers' supposed *influence* over you. And let me tell you a little secret: Mr. J wasn't the only one. Statistically speaking, you've been taught by gay teachers in this school sometime during your upbringing. All of you." Her gesture encompassed the entire room. "Along with history and math and science and literature, they taught you about respect and getting along with others. You just didn't know it.

"Some people in this town have certainly absorbed the scary buzzwords, the ones that those PPAW organizers taught them to say. Now they call ideas they don't understand 'indoctrination,' and they're labeling teachers and librarians you've known and trusted for years 'pedophiles and groomers.' Fearmongering, nothing more. And if you'd been paying attention in my class, you might actually have an idea what words like 'Marxist,' 'communism,' and 'socialism' really mean, because the way you're tossing them around tells me you haven't got a clue. Too bad it's too late to go back and change some of your grades.

"So, *shame on you* PPAW folks. Yes, shame on you for trying to suppress the free exchange of ideas. For trying to villainize and smear the good names of the people whose only goal is to educate your children, to broaden their horizons, and to prepare them for life in the United States of America and as citizens of the world."

Victor cleared his throat. "Ms. Hadlin, your time is—"

Ignoring him, Diana went on. "And, oh, let's talk about books for a minute, since you're here piling on a librarian and trying to get books removed. While you all were in school, you read books about other cultures, about slavery, about other lifestyles. You might not have enjoyed every single one, and lord knows I've heard plenty of complaints about them being boring or too old-fashioned or whatnot, but that was hardly the point. They were part of your school experience because you needed to know about them in order to become broad-minded adults.

"If there was anything you *should* have learned in my classes, it's how to think for yourselves. You should have also learned what happens to civilizations when a minority tries to control what the rest of its citizens are doing or thinking. What happens when they take books off the shelves and demonize the intellectuals. Reminder: It isn't pretty. It leads to the destruction of people's lives. *Sometimes* it's the first step to the concentration camps, and even as far down the road as genocide. Major Duquesne has it right: time to get back to the history books. The kids know it too. Students have been standing up for their right to read so-called objectionable books for generations. There was even a Supreme Court case about it back in 1982. Look it up: *Island Trees v. Pico*. Some of the same books involved in that case are on the PPAW list over forty years later, and—spoiler alert—the students won that one.

"So, I will not be a party to this. I'll be damned if I let some small-minded out-of-towners whip up another McCarthy Red Scare in my own hometown, the one my own great-great-great grandfather built."

Although the audience thought she was finished, amid the cacophony of both applause and jeers, she had one more thought for her fellow library board members, and addressed them directly, jabbing her finger at them to make her point. "We have a job to do in this situation, and we'd better get it right. Protect the librarians, protect the teachers. Protect the forward-thinking people of this town so we don't end up going backward to the Dark Ages.

"Do. Your. Job."

She returned to her seat, seemingly cool and unruffled despite the passion of her speech or the hubbub it caused.

"Well, that was, um . . . Yes. Thank you for your input, Ms. Hadlin,"

Victor said, apparently at a loss for words. He stood up from his spot and cleared his throat again. "And thank you all for attending. As we have reached the end of the public comment period, I call this meeting—"

A voice came from the back of the auditorium: "Hold up."

TWENTY-SEVEN

The voice belonged to Brianne Golding, now treasurer of the graduating class as well as a reliable supporting player in school theater productions. Victor had called out her name earlier in the evening, but she had failed to appear. Jessie had been disappointed at the time, as Brianne was the sort of person from whom she had hoped to hear, one whose opinion carried weight with her fellow students and who could provide the sort of positive testimonial she needed. Brianne strode into the room wearing the recognizable uniform of the local McDonald's.

"We have something we want to say."

And at that, a dozen students scattered throughout the room stood up and made their way down to the podium, causing a buzz of conversation. Some of the younger ones had come with their parents, but a good number whom Jessie recognized as juniors and seniors were on their own. Among them were those who had stood watch at the Wiltons' driveway, including Alanna Marshall, who ignored her father's vocal demands that she sit down.

The students made a rough semicircle behind Brianne as she walked up to the microphone. But as she adjusted it lower—she was a good deal shorter than Diana Hadlin—Victor said, "I'm sorry, young lady, but the public comment period is closed. If you had something to add to the conversation, you should have signed up to speak."

"I did, but, sorry, I just got off of work," Brianne said, addressing the board. "Maybe you've noticed my very fashionable outfit. And I think that if the library board is so concerned about *the children*, it might be helpful to, y'know, actually listen to some of the children involved."

"Several of your fellow students have *already* given their opinions, miss, and now the session is closed. I am hereby turning off the micro-phone." He nodded to someone at the control panel, who shut the amplification off with a click. The board members, looking relieved, began to gather the notes from the table in front of them.

"Fine," Brianne said, "no problem." With her voice booming out, louder than Jessie would ever dream of speaking, she added, "I don't need a mic anyway." Jessie gave silent kudos to Louise McCaffrey, the faculty adviser for the drama club. If nothing else, Brianne had certainly learned how to project.

Diana Hadlin stood up and, with the cool air of someone who knew she would not be refused, turned the mic back on. She walked back to her seat, one eyebrow arched, daring Victor to say something. He did not.

"Hi, I'm Brianne Golding, a senior at the high school. We here," she gestured behind her, "and a bunch of our peers who couldn't make it tonight, wanted to thank Pee-Paw and their members for the awesome work they're doing on behalf of the students of Hadlinsburg."

"What the fuck—" Cassandra looked ready to punch someone. Bill hissed out a breath.

"Oh, no," Jessie said, slumping down in her seat, her head in her hand. If she couldn't depend on people she knew to stand up for her, the children, she'd have no chance at all.

After a pause, Brianne continued. "Yes, without Pee-Paw's guidance, we wouldn't have this important and really comprehensive list of books they want removed from the school and our public library, books we shouldn't be reading." She held up the by-now familiar tally of challenges. "It's a great list," she said, looking at it and running her finger down the titles, "so you'll be happy to know that a group of us in school have started a book club to read them. We might not get to all of them, because some of us will be headed to college soon, but it's obvious to us that if a group like Pee-Paw wants them removed, they must be worth reading."

"I don't think my heart can take much more of this," Jessie whispered to Cass as hoots, applause, and some taunts erupted from the audience. Cassandra laughed, shaking her head.

"In case you can't figure it out, this is our way of telling the board that Pee-Paw doesn't speak for us. What's the point of school if you're going to cave and let some out-of-towners with a political agenda tell us what we can and can't learn about?

"But what we really want to say is that Ms. Wilton is getting a raw deal. Nobody said *anything* about her and her wife before the Pee-Paw people came to town. Now all of a sudden she's somehow a danger to the community, and it's all"—and here, putting into practice all her drama club training, she pressed the back of one hand to her forehead and used the other to clutch imaginary pearls around the collar of her uniform—"*Won't someone think of the children?*

"Well, that's crap!

"You know how I met Ms. Wilton? She and I moved to Hadlinsburg around the same time. I came here from Kansas City in eighth grade, and I knew nobody. I used to hide in the library after school, reading. Feeling like a total loser. But Ms. Wilton always came by to see how I was doing, to recommend books she thought I'd like. And after a while, I stopped feeling like I was all alone, and I made friends. I'll be going off to college next fall, and I'll be asking Ms. Wilton to write me a letter of recommendation."

Brianne gestured to the students behind her. "Everyone here has been around Ms. Wilton, asked her for help, for the past four years, and nobody has been turned gay. I mean, Benny's gay," and Benny, tall and skinny with heavily gelled, dark brown hair, smirked and gave a little wave to the crowd, "but he's always been gay; his family has known since fourth grade, the rest of us have known for years, and you can't pin that on Ms. Wilton. And Mia over here, who babysat for Eli and Micah for two years, has been groomed so hard that she goes to St. Mary's every Sunday and sings in the choir with her steady boyfriend. Scary, huh?

"On behalf of the students of Hadlinsburg High—and their brothers and sisters in lower grades—we're asking the library board to *reject* Pee-Paw's demand that Jessie Wilton step down or be fired.

"Thank you."

With a couple of hugs and high-fives, the students returned to their seats. Victor looked toward Diana, seeking her approval, and she gave a barely noticeable nod. He cleared his throat again. "As I was saying: Since we have reached the end of the public comment period, I call this meeting adjourned. Thank you all for attending."

The room did not immediately empty. People were slow to file out as conversations broke out among small groups. Jessie could hear strident voices, some raised in anger and disbelief. "Can you imagine?" "How dare she . . ." "All those years . . ." "Who would have thought . . ."

Once again Bill hugged Cassandra and Jessie in turn, bending over to embrace the latter, who found herself unable, for the moment, to rise to her feet. "You've got this," he said to her, touching her face with his fingertips, and headed toward the exit. "I'll catch you outside."

It seemed to Jessie that it took a very long time before she felt steady enough to stand up. There were only a handful of people left in the auditorium, and the few who tried to approach her were waved off by Cassandra.

"You all right, babe?" Cass asked as she helped Jessie to her feet, their theater seats bouncing back into the upright position. Someone started to shut off the lights. "It's been some night, and you look a little pale. Let's go home."

"Yeah, it's, um." Now that she was vertical, Jessie realized it wasn't only her breath that she'd been holding. "Wait for me, gotta go to the ladies' first."

"Do you want me to go with you?"

Such an unnecessary, yet completely Cassandra-like thing to say. "No, thanks, I'm good." They shuffled out of their row and headed toward the doors.

"OK, meet you in the lobby, then?" She pecked Jessie on the temple.

"Right."

Her single-minded look warding off the stragglers who might have planned on speaking to her, Jessie speed-walked out of the auditorium, down the nearly deserted, half-lit hallway covered with posters for clubs and events, and into the ladies' room. When she came out, sliding her arms into her jacket, she nearly collided with Dean, who had exited the men's room across the hall. His tie was loosened, the top button of his shirt unbuttoned, and he was walking with his head bent over his phone.

"Oh, excuse m—" Seeing who was in front of him, Dean cut short his apology and clapped his mouth shut.

"No."

He took a step back, his face an unpleasant smirk of surprise, bemusement, and anger.

Jessie leaned forward, closing the gap. Tilting up her chin, getting in his face, despite the height difference. "You know what, Dean?" she said, all the stress of the past few weeks boiling over. "I'm not going to excuse you. For anything."

"Wha—"

"For always, *always* being rude to me and my family, from the beginning. For accusing me of the worst crimes." Her voice shook, and she swallowed hard. But she pushed on. "For setting my own town against me and putting my career at risk."

He hitched up his pants with a swagger. "Now, you listen to me—"

"Nope. Not for another minute. Seems to me we've all listened to *you* long enough, your bigotry and your—your condescension, and I'm fucking tired of it. You know damn well that Cassandra and I want nothing more than to raise our children in peace, like every other parent in Hadlinsburg. There is no 'gay agenda,' so quit acting as if there is.

"Trish and I," she gestured as if his wife were standing there, "we get along. Eli and Quentin, they're best of friends. Even Alanna's been—"

"You leave my kids out of this!" he snapped, his face red.

"Why should I, since you've made *my* family your personal punching bag? Acceptance, Dean, that's all we ever wanted.

"You want to see 'grooming,' well, you take a good look at what you've been teaching your own children: hatred, prejudice—the things you and Pee-Paw are trying to push on them—and leave me, my wife, and *my kids* the hell out of it."

As she spun on her heel to walk away, she heard him call out, "Crazy bitch! This isn't over!" Without turning around, she flipped him the bird.

"Oh, hi, Trish," Jessie said as she turned the corner and passed her friend in the hallway leading to the lobby. Taken by surprise, Trish gave a puzzled, halfhearted wave. Jessie, chin raised, kept walking.

Cassandra was, as promised, by the front door, standing next to Bill and speaking to a couple of students who had supported them. Jessie stood off to the side, waiting until the students left before joining Cass and Bill.

"Well, someone looks relieved," Cassandra said, her eyes narrowed.

"In more ways than one." Jessie laughed to herself a little.

"What happened? Tell me."

"I got something out of my system."

Twenty-Eight

"When do you think we'll get the board's decision?" Cassandra asked Jessie on the ride home.

Between fatigue and stress, Jessie's mouth was so dry she could barely answer. She rubbed her forehead, wishing she'd thought to bring along a water bottle. "Shouldn't be long. This was an emergency meeting."

"True. I suppose they can hardly claim hair-on-fire emergency if they're not willing to act quickly."

And act quickly they did. Jessie's phone rang at eleven thirty the following morning. A familiar voice said, "Hello, Jessie, this is Diana Hadlin."

Jessie felt a lump form in her throat, and her palms grew sweaty. "Good morning, Ms. Hadlin."

"I'll spare you the small talk and cut to the chase. The board voted five-to-two to keep you on."

A small cry escaped Jessie's throat, and tears sprang to her eyes. She couldn't speak.

"I'm not going to tell you who the two holdouts were, or what I had to say to them. Furthermore, I have insisted that those fuckers issue you a written apology for the emotional distress they've caused you and Cassandra."

While it was shocking to hear this elegant, educated older woman express herself this way, Jessie appreciated her forthrightness and burst out with a snorted laugh.

"I can't thank you enough, Ms. Hadlin."

"Call me Diana. You've earned the privilege. You keep doing what you're doing, Jessie, serving the people of this town."

"But I—I don't know how I can. How I can ever forgive them. How am I supposed to go back to work knowing the Pee-Paw people are still out there, still believing their lies?"

There was a short silence on the line.

"I hear where you're coming from. I do. I've lived my whole life here, of course, and have had to spend an awful lot of time persuading myself not to move to a bigger city where I could find a more open-minded community, as Mr. J did. But I figured, this is my town, my ancestors built it, for God's sake. *We've* been here for generations. So, why should *I* be the one to desert it? Why should I let them chase me away? I did my best to educate them in school, and I've kept trying long after I retired. And you, who are doing pretty much the same thing, why should *you* give up the life you have here?

"I hope people like Dean have learned something. If not, well, you'll know who your real friends are. I hope you'll count me among them. And someday, I'll hope you'll trust me enough to tell me all about Micah's fascinating journey."

"Oh, I'm more than happy to do that," Jessie assured her. "Anytime." She licked her lips. "But what about the book challenges?"

"Still in progress, I'm afraid. There will be more board meetings and some conversations with Allison. But at this point we're looking at them more as a nuisance than a threat. Folks like PPAW are used to sauntering in and having the whole community roll over to their demands; they don't expect pushback, certainly not the kind we gave them, certainly not from the kids, God bless 'em. Now that we've taken the wind out of their sails by voting to retain you, I think you'll find that the Hadlinsburg PPAW chapter will lose a lot of its influence, at least in the short term. I've already heard from two of the members who told me they were walking away. They seemed embarrassed, as they should be.

"I'd still advise not letting our guard down, though, and keeping a close eye on the school board. Guaranteed PPAW is already considering how to get their candidates—maybe even Dean—elected next year, and people have short memories. When election time comes, we're all going to have to make some noise to remind the town about the division they've caused in our community.

"We also can't forget that they're determined enough in their ideology to learn from their mistakes."

"What do you mean?"

"I mean, going after Black narratives as well as LGBTQ ones. In a community like ours with a strong Black presence, that's a sure-fire way to lose. As we've seen. But they'll likely adapt and adjust their attacks accordingly.

"In the meantime, though, I'm glad Hadlinsburg still has you, Jessie."

After saying goodbye to Ms. Hadlin, Jessie collapsed onto the couch, the nervous tension that had been holding her upright for the past two days gone. With shaking hands, she took two deep breaths, and she phoned Cassandra at work to give her the news.

"That's great, Jess! Woo! Yeah." Cassandra paused briefly. "So, what do you think, babe? Do you want to stay in Hadlinsburg . . . or?"

The unspoken question remained: *Or move to Queens?*

The line held silence for a few ticks while Jessie considered the question. "I guess we stay? I mean, I don't know yet. The people in town who support Pee-Paw, they're still here, aren't they? Probably retreating to lick their wounds to fight another day. Not that I want to decide anything right now, but it's something we're going to have to talk about a little more. See what the next couple of months bring."

Jessie's next call was to Bill, who answered on the first ring.

"I'm so happy to hear that, Jessie," he said. "At least we know that most of the town can appreciate what they have here.

"Well . . . I suppose that means I'll be heading back home tomorrow." Despite the relief occasioned by Jessie's announcement, his voice also contained something that sounded like regret. Jessie suspected that she knew why: As he had made no further mention of his invitation for them to live with him in Queens, he'd had to resign himself to returning to an empty home filled with memories of Keith, all the while aware that a remnant of his son still existed over six hundred miles away in someone else's three-year-old. It had to be hard on him. "Can I take you, Cassandra, and the boys out to dinner tonight to celebrate?"

"We'd like that very much."

They ended up at a Japanese hibachi restaurant in East Daniston, where the adults hoped that the boys would be entertained enough to ignore the more serious conversation that was going on over their heads.

"There's something I've been meaning to tell you, Bill, and I hope it doesn't make you sad," Jessie said as the chef dazzled the children by creating a smoking volcano out of onion rings on the cooking surface in front of them. Squeals of delight and applause ensued. "You are part of our family now and are welcome to join us anytime—with enough notice, of course. But what I've learned from Dr. Abernathy and his research is that within a few years Micah will almost definitely forget all about Keith. And that means he's going to forget about *you*. Well, as Keith's father anyway." She searched his face to assess the impact her words were having. "I don't want you to feel as if you've lost Keith all over again."

Bill's eyes turned to the action on the cooking surface and then to Micah, sitting next to him with his gaze fixed on the chef. Bill drummed his fingers on the polished wood table in front of him. "I know, and I've been thinking about it," he said. "I've come to the conclusion that knowing it's going to happen will make it easier when it finally does. It's not going to . . ." Here he paused, and Jessie could feel the emotion behind it. Biting his lip, he completed the thought: "It's not going to come as a shock this time."

Jessie immediately regretted bringing up the subject during their last evening together. But Bill smiled and nudged Micah, whose face blossomed into a huge grin when he looked up.

"Dis is fun, Dad!" Micah exclaimed, bouncing a little in his booster seat.

"Sure is, buddy," Bill replied.

Even Eli, who had been impossibly moody for the past month, shouted his approval of the chef's performance.

Back at the house after dinner, Bill helped Micah get ready for bed, tucking him in with tears shining in his eyes.

"I have to go back to New York tomorrow, Micah," Bill said.

"No!" Micah cried, kicking off the covers and throwing his arms around Bill's neck. "Don't go, Dad! Stay wif us!"

"I really do have to go home, buddy." Gently prying Micah's arms off, Bill settled him back into bed. "But your moms have given me permission to visit as often as I'd like, and I'll be joining you all for Thanksgiving. That's not too far away."

"Before you know it," Jessie added, already imagining creating an Advent-type calendar for the boys to count down the days.

"And then Christmas after that," Cassandra said.

"And then Christmas after that," Bill agreed. "And guess what! In the spring, as soon as I can, I'm going to get tickets for *all of us* to go see the Mets play. Together. How's that?" He looked at Jessie and Cassandra, watching from the doorway. "If that's OK with you, that is."

They both nodded their approval.

"Let's go Mets!" Micah yelled.

"Wait till Micah finds out that Shea Stadium doesn't exist anymore," Cassandra said to Jessie under her breath.

"Actually, that might be kind of interesting," Jessie replied. But her mind wasn't on Citi Field: She was thinking of Ground Zero and the 9/11 memorial. It was a question she had never asked Dr. Abernathy, and probably should before taking the children to New York: Would Micah be better or worse off if he went to the scene of Keith's death? Would he have any reaction at all outside of the typical preschooler's awe at the big buildings? Would it bring him peace or trigger more nightmares? She imagined bringing him to the memorial panel where Keith's name was inscribed, to see it, touch it, even make a crayon rubbing to be taken home and framed. Joey's name, too, to ensure that he—and their love, a love that had somehow outlasted death—would never be forgotten.

All on that tombstone-like slab above a waterfall, where water endlessly flowed like the tears of those left behind, down into the gaping hole, as big as the one left in their hearts.

After the boys were finally asleep, Bill prepared to take his leave. He hugged Cassandra, then Jessie. He stood with his hand on the doorknob.

"It's hard to leave Micah," he said, shifting his weight from one foot to the other.

"Well, we'll see you next month for Thanksgiving. And in between there are video calls," Jessie said. "Though we can't promise that Micah will cooperate, much less that Keith will put in an appearance."

"I'll take what I can get. Thank you both"—Bill opened the door— "for everything. And if you ever need me, you know where I'll be."

Without warning, Cassandra flung herself at him before he could step outside. "Don't go, Dad! Stay wif us!" she exclaimed in perfect imitation of Micah. Jessie was moved to laugh, but she realized with a start that Cass was only half-kidding. As Bill wrapped his arms around her, Cassandra broke out sobbing.

Jessie stared. Her own, dear, unemotional Cass, crying so hard that Jessie feared for her health. The demand that Bill stay might have started out as a joke—perhaps a bit out of character for Cassandra, but a joke nevertheless—but somehow it had become an outlet for her to pour her anger, her loneliness, her grief at the cruelty and dismissiveness of her own family and all that she'd missed out on growing up. Jessie backed up a couple of steps to give them space, her eyes welling with tears.

"I would have been proud to have you as my daughter," Bill said in a low voice, his cheek against Cass's hair. His tenderness provoked a fresh round of sobbing, and the three stood as if in a tableau while Cassandra cried herself out. After a minute or two, when Cass had quieted and everyone had availed themselves of a tissue, Bill kissed her on the forehead and headed out, with the promise of calling as soon as he got back to Queens.

"You OK, babe?" Jessie asked, smoothing a thumb over Cass's tear-streaked cheek.

Cassandra covered Jessie's hand with her own and nodded. "I think I will be."

For Halloween, Eli opted to be Iron Man, and Micah once again chose to be a firefighter, requiring a new outfit as he'd already outgrown last year's. To Jessie's and Cassandra's relief, though, his nightmares had stopped almost completely. On the rare occasion when one did wake him (and therefore, his parents), the mother "on call" would comfort him with the framed photo Bill had given him, of Keith and Joey at their backyard barbecue, the two men smiling into the camera and into eternity.

As the weeks passed, Micah began using his *th* sound more and more consistently, and Jessie figured it was likely to be in place permanently by the time his fourth birthday rolled around. (She admitted to herself, though not to Cassandra, that she was going to miss this last vestige of his babyhood.) While Keith continued to be a constant background presence in his life, Micah was finally starting to come out of his shell at preschool, and his conversation—with increasing complexity and a growing vocabulary—reflected that.

"Mama! Look!" he cried, running into her arms after class, carrying a worksheet with enthusiastically, if not precisely, colored shapes: a red circle, a yellow square, and a blue triangle. At the top of the sheet was a big gold star sticker. "I got a star for my shapes! Look!"

"Wow, you did!" Jessie said, taking the sheet and admiring it appropriately. "Good job!"

"An' know what else?" he said with equal excitement. "Emma is going to New York for vacation. Dat's where Bill lives!"

"That's true. Ooh, what fun!"

"I told Emma what Bill looks like. She's gonna look for him dere."

Trying not to laugh, Jessie said, "I hope she finds him."

Jessie or Cassandra reached out to Bill via a video call whenever Micah demanded it, and Bill called whenever the mood struck him. The contact never lasted long, but both of them seemed to be refreshed by it. The two women found themselves looking forward to seeing Bill on-screen, maybe for different reasons. As much as Jessie appreciated Bill and enjoyed seeing him slip into the role of doting grandfather, she suspected that Cassandra's affection for him went deeper. Watching the two of them interact, Jessie saw a woman who finally had the love of a father she had been lacking most of her life.

She and Cassandra privately had started to look at the calendar to decide when their own trip to New York could be arranged. Thanksgiving was only days away, and they wanted to be able to discuss their spring visit with Bill in person. Or maybe, Jessie thought with growing excitement, instead of giving gifts, they could use the money to spend Christmas in New York. The idea of introducing the boys to the spectacle of the tree at Rockefeller Center and the displays up Fifth Avenue was irresistible. It had been a holiday tradition with her parents, one that now caused a pang of nostalgia every year when she saw photos and news reports.

Sometimes at night, when they were alone, the two of them continued to debate whether to stay in Hadlinsburg. More often now it was Cassandra who made what she thought was a good case for returning east, even going so far as to find some job listings—including one near Bill—that might be suitable for both of them. Jessie could understand why. But she was the one who now leaned toward staying, wondering at the wisdom of uprooting the boys just when things had started to get back to normal, when their friendships had started to recover . . . and particularly, she reminded Cassandra, when Trish had finally stood up to her husband, allowing Quentin and Eli to spend time together again. At least as long as Dean wasn't around.

"Would you look at that?" Jessie said to Cass as Eli dashed off to his most recent playdate at the Marshalls' without glancing back. "It's almost as if kids don't need 'protecting' from people different from them."

"Or to be told who they can love." She grinned at Jessie. "What a concept."

Their routine work lives had returned as well. Although PPAW still held sway over a handful of families, many parents who had been avoiding Jessie started to come back to the library, and, with permission restored, their children began asking for help again. One of them was Alanna Marshall, who, Jessie heard, had celebrated her sixteenth birthday at the beginning of November with a massive party at the town's finest restaurant. The Wilton family hadn't been invited, naturally, but they'd heard all the details from classmates who had attended. It sounded like quite the extravaganza, complete with a DJ, a sushi station, and a sundae bar. Jessie was happy for her.

She watched Alanna saunter into the library in a pair of what, thanks to Trish, Jessie could now recognize as very expensive jeans and a large designer purse worth several weeks of Jessie's salary that Alanna's parents had given her on her birthday. The girl carried herself with that world-conquering confidence Jessie so admired, so different from the way she'd held herself when she was Alanna's age.

"It's nice to see you, Alanna," Jessie said with a welcoming smile.

"Same here, Ms. Wilton."

"Everything OK?"

"Oh, yeah, for sure."

"How's school?"

"OK, I guess."

Having read that asking about school was a losing strategy for getting a teen to talk, and guessing that it was now proven accurate, Jessie went right to the point. "What can I do for you?" She looked past the girl's shoulder. "You didn't come with your mother today?"

"Nope," she said, grinning. "I drove myself."

"You got your driver's license!" And, no doubt, a brand-new car from her grandparents to go along with it. Jessie begrudged her none of it. "Congratulations!"

"Thanks. Mom knows I'm here, though."

Jessie and Trish had started to talk again, and their conversations now went deeper. Trish still wanted to talk cosmetics, fashion, and local gossip—some things never changed—but she also asked sincere questions about Micah and bemoaned how independent Alanna had become, how quickly she was turning into her own person. She made a sincere effort to get to know Cassandra better—and understood that they would not be reciprocating with Dean. Every now and then, Trish let slip about an argument she'd had with him—declaring "He can be such an idiot!" on more than one occasion—and Jessie tried to listen without judgment, determined to be supportive even though her inclination would be to put the blame on Dean every time. If Trish needed a friend, that friend was going to be Jessie.

"Is there something I can help you with?"

"Nah, just saying hello. Here to pick up some reading material." And with a playful side-eye Alanna flashed the PPAW list of challenged books. She was, it appeared, part of the "Forbidden Books Club" at the high school.

Jessie beamed. "How about this one?" She pointed to one of the titles that she thought would be a good intellectual challenge for a junior and then gestured to the teen section. "Right over there."

With a nod, Alanna made a beeline to the shelves and started scanning by author. Jessie looked on in satisfaction, knowing that, like the other books on the list, this particular title was still on its shelf, right where it belonged.

Thinking about their lives in Hadlinsburg now, she guessed that they would end up staying after all. There was still work to be done, and people like Dean and the PPAW-faithful would still be around; she'd won a battle, even as the war continued. Without a doubt, there would be more, perhaps even greater, ugliness ahead. But for now, weighing those negatives against the support of Alanna and the other students, and even from surprise quarters like the Rev. Robinson, she had begun to think they were going to be OK in Hadlinsburg. All of them. Particularly with Eli newly returned to the comfort of his friendship with Quentin, and Micah becoming more and more grounded in the here-and-now, Jessie was increasingly sure.

They, too, were where they belonged.

*****

If you enjoyed this story about the fragile and sometimes blurred line between the known and the unknown, you might like my 2023 novel, *The Hand of Miriam.*

I hope you'll consider leaving a review on Amazon, Barnes and Noble, Goodreads, or wherever you track your reading.

Author's Notes

On the morning of September 11, 2001, I was driving to my job at a cable TV company on Long Island, listening to the radio, when the DJ announced that "a small plane" had hit one of the Twin Towers. A quick glance at the intensely blue, cloudless sky told me that it had been no accident caused by low visibility. Over the course of the day, my coworkers and I watched in horror as the terror attacks unfolded in real time on the many TVs in the building. The town where my family and I lived was home to many courageous FDNY first responders who never returned from their shifts. This book is dedicated to them and to others who put their lives on the line for the greater good.

I'd also like to shout out to a different sort of hero: librarians. Public libraries are one of civilization's greatest ideas, and librarians, in their quiet way, are often on the front lines of defending democracy.

When I was growing up, my parents owned a copy of *The Search for Bridey Murphy*, likely the 1965 re-release of the 1956 (purportedly) nonfiction book by hypnotherapist Morey Bernstein. As a pre-teen terrified of death, I read with avid interest about Bernstein's "past-life regression" work with an American woman who, he claimed, had lived a life in Ireland in the 1800s before being "reborn" here. The book was a sensation at the time of its release.

Although that particular story has since been debunked, the topic of reincarnation continues to fascinate. To those who follow Eastern religions such as Hinduism, it is not remarkable at all, just a part of the life cycle. But among those of us in the West, the idea faces scrutiny and skepticism. An article published in the May 2, 2024 edition of *The Washington Post* renewed my interest in reincarnation, and I read two books by the article's subject, Dr. Jim B. Tucker, a now-retired child psychologist. Dr. Tucker made it his life work at the University of Virginia School of Medicine to use scientific methods in the investigation of apparent past-life claims by young children. The entirely fictional character of Dr. Vince Abernathy in this novel is inspired by the work done by Dr. Tucker.

The character of Bill Weyerhauser is an affectionate homage to my late friend William (Bill) Munch. Billy, as his many friends called him, and I knew each other in high school, grew apart, found each other in our professional lives, lost track again, and then reconnected via social media many years later. Separated by geography, we messaged each other frequently about the things he was passionate about: art, music, literature, politics, and above all, his beloved family. A writer, artist, and philosopher, Bill was a true Renaissance man. His untimely passing in 2023 shook me to my core. I hope that his wife and children approve of my portrayal of Bill Weyerhauser, as it was done with love and the utmost respect.

The group I invented for this book, Patriot Parents Against Woke, is fictional, but it is modeled after real so-called parents' rights organizations. These right-wing, often religion-based extremists want to decide what books and information should be available to the public in schools and libraries. Under the disingenuous guise of "protecting children," they focus on removing books they find objectionable, largely because of LGBTQ+ content but also due to history and facts which conflict with their personal beliefs. In the process, they often besiege teachers, librarians, and administrators who push back, causing conflict and chaos in public school systems. This is censorship, pure and simple, and it is one of many unfortunate attacks on American values that have accelerated in recent years. The speed with which otherwise sensible people turn on their neighbors or give up their own rights under the cult-like influence of these groups is terrifying. Children growing up in the United States—everywhere, really—should have the opportunity to expand their knowledge of the world without being subject to the bias of strangers with a bigoted, intolerant agenda.

Acknowledgments

As I turn sixty-five this year, more than ever I consider how lucky I am to be surrounded by supportive family and friends. I'm abundantly grateful for my husband, Roy; my son, Daniel; my daughter, Brynn and her husband, Adam; and my mother, Sandy, still vital at ninety-one. Some of my friendships date back over half a century, while others are comparatively recent but just as important. The love and encouragement you bring keep me going during the most trying times. Thank you all!

Writing about people whose lives differ from one's own can be a delicate business, and I cannot claim to fully appreciate the challenges facing other communities, particularly marginalized ones. With the understanding that no group is monolithic, and that opinions on my portrayals will vary, I'd like to thank Bri P, my sensitivity reader, for her insights.

I research all my novels as thoroughly as possible, and I always receive help from experts in the field. This time around, I checked in with my friends Lori Ellis, a speech and language pathologist, and Dr. Sirish Veligati, a child psychiatrist, to ensure an accurate depiction of three-year-old Micah Wilton and his unusual situation. I appreciate the generous gift of their time.

For *The Librarian's Son*, I had yet another new editor, Heather Hudec at Simply Spellbound Edits. She was the ideal choice for this project, and I'm grateful for her expert guidance in making this novel the best it could be. I hope we have the opportunity to work together again.

And, last but never least, I extend a great big thank you to my dear friend of over thirty years, Dr. Debra Blaine. A physician, a resilience coach, and a talented author in her own right, she not only provides me with practical help getting my books published but acts as my #1 cheerleader, giving me pep talks and talking me off various (metaphorical) ledges. Read about Debra and buy her books at AllThingsWriting.com.

About the Author

Ellen Gardner Gelerman grew up on Long Island, New York, and spent much of her adult life there. She received her BA in English in 1980 from Indiana University, Bloomington, leading to a lifelong love of English literature as well as a copywriting career in advertising and promotion. Beginning with Grey Advertising in Manhattan, and moving on to Newsday (Melville, NY) and Cablevision (Bethpage, NY), Ellen wrote television, radio, and print advertising copy as well as brochures and marketing scripts.

Though Ellen is retired from her formal career, writing is still her passion. A short story of hers appeared in *The Road to Pemberley: An Anthology of New Pride and Prejudice Stories* (Ulysses Press, 2011). Her debut novel, *The Book of Hannah: A Tragicomedy in Three Trimesters* (2019), won the 2021 NYC Big Book Award in the Chick-Lit category. She is also the author of *The Hand of Miriam* (2023), a Jewish coming-of-age novel, and *Hannah and Her Daughters* (2024), the sequel to *The Book of Hannah*.

Ellen and her husband, Roy, who have two adult children, currently live in Michigan with their dogs. Ellen teaches Zumba for the fun of it and works as a political activist because the times demand it.

The Book of Hannah: A Tragicomedy in Three Trimesters

Hannah and Her Daughters

The Hand of Miriam